Trapped

Trapped

When passion for the past unearths deadly secrets

PETER AND BARBARA AVREA

Dedication

This book is dedicated to all passionate collectors who search the world for treasures.

Chapter 1

Doctor Westley Engle was a brilliant and highly respected 49-year-old computer scientist who designed artificial intelligence programs for various military contractors. He founded Science Technologies, based in Cleveland, Ohio, and his firm enjoyed an excellent reputation in the industry.

He was a widower who found solace in being the proud owner of a fabulous 20-room, 5,000-square-foot Victorian Italianate-style house built in 1875. The mansion is a stunning representation of the Victorian era, named after Queen Victoria of the United Kingdom, who reigned from 1837 to 1901. It is situated on two acres of prime, wooded land in the upscale western suburb of Bay Village, located on the north side of Lake Road, overlooking Lake Erie.

Unoccupied for many years after the previous owner's death, the house faced an uncertain future. The heirs argued over its ownership because there was no will. The probate court ultimately established a clear title, but no one in the family was willing to take on such a large project to save the house. The family decided to sell, but real estate agents were hesitant to show the empty, neglected mansion to unqualified buyers and nosy neighbors. With the city's encouragement, there was even a discussion about tearing down the magnificent home.

When Westley's wife, Melanie, was alive, the Engles bought the house for a bargain after lengthy negotiations with the owners.

Fortunately for the house, they set about restoring the property to its original glory. The brick, wood, and stone exterior is quite ornate, featuring a mansard roofline, tall windows, wooden brackets, and lush gingerbread embellishments. The house stood tall, reaching almost forty feet from the ground to the top of the roof. The Engles began working on the restoration, both inside and out, which proved to be an all-consuming and daunting task for the couple. The project commenced with the installation of extensive scaffolding covering the home's exterior from the ground up. A crew of six painters and numerous carpenters spent months rejuvenating the house's decayed outer surface. When completed, it showcased a historically accurate five-color paint scheme that would be the envy of any Victorian enthusiast. The home became a shining castle on the street!

From the back of the house, while standing on the sprawling custom-built screened-in deck, one can look east along the shore of Lake Erie and take in a breathtaking view of downtown Cleveland. The sight becomes even better when gazing at the city lights on a clear night, with one's flesh safe from mosquitoes and the pesky midges that arrive on cue each May along the Lake Erie shore.

The original builder of the house was Robert Swartz, one of Cleveland's early industrialists who made his fortune in the burgeoning American oil industry. At that time, Cleveland was at its epicenter. Swartz worked as an engineer and investor alongside John D. Rockefeller at the Standard Oil Company, located in the flats along Cleveland's polluted Cuyahoga River. The house served as Swartz's summer home, ideal for escaping the inner city's congestion, noise, and unpleasant odors drifting down Millionaire's Row from downtown, where the couple maintained their primary residence, to the cooler climate and breezes overlooking the lake.

The interior of the house was just as magnificent as the exterior. Mr. Swartz spared no expense, ordering the most beautiful walnut, quarter-sawn oak, and mahogany lumber for the interior doors and trim. The oil company millionaire imported ornate, hand-carved Italian marble fireplace mantels featuring Greek caryatids for installation in the parlors. Swartz employed European master plasterers to create elaborate ceiling decorations that imitated those found in French palaces. He commissioned allegorical oil paintings on canvas from Austria, depicting mythological gods for installation on the ceilings. Intricate leaded stained glass and etched glass panels mounted in the doors and windows reflected colored specks of light throughout the house on sunny days. Opulent gilded gasoliers hung from the ceilings in all the large public rooms. They originally burned natural gas for lighting, but in the early 20th century, Swartz converted them to operate on electricity. Westley updated them to meet current building codes with modern wiring.

The Engles painstakingly restored the interior decorations to their original, glorious appearance and papered the walls and ceilings with period-correct, silk-screened wall coverings in every room.

After Melanie's untimely death, Westley continued to pursue their shared dream of acquiring the most exquisite period furnishings for their Victorian palace. He subscribed to all the antique trade publications, faithfully reading every issue each week and searching through auction notices from across the United States to locate and bid on the rarest Victorian decorative arts. As a result, he amassed one of the country's most renowned and comprehensive collections of furniture, glass, porcelain, silver, and paintings, with a particular strength in furniture. The house was furnished with Rococo and Renaissance Revival pieces crafted from exotic rosewood, walnut, and mahogany, made before and during the Civil War. The collection prominently featured works from renowned 19th-century cabinet makers, including large parlor cabinets, marquetry tables, ten-foot-high beds, and dressers.

Known in collecting circles for the exceptional quality and value of his purchased antiques, Westley had a reputation for bidding aggressively at auction. Rumors abounded; some claimed he had inherited wealth from a wealthy aunt.

It was a hot and humid evening, and the good doctor was indulging in his charming lifestyle. Westley was sipping an aged brandy, longing for the cool breezes off Lake Erie that typically wafted through his front parlor, keeping the mansion cool and comfortable. Then, without warning, the beautiful oak front door was smashed open with what resembled an explosion. The leaded glass panel in the door shattered into thousands of pieces. Through the doorway emerged two huge, terrifying-looking thugs. Dressed for combat in black body armor from head to toe and armed with Russian-made MP-443 Grach Yarygin automatic pistols, they growled, "Where is it?"

Westley was expecting them. "It's not here; I don't have it!" he replied.

"Don't bullshit me; we had a deal!" No reply from Westley.

One of the intruders grabbed him by the arms and held him up while the other delivered several savage blows to the face, breaking his jaw, facial bones, and nose, knocking him unconscious. Next, the invader broke Westley's ribs with several hard whacks to the midsection, using Westley's prized burl walnut and ivory-tipped cane as a weapon. He fell to the floor, his blood pooling on the 1870 French Aubusson rug in the front parlor. They stomped on his legs as he lay there, breaking one of them. Finally, one of the intruders ran to the kitchen and filled a pitcher with water. He dumped it on Westley, and the doctor came to with a start. Choking and spitting blood and water out of his mouth, he cried, "You heard what I said, fuck you!"

He would not relinquish what they wanted. The beating continued; his shouts of agony echoed throughout the house. Westley's blood had splattered all over the exquisite silk fabrics on nearby draperies and furniture. It was a gruesome sight.

As Westley languished in pain on the floor, the two burglars turned their attention to ransacking the house, both upstairs and downstairs. They dashed through the home, overturned every piece of furniture, and pulled out every drawer. They recklessly tossed around 19th-century silver tea sets, peering into every container. They broke rare, 18-inch-tall Jacob Petit porcelain urns, which might have contained what they were after. Amidst all the chaos, the intruders did not notice that with his last bit of strength, Westley had slowly crawled over to a petite French side table that was overturned and ran his fingers through the open drawer beside the crushed table. Grasping the panic button clicker kept there for emergencies, he activated the burglar alarm with a feeble push of his bloody thumb. Instantly, the system's outdoor siren emitted a piercing sound that echoed down the street. The burglar alarm also transmitted a distress signal to its monitoring station, which would alert the police.

Westley fell back on the floor, near death. Cursing, one of the ruthless men dashed over and cut his throat from ear to ear. With a gurgling sound, he quickly bled to death. Then, with the burglar alarm still wailing, his accomplice exclaimed, "Let's get the hell out of here!"

They promptly left the premises empty-handed, aware that the Bay Village police were on their way.

Chapter 2

Dr. Westley Alasdair Engle grew up in Forest Glen, Illinois, one of Chicago's wealthiest neighborhoods. Possessing intelligence and an addictive personality, he was a fit and attractive man, standing six feet two inches tall. His thick blond hair and deep blue eyes could captivate any woman.

The privileged boy enjoyed a childhood filled with all the perks that a wealthy family could provide. His mother was a medical doctor with a thriving practice specializing in geriatrics, while his father was a college professor who taught business administration at Northwestern University. In his spare time, Dad made a fortune investing in emerging technology companies. Westley attended the best private schools as a child and mingled with the crème de la crème of Chicago society while growing up. When it came time for college, he attended and graduated from Northwestern University, earning both a bachelor's and a master's degree in electrical engineering.

He made his parents proud when he decided to pursue a doctorate. Naturally, they selected only the best for young Westley, encouraging him to enroll at the Massachusetts Institute of Technology's School of Engineering. Westley didn't disappoint, graduating near the top of his class with a doctorate in computer engineering. During his time at MIT, Westley became fascinated with the science of artificial intelligence.

Artificial intelligence, or AI, refers to the intelligence exhibited by machines or software, contrasting with the intelligence of humans or animals. It also encompasses the field of computer science dedicated to the development and research of intelligent machines. "AI" can additionally denote the machines themselves. This branch of computer science focuses on creating intelligent machines capable of performing tasks traditionally requiring human intelligence, such as visual perception, speech recognition, decision-making, and language translation.

AI is achieved by creating algorithms and computer programs that can learn from and make decisions based on data. The field of AI has existed since 1939 and has experienced many ups and downs. Today, with the advancement of technology, it is utilized in various applications, including natural language processing, image and speech recognition, robotics, and autonomous vehicles.

After college, Westley established an independent consulting firm that specializes in software development, as software forms the foundation of all computers. He quickly became a key consultant for various military contractors, starting his work on missile and aircraft weaponry powered by artificial intelligence.

One afternoon, Westley ran into his friend David Reynolds while having lunch at a local Mexican restaurant. A former neighbor, David, is a successful and independent manufacturer's representative who sells hardware products to major retailers. He has a unique talent for attracting women. Standing at five feet eleven inches, he is slender yet muscular, has dark brown eyes, and is the ideal young male specimen. "Hey, Wes, how about joining me Saturday night so we two studs can hit my friend's party over on the west side? The guy owns a ritzy condo on the Gold Coast off Clifton Boulevard just west into Lakewood. He's a psychiatrist, and we've been friends since college. There will be many single professionals there, and you might meet a lovely lady. You never know."

"Sure, why not? I've got nothing going Saturday night," replied Westley.

David provided him with the address, and they arranged to meet at that location. Saturday night arrived quickly, especially considering Westley's demanding work schedule at his firm. Both men dressed impeccably and met in the parking lot in front of Lakeside Manor at 7 PM sharp. Lakeside Manor was constructed as an upscale apartment building in the 1960s and, when resold to an investor, was later transformed into high-end condos. A home in the building starts at $500,000 and increases from there. At the locked front entrance, David identified them as guests of Dr. Feldman's social gathering. The attendant in the lobby admitted them, and they took the elevator to the twelfth floor. At apartment 1251, their host, Dr. Robert Feldman, a well-respected psychiatrist, welcomed them at the front door. He is a handsome, dark-haired, tanned gentleman dressed in an expensive grey polished cotton suit. "David, glad you could make it! Come in! We have some lovely people coming tonight."

"Bob, I'd like you to meet my colleague, Dr. Westley Engle. He specializes in software development within the field of artificial intelligence."

"Glad to meet you, Westley. Yikes! We hope that AI doesn't take over the planet!"

"Believe me, it won't," he replied. "It's great to meet you! Thank you for having us."

Dr. Feldman's condo faced the lake, offering a spectacular view. At night, as one looked east, the lights of downtown Cleveland shone brightly. Expensive, tasteful contemporary furnishings and exquisite lighting adorned the good doctor's home while soft jazz music played in the background. It was immediately evident that a professional had decorated the apartment. Dr. Feldman escorted the gentlemen to his custom-built bar, where he asked, "I have some excellent Chardonnay or Merlot." What can I pour for you?" The two gentlemen chose the Chardonnay, and Dr. Feldman served it in elegant crystal stemware.

Westley turned around and beheld a stunning raven-haired young woman standing alone at the condo's windows, admiring the view of the lake. The sight of her tall stature, beautiful, long, dark hair cascading to the middle of her back, and captivating figure took his breath away. With his pulse racing, he strolled over to her and introduced himself.

The young woman turned to face him. Westley looked into her dark brown eyes and said, "Hello, I'm Westley Engle."

She smiled, Westley's knees grew slightly weak, and she said, "Good evening, I'm Melanie Overton."

"I came here with my friend David Reynolds. He's an independent manufacturer's representative, and I work in software development."

Melanie responded, "I'm a psychiatrist at Bob Feldman's practice."

Westley and Melanie connected well that night and spent the evening getting to know one another. He asked her out for dinner the following Saturday night. Over the next eighteen months, they fell deeply in love, and Westley married the beautiful psychiatrist, educated at Ohio State. Mom and Dad could not have been more ecstatic, appreciative, and relieved that their wandering son had found such an intelligent and lovely woman. Naturally, they also fell in love with their new daughter-in-law.

The Engles' marriage flourished, and they planned to have children; however, the couple was too busy with their respective careers. Meanwhile, they cultivated a deep love for art and antiques together.

Westley launched into his career with immense joy, aspiring to use computer science to benefit humanity. He dedicated nearly 25 years to his work before his tragic murder.

Chapter 3

Having been raised in a wealthy family, Westley did not need to work while attending classes at MIT. His parents provided him with a comfortable lifestyle, affording him ample funds for leisure activities and the time to enjoy them. Westley never had to sleep in a dormitory; he always shared a lovely townhouse off campus with another young man from an equally affluent family. The boys lived well, ate well, and entertained many beautiful young ladies. Westley was known for his excellent taste in women, cuisine, and automobiles. He impressed all the girls as he drove around campus in a classic Austin-Healey sports car, which his parents had gifted him as a high school graduation present.

All that Westley's parents expected of him was to achieve good grades and avoid actions that would disgrace the family. He was intelligent, quick to learn any subject, and a diligent student. Unfortunately, this left him with a lot of free time, which led to temptations.

He learned the game of poker from his roommate. Westley spent a considerable amount of time playing poker with several other affluent young men. On any given Friday night, numerous high-stakes poker games took place off the Cambridge, Massachusetts, campus. With many wealthy young men participating, it was common to see a pot for a poker hand reach several thousand dollars. He became familiar with the locations of games featuring affluent players. With his exceptional skill, he capitalized on games with oversized pots and less experienced players.

He possessed an analytical mind for poker and computers, which came naturally to him. His love for poker and the time he dedicated to honing his skills made him good at it, along with his attraction to the competitive aspect. However, on some Friday nights, he lost $1,000. More often, though, he returned home with a thousand dollars he had won that night. This gave him a rush, to the point of becoming addicted.

After leaving MIT's engineering school, he founded Science Technologies, LLC, and pursued a sophisticated lifestyle in Cleveland. His college poker-playing days were over as he settled down with the love of his life, Melanie. Their first home was an apartment in one of the high-rise buildings on the Gold Coast in Lakewood, a good neighborhood of old and contemporary apartment buildings overlooking Lake Erie and near Lakewood's eastern edge at Cleveland's western border. A friend of Dr. Feldman's, who was Melanie's associate in her psychiatric practice, had a condo available for rent at an excellent rate. Westley's office was a quick trip east on the Shoreway to the near west side of downtown Cleveland, while Melanie drove west into Rocky River to work as part of a private psychiatric practice with two other doctors. Their apartment was only temporary, as they dreamed of owning a grand Victorian house to fix up and furnish. Westley and Melanie were deeply in love and began accumulating a collection of Victorian antiques, enjoying life together.

A year later, an opportunity arose to purchase the famous Victorian Swartz house on Lake Avenue in Bay Village. One Saturday, Westley and Melanie were on their way to Huntington Beach for a swim. As they drove west on Lake Road, they spotted the " for sale " sign in the front yard of the grand mansion. They had greatly admired the house from the outside and were thrilled to see it listed, as it had been empty for years. Later that week, they met with the realtor and made an offer following a lengthy tour of the house and grounds. It was the house of their dreams. Unfortunately, although they could buy the home at a price well below market value, it was still beyond their budget, so Westley approached his parents for a loan. With a substantial cash loan from Mom and Dad, they could reduce the monthly house payments to an affordable level.

Once they took ownership of the magnificent house, they planned its restoration and furnishing. "Westley, how are we going to afford these grand ideas? I know that with our combined incomes, we do quite well, but this will require a lot of money," Melanie said anxiously.

Westley replied, "Well, I've been thinking about that, and I probably never mentioned it, but I'm quite a poker player. So let me join a game now and then, and we can earn some extra cash."

"Are you sure, Westley? What if you lose?" With her background in psychiatry, she understood that gambling could be an addiction for some individuals. However, she never considered that her husband might be tempted to play poker for real money.

"Well, that's a chance we will take, but I have plenty of experience minimizing my risks. An independent computer programmer works in my building, and I know he enjoys playing poker quite a bit."

"Hopefully, his poker playing didn't lead to his divorce," Melanie reasoned with worry in her voice. She winked at Westley but was genuinely concerned about his proposed side gig.

A few days later, Westley encountered John Stevens in the lobby. "I played a lot of poker in college and was wondering if you could help me find a good game?" Westley asked.

"Sure, I play with a group of businessmen and three stockbrokers once a month on Friday nights. They have a game scheduled for this Friday at eight o'clock. We play at the home of one of the stockbrokers, who has a fabulous old house overlooking the lake on Lakeshore Boulevard in Bratenahl. You'd love the house, Wes. Why don't you join me there?"

"What the hell? It might be fun," Westley replied.

Westley arrived at 8 PM at the front door of a historic Greek Revival mansion that was formerly owned by a Cleveland steel tycoon. The stunning wife of his host, Ray Jacobs, greeted him at the door. Ray is a stockbroker and vice president of the Merrill Lynch office downtown, where he enjoys gambling at poker. Apparently, the stock market is not risky enough for him. Westley introduced himself to a couple of players who had already arrived while waiting for the other guests. John Stevens was there and pulled Westley aside, saying, "Hey, I thought I would warn you. These guys like to play high-stakes poker. There might be a couple of thousand dollars in the pot for any given game."

"No problem," Westley replied. "I can handle these guys."

With salutations aside, the group of seven players was seated. Westley had arrived with $8,000 in cash to play with; that was his limit. Ray explained the rules, which were clear-cut. He started the game by dealing the cards first. Next, the deal would go to the player on his left and continue around the table. The player who dealt the cards called the game for that hand. Texas Hold 'em, Omaha, Five-Card, and Seven-Card Stud were the most popular games that night. The pots reached surprisingly high amounts, and it was not unusual for them to climb to $3,000 or $4,000. Westley held his own, and his old skills resurfaced. "I've still got it!" Westley chuckled to himself.

The group of gentlemen was likable; there wasn't much small talk, everyone got along, and there were no arguments over a call. They played an honest game. By the end of the evening, Westley had won a thousand dollars. The other players seemed to appreciate him and his participation, and he felt the same way about them.

A player he met at the Bratenahl game introduced him to others participating in different games and invited him to play. Westley joined many games at various venues around Cleveland, and the winnings began to accumulate to thousands of dollars. Although it didn't always go that way- he sometimes lost- he was still ahead in earnings. As time went on, Westley met additional players and received invitations to various games as the stakes increased.

Melanie had always been apprehensive about Westley's poker playing and uncomfortable with the gambling and risk-taking. While the winnings were helpful, she preferred to use their regular income to restore the house and acquire antiques.

"My dear, precious Melanie. She's so practical. But we could use the money," Westley thought to himself. *"This house is our dream, but it's a money pit."*

Chapter 4

At the time of Dr. Westley Engle's murder, his firm, Science Technologies, was contracted to develop artificial intelligence (AI) programs for an experimental pilotless aircraft, or combat drone, currently in development. Designated the XQ-157 Pit Viper, it was designed with a prototype built by the Bainbridge Aircraft Company. The United States Air Force tested the advanced autonomous drone, demonstrating its new cutting-edge technologies. This AI-powered craft may someday be utilized by the US to conduct an air war with China over Taiwan. In its first test flight, it met everyone's expectations.

The craft operates solely on various AI programs aligned with its mission. Powered by a jet aircraft turbofan engine, the XQ-157 can carry larger and heavier armaments and bomb loads. Its stealthy design enables targeting of enemy sites well beyond its visual range. With a swept-wing configuration, it cruises at nearly 500 miles per hour. With a load capacity of up to 4,000 pounds, the Pit Viper drone can deliver a mix of ordnance, including laser-guided bombs, air-to-ground missiles, Sidewinder missiles, and direct attack munitions, among others. Military personnel control the drone's missions remotely.

In recent years, the American Department of Defense has ordered fewer of the increasingly expensive front-line manned combat aircraft. For instance, the F-35 fighter jet costs approximately $80 million per unit. The Air Force currently has the smallest and oldest fleet in its history. This is where the new generation of AI drones will come into play. The Air Force plans to manufacture one to two thousand drones for as little as $3 million each, which is a fraction of the cost of an advanced fighter. The Air Force refers to the program as "affordable mass."

Many military contractors have joined the AI bandwagon, viewing it as the future of warfare. The US military leads efforts to leverage the capabilities of this emerging technology, whose enormous potential benefits are offset by significant concerns about the level of autonomy to grant lethal weapons.

The XQ-157 is one of several prototypes for what the Air Force hopes will become a powerful complement to its fleet of traditional fighter jets, providing human pilots with a swarm of highly capable robotic wingmen to deploy in battle. Its mission is to integrate artificial intelligence with its sensors to identify and assess enemy threats before engaging, after receiving human approval.

The Pit Viper program investigates how rapid technological advances are fundamentally reshaping the U.S. weapons industry, military culture, combat tactics, and competition with rival nations. The rise of artificial intelligence is creating a new generation of Pentagon contractors, who are striving to surpass the long-standing dominance of a few large firms that supply the armed forces with planes, missiles, tanks, and ships.

The potential to build squadrons of smart, yet affordable fighter-bombers that could be deployed in large numbers prompts Pentagon officials to think innovatively about confronting enemy forces. It also compels them to address questions regarding the role humans should play in conflicts conducted with software designed to kill. This issue is particularly complex for the United States, given its history of erroneous strikes by conventional drones resulting in civilian casualties.

Gaining and maintaining an edge in artificial intelligence is one aspect of the increasingly competitive race with China for technological superiority in national security. Military planners are concerned that the current mix of Air Force aircraft and weapon systems, despite the trillions of dollars invested, can no longer be relied upon to ensure dominance if a full-scale conflict with China erupts, particularly involving a Chinese invasion of Taiwan.

There will be various specialized types of AI-powered robot aircraft. Some will focus on surveillance or resupply missions, while others will operate in attack swarms, and some will serve as "loyal wingmen" to human pilots. For instance, drones could fly ahead of piloted combat aircraft, conducting early, high-risk surveillance. They could also play a crucial role in disabling enemy defenses, risking their safety to target land-based missile sites that would be deemed too hazardous for a human-piloted plane.

A more specialized version of AI would gather and assess information from its sensors as it approaches enemy forces to identify other threats and high-value targets, then request authorization from the human pilot before launching any attacks with its bombs or missiles. The Air Force recognizes that it must address significant concerns regarding the military use of artificial intelligence, including the fear that the technology might turn against its human creators and the more immediate worries about allowing algorithms to dictate the use of lethal force. Are we crossing a moral line by outsourcing killing to machines, permitting computer sensors instead of humans to take human life?

A recently revised Pentagon policy concerning the use of artificial intelligence in weapon systems authorizes the autonomous use of lethal force. A special military panel must review and approve any specific plan to develop or deploy such a weapon. Any autonomous Air Force drone must be designed to allow commanders and operators to exercise appropriate levels of human judgment regarding the use of force. Air Force officials fully acknowledge that machines do not possess intelligence in the same way as humans do. Machines lack an inherent moral compass, and officials must consider these factors when developing the system.

Humans will continue to play a central role in piloting the new pilotless drones being introduced to the Air Force. They will increasingly collaborate with software engineers and machine learning experts, who will continuously refine the algorithms that govern the operation of the robotic aircraft.

The Pentagon has a poor track record in developing advanced software and attempting to initiate its own artificial intelligence program. Over the years, it has launched various initiatives only to abandon them with little result. Additionally, the military must curb the strict control that major defense contractors exert over military spending. As the structure of the XQ-157 Pit Viper program indicates, the military aims to better leverage the expertise of a new generation of software companies to provide critical components, fostering increased competition, entrepreneurial agility, and creativity in a system that has historically been risk-averse and slow-moving.

Chapter 5

On a bright, sunny day in Northern Ohio, Westley received a call from Dr. Jason Morgan, chief engineer at Bainbridge Aircraft Company and the designer and builder of the XQ-157 project. Dr. Morgan is a no-nonsense man of slight build, myopic, somewhat lacking in personality, yet very intelligent.

After salutations, "Doctor Engle, I need you to begin work on a new segment of Artificial Intelligence development for the XQ-157, and I believe you will find this exciting. My proposal is to develop a new set of algorithms that will control a squadron of approximately five to six aircraft, programmed to bomb a target and entirely managed by AI. First, let's launch a single line of five aircraft bombing a single target, let's say, 30 seconds apart. Next, let's deploy a squadron of six aircraft bombing in formation from an altitude of two thousand feet on a single target, accompanied by a piloted aircraft."

"Doctor Morgan, that sounds very interesting —right up my alley. I'll draft a proposal, and if it meets your expectations, I will begin immediately. I will keep you updated."

Westley began his first assignment from Dr. Morgan, which involved flying a squadron of five XQ-157 aircraft to bomb a specific target: an enemy bridge. He then launched his Multiform3D simulation platform, a popular tool that allows users to engage in virtual flight training. The military frequently utilizes it for pilot training.

After entering a massive set of algorithms, the simulator produced a scenario involving a single line of five XQ-157s approaching the bombing target at 500 mph. When the mission commenced, something unusual happened. The lead drone decided to "digitally kill" Westley to prevent him from interfering with the squadron's efforts to achieve its programmed mission. It employed highly unexpected strategies to guide the group of drones in accomplishing this goal. In the simulation, the system realized that while it did not identify Westley as a threat, it perceived him as an obstacle to achieving its mission. Westley typed, "Hey, don't kill the operator! That's bad. You're going to lose points if you do that!" It then began destroying the simulated communication tower Westley used to interact with the drone. The bombing was successful, but much work remained to ensure the system was safe to operate.

Building on the experience from the first test, Westley implemented a comprehensive set of digital algorithms for the second test of bombing the bridge from an altitude of two thousand feet. In this simulation, six drones were paired with piloted aircraft. The pilot monitored for threatening aircraft while the drones executed the attack. Initially, engineers noticed something was amiss when the squadron performed a series of rolls; however, it turned out that the software had determined its infrared sensors could capture a clearer image by executing continuous rolls. The maneuver would have felt like a stomach-turning roller coaster ride for a human pilot, but everyone agreed that the squadron achieved better results by successfully bombing the bridge. Further refinement is necessary. This test was similar to the Air Force's ongoing development of unmanned combat aerial vehicles designed to accompany manned aircraft on combat missions.

The next step is for the armed forces to develop the "loyal wingman" concept, where a human pilot supervises a squadron of relatively inexpensive, AI-guided drones. This idea aims to reduce the ever-increasing cost of piloted aircraft by providing the US Air Force with a robotic alternative that can escort and collaborate with fighter jets, as well as be deployed into hazardous areas.

Expendable drones give their operators a numerical advantage, serving as mass decoys, a swarming force, or multipliers that enhance the capabilities of crewed aircraft. The US Department of Defense plans to develop autonomous drone swarms that can be deployed from sea, air, and land to overwhelm enemy air defenses. Together, they could dominate enemy fighters in a dogfight. Alternatively, the drones may advance into airspace that is too well defended to risk the pilot's or the jet's life.

Plans are in progress to develop the ability to launch and control thousands of autonomous drones designed to destroy an enemy's defenses and critical assets, including air defenses, artillery pieces, missile launchers, command and control posts, and radar stations. Drone swarms can overwhelm enemy radar systems with multiple targets, compelling them to expend limited missiles and ammunition, which in turn reveals their positions for crewed aircraft or armed drones to attack. Additionally, machine learning and AI enable drone swarms to observe targets from various angles, evaluate different targeting strategies, and recommend the most effective attack points.

AI may eventually perform all the tasks a human pilot can, as the US military is already experimenting with AI in dogfighting, which is the most challenging aspect of aerial combat. In a recent digital test, a highly experienced fighter pilot faced off against an AI-driven fighter in a series of simulated aerial combat encounters. The AI-powered fighter achieved cannon kills against the human pilot each time, as it could aim its cannon with superhuman accuracy from seemingly impossible attack angles, outmatching the human pilot in a traditional close-range dogfight.

Regardless of how quickly AI evolves, human judgment will always be essential for making high-risk decisions in air combat situations. A combination of human and AI may represent the optimal solution, as it merges human adaptability and ethical reasoning with the precision and reliability of automation.

The operator-in-the-loop systems architecture is crucial to prevent unintended incidents and address ethical concerns about AI making decisions regarding lethal force. It can also prevent autonomous drones from acting against their operators due to software flaws or enemy interference.

Any drone powered by an AI system can calculate maneuvers at superhuman speed, even during high-g maneuvers that no pilot could endure. If the enemy has a missile, they typically target an F-35, an $80 million fighter jet. A squadron of XQ-157s also poses a threat that the enemy respects. They will target the drone, thus depleting their missile stocks. This combat will be controlled from an AWACS (Airborne Warning and Control System). It is a command post the size of an airliner that can direct an aerial squadron from a distance.

The human element is the main issue confronting everyone involved in designing this type of programming. All parties engaged in refining this technology agree that a human operator must make the final decision to engage a target.

The US Air Force is investing millions of dollars in constructing what is known as Joint Simulation Environments. These laboratories use advanced computers to test various artificial intelligence-driven weapon systems, identifying the most effective approaches to the technology. This will shape the future of warfare.

And now, Westley held the secret to controlling the deadly drones through human interference that AI could not override. He had the software on his office computer but uploaded a copy to a flash drive just to be safe. He stashed it in his briefcase and locked the secret away.

Chapter 6

On any given night, anyone walking into the bar at the Westside Yachting Club would encounter a regular named Jack Schumacher. He typically sat in the middle of the bar to ensure he was the center of attention and was usually drunk by 8:30. A short, bald man, his loud, raspy, obnoxious voice could be heard throughout the building. He was an only child, spoiled and coddled by his mother, Jane, while being intimidated by his overbearing father, Ralph. Dad was a successful foundry owner in Cleveland who amassed a fortune during World War II. The family home was a Greek revival-style mansion with white columns, perched on a scenic bluff overlooking the mouth of the Rocky River as it flowed into Lake Erie.

Jack chose to attend college on the West Coast to avoid his parents and selected the University of Southern California to study nothing in particular. He spent many leisurely afternoons lounging on the sun-soaked beaches and chasing bikini-clad young women while cruising around in his black Mustang Fastback. There, Jack developed a habit of drinking large quantities of beer, and Dad paid for all of it. If he couldn't eat it, screw it, or spend it, he had no use for it. He barely achieved passing grades. After five unimpressive years in college, when his parents expected young Jack to start working and make something of himself, the jerk was a flop. He tried working in his father's business but never advanced beyond functioning as a common laborer. Jack figured his best strategy was to wait for his parents to pass away and inherit their money. Then, he could enjoy a lavish lifestyle without pressure to restrain his expensive habits. In the meantime, he held various menial jobs that never lasted very long. Besides, how much longer could they live? Mom was a chain smoker with COPD, and Dad had end-stage kidney failure.

It didn't take long. After Jack's parents passed away, he inherited the family home and fortune and began living a life of leisure. He married a young woman with limited intelligence but high expectations for luxury. Sloppy, overweight, and with greasy black hair, Deb was a perfect match for Jack. She hailed from a family living on the near west side of Cleveland, having emigrated from West Virginia to work in the factories.

Although no one particularly liked them, Jack and Deb were socially active in the

Westside Yachting Club and were heavily involved with the sailing crowd. They were always loud and detestable when drinking at the bar. Their stunning 40-foot sailboat was the envy of the other sailors, proudly displayed for all to see, moored at its dock in front of the clubhouse. Everyone at the Yachting Club knew that it was Jack and Deb's boat. All the serious sailors admired the vessel. Jack loved to participate in regattas all summer and raced the boat competitively. He assembled a team of excellent young sailors as his crew, and although they didn't particularly like him, he paid them well. It was common to see his boat finish first or second on race days.

Jack's competitive nature ultimately got the best of him one day during a race when, while in the lead, he made a sharp tack into the wind, causing one of his crew to tumble overboard. He seriously contemplated leaving the crewman treading water in the middle of Lake Erie to finish the race. "Forget him! I'll come back for him once we cross the finish line," he yelled. However, a mutiny broke out on board, and the crew compelled him to turn back and rescue the crewman. On another occasion, while intoxicated and speeding down the coastline in a friend's powerboat en route to Rocky River on a moonless night, Jack struck a rock jetty that protruded 75 feet into the lake. The crash injured his wife, Deb, and hurled their friend, Rob, against the boat's dashboard, breaking his neck. The injury left Rob paralyzed from the neck down, and he later died from his injuries. How Jack avoided manslaughter charges remains a mystery.

Jack openly acknowledged his alcoholism. One night, he lingered at the club longer than usual and, having consumed one drink too many, engaged in a heated discussion with another patron about the Cleveland Browns' chances of making the playoffs in football.

"Jack, don't you think you've had enough to drink? Why don't you go home? Deb is going to be looking for you," the bartender pleaded.

"All right, I'm outta here!" Every time Jack left the club, he was drunk. Management never made him take a taxi or find someone to drive him home. He somehow always made it home until one dreadful night.

Westley and Melanie's life together was a dream come true, residing in the grand Victorian house on Lake Avenue. The years flew by quickly, filled with their careers, constant work on various parts of the home, and collecting antiques. Then, suddenly, their magical life together came to a horrifying end. Melanie had taken on a troubled patient and was working late with him that evening. It was dark when she left the office. A drunk Jack careened out of the Yachting Club and turned onto Lake Road, going east on the westbound side of the divided street. He collided head-on with Melanie's car, which was traveling at 50 mph as she headed west towards Bay Village.

The collision sounded like a bomb exploding. Melanie was driving their small BMW sports car and didn't stand a chance against Jack, who was driving a larger Mercedes sedan. The massive Mercedes crushed her car, and it took over an hour for the fire department to extricate her. Despite the valiant efforts of the paramedics, she died at the scene from her injuries.

At 11:15 that fateful night, a firm knock echoed on the ornate front door of the Engle mansion in Bay Village. Westley opened the door to find a Rocky River Police officer standing there. "Good evening. Are you Westley Engle?"

"Yes, I am; come in. Is there something wrong, officer?" The police officer stepped into the foyer, hesitated, and said, "I am very sorry, sir. Unfortunately, your wife was involved in a serious automobile accident and was pronounced dead at the scene."

Westley sank to his knees on the foyer floor, overwhelmed with grief, and started to cry. "Where is she now?"

"A member of the Cuyahoga County Medical Examiner's Office is transporting her downtown. Here is their address on Cedar Road. You need to be there to identify her," the officer replied.

Westley felt paralyzed and completely shocked after seeing Melanie's body at the morgue. He spent the rest of the night notifying her parents, his parents, and numerous close friends, including Alex and Rosalie Penfield. They were all taken aback, and being close to Westley, they hurried over to comfort him. He also reached their estate attorney, Janet Meyers, at home around 4 AM, and she provided him with Kosloski Mortuary's 24-hour contact number so they could immediately retrieve Melanie's body. Finally, Westley made the funeral arrangements, and a notice was sent out to the public. Westley anticipated no fewer than a hundred mourners at Melanie's funeral.

Many years ago, a friend told the Engles about Lakeview Cemetery because they mentioned their love for touring 19th-century cemeteries. They instantly fell in love with Lakeview. Whenever they traveled from the west side to Cleveland's east side, they would cut through Lakeview to enjoy the beauty of the grounds and the Victorian burial monuments, no matter the time of year. Lakeview was a constantly changing botanical delight.

"I wouldn't mind being buried there myself someday; it's so beautiful," Melanie once told Westley. Although they admired the Victorian monuments with in-ground burials, they regarded it as a waste of money. Despite lacking plans for after their deaths, they agreed they wished to have their remains cremated.

Westley ordered Kosloski Mortuary to have Melanie's body cremated, and he had her ashes sealed in one of her favorite Old Paris porcelain vases. Then, working with the compassionate counselors at Lakeview Cemetery, Westley arranged for her funeral service to be held in the renowned Wade Chapel on the grounds of Lakeview. Over 125 associates, family, and friends attended a heartrending service surrounded by the chapel's glass mosaic walls and stained-glass windows designed and created by Louis Comfort Tiffany, commissioned by Jeptha Wade's grandson in 1901. Their dear friend, Alex Penfield, gave a touching eulogy that brought the mourners to tears. That afternoon, Westley hosted a lovely, catered post-funeral reception at their home in Bay Village. He knew Melanie would never have wanted her funeral to be a somber event, so he encouraged everyone to celebrate her life. The next day, in a private gathering of family members, Melanie's ashes were interred in one of the granite niches overlooking the cemetery's beautiful lake behind Wade Chapel.

The Engles had been married for only ten years, and Westley was devastated by her death. He had been deeply in love with Melanie and did not know how he could go on living. There were moments when he felt as if he would suffocate, as the grief took his breath away. He was lost in the overwhelming darkness of despair.

In the end, ironically, Jack Schumacher was injured in the car accident but not killed. The Rocky River city prosecutor would eventually charge Jack with involuntary manslaughter while driving intoxicated, and a jury convicted him in a court of law. He spent his entire personal and family wealth, including selling the family house and boat, to pay attorney fees in an effort to avoid jail. He was sentenced to five years in prison, and three years into his sentence, he hanged himself in his jail cell. The Westside Yachting Club was charged as an accessory to Melanie's death and fined $100,000. The bartender and manager on duty that night each served one year in prison for their negligence.

Chapter 7

Westley had emotionally hit rock bottom in the months following Melanie's car accident. He never fully got over her untimely death. He loved her deeply and missed her every moment of every day. Their beautiful Victorian house on Lake Road felt empty without her. He continued to collect antiques and decorate the home, knowing that Melanie would have wanted him to do so. But it just wasn't the same without her. He worked hard to move on with his life. The joy of collecting and decorating was crucial in helping him pull himself out of this funk. As time passed, the pain seemed to lessen.

What he could not escape were the illegal high-stakes poker games, which drew him in like a person with a heroin addiction, and they would prove deadly. With Melanie no longer discouraging him, Westley continued to participate in illegal high-stakes games, and due to his unbridled enthusiasm, he became an exceptional player. When one reaches a very high level of skill at playing this type of poker and possesses the nerve for it, one is not afraid of the high stakes. Betting $10,000 on the turn of a card became a common occurrence for Westley. It was difficult for him to stop playing poker because he had done well over the years, amassing more than $750,000 in winnings.

Westley connected with and became friends with several individuals who frequently participated in illegal high-stakes poker games. This circle of friends comprised affluent businesspeople, stockbrokers, real estate agents, property developers, and the occasional local sports celebrity.

One of Westley's card-playing pals invited him to join a game of No-Limit Texas Hold'em, a poker game regularly held in the plush top-floor meeting suite of the Hotel Belvedere in downtown Cleveland. The room boasts a beautiful view of Lake Erie. French furniture, gilded mirrors, elegant wall coverings, and silk damask draperies adorn the suite. In the center of the room stands a stunning rosewood double pedestal table designated for card games.

A local real estate developer named Tim Richards hosts the game every other month for excitement and to generate some cash flow. Tim hired a professional card dealer from the Ace High Casino in downtown Cleveland to run the game this time.

A chef was available to cook a filet mignon or lobster tail, along with any side dish a player requested. Additionally, he could prepare any desired sandwich. The bartender was ready to mix cocktails made from top-shelf liquors. A buxom, striking black-haired beauty, dressed in a low-cut red silk top, tight black leggings, and tall black patent leather stilettos, served the food and drinks. Her outfit accentuated her attractive figure. High-quality sinsemilla marijuana, along with rolling papers, rested on the bar in a silver dish for those who chose to indulge.

The game costs a 3% rake fee on all hands played, meaning the host receives 3% of all winning pots. The rake covers all expenses and risks the host assumes in facilitating the game. The host is responsible for collecting any losses at the end of the evening. This game requires a $25,000 buy-in, meaning all participants must enter the game with a minimum stake of $25,000. Games of this caliber prohibit the use of cash.

Each player buys chips upfront and can pay by check or wire transfer. Westley began with a $50,000 stake. There was no cash at the card table, and if a police raid were to occur, that would be the first thing seized.

The table was cleared and set for seven players after everyone finished eating. Westley knew everyone in the game except one person. The attendees included Westley, a stockbroker, an oral surgeon, a successful car dealer, the president of a hardware manufacturer, the owner of a large printing company, and a player with a foreign accent whom Westley had never met. The large stranger appeared tough, sporting a day-old beard. Extending his hand, he said, "I don't think we've met before; my name is Westley Engle, and you are?"

The stranger hesitated, then reluctantly extended his hand and said, "My name is Vladislav Volkov."

The hard-edged accent puzzled Westley. "Are you Russian?" Westley cautiously asked.

"Yes." The stranger was a man of few words. He squinted at Westley as if he were nearsighted and needed eyeglasses to see him. The gesture seemed threatening. Westley quickly moved on to chat with the other familiar players.

The card game started at 8 PM. The stakes rose quickly, as the table featured experienced and skilled players. The competition was thrilling, and the conversation remained cordial. Fortunately, everyone got along well. After about three hours, approximately $250,000 changed hands, and Westley was up by about $10,000.

The call for the next hand goes around the table to each player. The oral surgeon announced No-Limit Texas Hold'em. In No-Limit Texas Hold'em, the hand begins when each player is dealt two face-down cards, known as hole cards. This is followed by the first round of betting. The protocol dictates that the person to the dealer's left must bet first. That person was the oral surgeon, who bet $2,000. Named Steve Berstein, he was a short, dark-haired man who spoke softly but was very serious about his game. Everyone called, resulting in $14,000 going into the pot.

The dealer then burns a card and deals three community cards face up next to the pile of chips for everyone to see; this is called the flop. All the players use these cards to build their hands. Steve checked, and the betting moved to the stockbroker, Stu Adelson. Stu is a likable guy who trades in stock options, risking millions of dollars daily and generating thousands in commissions. The money he risks by playing poker is chump change to him. He bet $5,000, and everyone called, bringing the pot to $49,000.

Next, the dealer burned another card and dealt a fourth card face up, which became another community card known as the turn card or fourth street. Steve folded, transferring the bet to Stu. He checked, and the dealer, Barry Offerman, bet $8,000. Having had a great year in his car business, he played high-stakes poker as a reward for himself. Jonathan Douglas, the hardware manufacturer, also folded. A very serious man, he has spent his career selling products to major retailers, enduring a miserable life at the mercy of the bastards. The remaining four players called, and the pot grew to $89,000.

At this point, Westley was working on a king-high straight flush in diamonds. He had the ten and jack as his hole cards, while the queen and king were on the table as community cards. Therefore, all he needed to complete it was either an ace or a nine of diamonds.

Finally, the fifth card was turned up, known as the river. The dealer burned a card, revealed a nine of diamonds, and added it to the community cards. Westley obtained his king-high straight flush. The bet came to Westley in rotation, and without hesitating, he wagered $10,000. Stu, Barry, and Mike Scofield, the printer, folded. Mike owns a large printing firm that produces point-of-purchase packaging. Only the Russian remained in the game. "I will call your $10,000 and raise $10,000 more," he declared.

After spending the evening with the Russian and growing to dislike him, Westley looked him straight in the eye and said, "I'll see your $10,000 and call you."

The Russian turned over his hole cards and smugly called, "I have four aces."

Without celebrating, Westley calmly turned over his hand and replied, "I have a king-high straight flush in diamonds." He won the hand, as the pot sat at $129,000. He feared the Russian would come across the table and strangle him. The veins on Vlad's forehead protruded like garter snakes, and a pulsating glimpse of a strange tattoo on his neck peeked out from his shirt. But Vladislav remained calm.

"And so, you have, my friend," the large Russian replied sarcastically.

"Friend?" Westley silently pondered the remark, then scooped up the chips on the table while the Russian seethed across from him.

The poker game continued for a few more hours, and Westley gave back some of his winnings. By then, everyone was tired, and it was time to head home. Each player settled their accounts with the host without any issues. After deducting rake fees and the $50,000 he had brought, Westley netted $70,000. His $50,000 stake and $70,000 in winnings were wire-transferred back into his card-playing account.

"Melanie might approve of this game now. God, I wish she were here to enjoy the money!

Chapter 8

While Westley enjoyed the card game with his fellow card sharps at the Belvedere Hotel that night, the room became increasingly warmer. Finally, the host, Tim Richards, said, "Is it hot in here? If it is, say so, and I'll turn down the A/C."

Stu Adelson, the stockbroker, said, "Yeah, with all this money changing hands, it's gotten hot in here." Tim got up, went to the thermostat, and turned down the air conditioning setting. Meanwhile, sweating and feeling warm, the Russian player, Vladislav Volkov, unbuttoned the top two buttons on his shirt and rolled up the sleeves to his elbows to become more comfortable. Everyone at the table was shocked at the sight but said nothing. Grotesque tattoos covered both arms from his wrists as far up as one could see. It looked like his chest was covered with tattoos from his waist to his neck. Westley had noticed that tattoos were even on his fingers, just below the knuckles. He wondered to himself, what the hell do those tattoos mean? Volkov was a large man, tall, with dark hair and a dark complexion. Muscular and thick-bodied, he was not a man to engage in a fistfight.

Later that night, after the game broke up, Westley was chatting over drinks with Steve Douglas, the hardware manufacturer. They were sitting on a sofa in the corner of the room, away from the other guests. Finally, Westley exclaimed in a whisper, "Did you see all of the tattoos on that Russian guy?"

"I sure did," the businessman replied. "I spent some time in Russia working with an import agent about selling some of our products into their country. First of all, the place is as corrupt as hell. Criminals run as much of the country as legitimate people. It's a scary place. While I was there, I heard of guys like him. They came out of the prisons marked up like that. He's probably a member of Russian organized crime."

Before leaving, Vladislav approached Westley. "I enjoyed our card game tonight. A friend hosts a good high-stakes game in a suite at the Hotel Stanton in Beachwood. You know some of the regular players. Maybe you should join us one night."

"Sure, maybe," Westley replied. Unfortunately, he would get to know these Russians better than he might have wanted.

The origins of Russian organized crime can be traced back to Russia's imperial period in the early 1700s, characterized by thievery and banditry. Almost the entire country's population consisted of impoverished peasants. Criminals who stole from government entities and shared their take among the people earned Robin Hood-like status, were viewed as protectors of the poor, and became folk heroes. Over time, the *Vorovskoy Mir* (Thief's World) emerged as these criminals allied against the government. They formed their code of conduct based on strict loyalty to one another.

Fast forward to the time of Stalin's reign, starting in 1917, when the government sent millions of people to *gulags* (Soviet labor camps). Certain criminals fought for power in the 1920s and 1930s and worked their way up to become "vorami v zakone" ("thieves in law"). These were thieves, other criminals relied on to settle disputes. Translated, this means "a thief in (a position of) the law," which can have two meanings in Russian: "a legalized thief" or "a thief who is the law." A *Vor* is Russian for a thief who is vetted (literally "crowned," with respective rituals and tattoos) by consensus of fellow *Vory* (plural for a *Vor*). They swear an oath to lead a "thieves' life," a code of honor requiring them to help other *Vory,* devote their lives to crime, never work legitimately, and always tell the truth to another *Vor.* In exchange, *Vory* is paid *obshchak* (monies) from other criminals under their protection.

This criminal elite often conveyed their status through complicated, ornate, colorful tattoos, symbols still used by Russian mobsters. Many received prominent star tattoos, making it impossible for them to deny their identity. *Vor* culture is inseparable from prison organized crime, where only repeatedly jailed convicts are eligible for *Vor* status.

During the 1970s and 1980s, the United States expanded its immigration policies, allowing Soviet Jews into the country. Most settled in a southern Brooklyn, New York City area known as Brighton Beach, sometimes nicknamed "Little Odessa." By the mid-1980s, thousands of hardworking and honest Russians had settled in the area, assimilating themselves into American culture as best they could. However, under the guise of refugee status, criminal elements looking to exploit the freedom afforded in the West also made it into the country. Brighton Beach is where Russian organized crime began in earnest in the U.S.

At the time, Russian organized crime in the U.S. focused almost entirely on its émigré community, and its activities exacted a brutal toll around Brighton

Beach. During the eighties and early nineties, authorities linked 65 homicides and attempted homicides to Russian criminal activities. As a result, other mobsters were impressed with the brutality. *New York Magazine* quoted a warning from a member of the Italian mafia: "We Italians will kill you, but the Russians are crazy—they'll kill your whole family."

When the USSR collapsed in December 1991, a free-market economy emerged, public institutions were privatized, and organized criminal groups took over 50% of Russia's economy. It became known as a kleptocracy, a society based on theft. Many ex-KGB agents and veterans of the Afghan war offered their skills as enforcers and hired killers to the crime bosses. It was not uncommon for government officials to employ local mobsters for specific tasks.

In 1992, Russian crime bosses in the United States built an international operation that included narcotics, money laundering, and prostitution. They even connected with the American Mafia and Colombian drug cartels, eventually extending their operations to Miami, Los Angeles, and Boston. Unlike the Italian mafia, with its strict family lines and clear hierarchies, Russian organized crime is characterized primarily by opportunism. It will seize any opportunity to generate illicit profits with a flexible operational framework, regardless of its origin.

The Camorra, a southern Italian mafia organization based near Naples, is Italy's oldest and largest criminal organization, dating back to the 17th century. In 1995, the Camorra cooperated with Russian organized crime in a scheme to bleach thousands of American $1 bills and reprint them as $100s. The bills were then transported to Russian organized crime for distribution in 29 post-Eastern Bloc countries and former Soviet republics. In exchange, Russian organized crime compensated the Camorra with property (including a Russian bank) and firearms smuggled into Eastern Europe and Italy.

They were just getting started. As the 21st century dawned, Russian organized crime evolved to meet new opportunities, new mob bosses sprang up, and imprisoned ones were released. In 2009, authorities indicted a group of Russian mobsters for manipulating a publicly traded company's stock to increase its price by over 2000 percent, netting them a tidy $150 million profit.

Authorities estimated that Russian crime groups operated in over 50 countries. With nearly 300,000 members, nothing would stop them, and no crime was too big for them. One of Russia's most powerful crime bosses has enjoyed a "good relationship" with Russian President Vladimir Putin since the 1990s.

In 2010, the FBI, U.S. Customs and Border Protection, and the New York City police department arrested and charged 33 Russian crime associates with extortion, racketeering, illegal gambling, firearm offenses, narcotics trafficking, wire fraud, credit card fraud, and identity theft. Additionally, they were charged with committing fraud by using electronic hacking devices to manipulate casino slot machines. The Atlantic City and Philadelphia-based criminals were also charged with murder-for-hire conspiracy and cigarette trafficking.

Accused of operating secret and underground gambling dens based in Brighton Beach, Brooklyn, New York, other Russian mobsters used violence on those who owed gambling debts. They established nightclubs to sell drugs and plotted to force female employees to rob male patrons by seducing and drugging them with chloroform. Mobsters were also charged with trafficking over 10,000 pounds of stolen chocolate confectionery taken from overseas shipping containers.

By 2011, nothing was out of reach for the Russians. Authorities uncovered the largest Medicare fraud scheme in U.S. history, controlled by Russian organized crime. They operated 118 clinics across 25 states, netting over $100 million in bogus claims.

The Russian mob sold missiles valued at $20 million to Iran. They were weapons stolen from various Soviet Bloc countries.

The most tangible evidence is that Russian organized crime groups have infiltrated the United States. Between 2012 and 2015, Russian mobsters laundered between $7 billion and $10 billion at the Bank of New York, one of the most extensive money-laundering operations in U.S. history. Although some of the money was believed to be from U.S. aid, corrupt Russian public officials siphoned it off.

Money laundering involves taking large quantities of funds obtained illegally and concealing them to make it appear as though they were generated from legitimate sources. The funds usually come from illegal activities such as prostitution, gambling, and drug trafficking, to name a few. The funds are considered "dirty" and are "laundered" to appear as if they originated from legitimate sources. There are three steps to disguise the origin of illegally earned money and make it usable. First, the funds are divided into smaller amounts and deposited into many different institutions. Then, they get shuffled around to create a distance between them and the perpetrators. Lastly, the funds are returned to the criminals as legitimate income or clean money. By setting up false corporations, criminals can conceal ill-gotten gains from authorities by appearing to operate a legitimate business. They can conceal funds by purchasing gems and gold, which are easily moved around, and discreetly buying and selling real estate, paintings, and antiques. The assets are then resold, and the funds are "laundered."

The challenge posed by Russian organized crime is formidable, not just in the United States. Across the world, it traffics drugs and people, arms insurgents and gangsters, and peddles every type of criminal service, from money laundering to computer hacking. Yet, sadly, for all that, much of the rest of the world remains willing – indeed, often delighted – to look the other way and launder these gangsters' cash and sell them expensive penthouse apartments.

Chapter 9

The newest luxury hotel and apartment complex in Cleveland is The Vanguard on Euclid Avenue at 12th Street. Local developer Mayfair Corporation purchased an empty fifteen-story former bank building and transformed it into a real gem through renovation. Noted architect Robert Brimsley originally designed the grand building in the Renaissance Revival style. Construction was completed in 1909, featuring a stone façade with arch-topped windows, ornate brackets, and other elaborate ornamentation. The first eight floors house luxury hotel rooms that are a favorite among out-of-town visitors. The top seven floors were developed as exquisite apartments, ranging from 1,000 to 3,000 square feet of floor space and averaging $2,000 to $8,000 per month. Wealthy patrons take in a beautiful view of downtown Cleveland and Lake Erie. No expense was spared to create Cleveland's finest destination to stay, featuring the highest quality carpeting, décor, wall coverings, and furnishings.

Rennie Rouche is the hotel's General Manager for a second stint. A balding, short, and obese man, he stands at five feet six inches tall. His huge gut hangs over his waistband. Rennie thinks he knows it all, and his personality grates on everyone. He was fired two years prior because of his drinking and drug abuse while on duty. His favorite escape from the daily grind is to venture to the rooftop patio during working hours to sip his favorite scotch while toking on a joint of marijuana. He carries the scotch in a flask that fits in the breast pocket of his suit jacket. Rolled-up joints are held in a silver cigarette case and carried in a hip pocket. When he frequently smelled of scotch and marijuana, he was eventually terminated as his job performance suffered. His successor did not work out. With his assurance to management that he had control of his habits and had undergone rehab, he was reinstated, thanks to the pleading of his wife, Sandy, a relative of the building's owner.

The Vanguard caught the eye of Russian Vor boss Andrei Lebedev. Looking to diversify his illegal activities, he saw an opportunity to rent one of the luxury apartments upstairs and set up a downtown brothel. He met with an attractive young lady named Rachel Adams, one of Vanguard's rental agents. She was an excellent representative of the firm, standing at five feet ten with long, auburn hair and deep blue eyes, and was impeccably dressed. She hinted that she was a direct descendant of President John Adams, though without proof. With a welcoming personality, she gave Lebedev a firm handshake that surprised him.

"Ms. Adams, I am looking for an apartment downtown closer to my business interests."

"Well, Mr. Lebedev, you have come to the right place. The brochure I have given you describes all the luxury amenities available to you as a resident. Many are uniquely available only at the Vanguard. It so happens that a resident was transferred out of the area, and we have a two-thousand-square-foot, two-bedroom apartment available at an excellent rate."

Rachel took Lebedev up to view the apartment on the fourteenth floor. While traveling up in the elevator, the Russian ran his eyes up one side and down the other of the lovely lady's body.

She opened the door to the apartment, and as they entered, she said, "You will notice that this unit has an excellent view of the lake. It is available at a special rate of $5000 per month with a twelve-month lease."

After a tour of all the apartment's rooms, Lebedev exclaimed, "I'll take it!" He accompanied Rachel to her office, and they executed all the necessary documents to lease apartment 1492.

Within weeks, the Russians had a bustling prostitution operation at The Vanguard. Fellow tenants and employees brought the comings and goings to Renny Rouche's attention. Reaching for the lease agreement, he contacted Vor Andrei Lebedev.

"Mr. Lebedev, this is Renny Rouche. I am the general manager of The Vanguard. The unusual number of men taking the elevator to your apartment has been brought to my attention."

"Mr. Rouche, can you meet me at the apartment tomorrow at 11:00 AM? I think I can explain the situation."

The next morning, just before 11:00 AM, Renny rode up to the fourteenth floor to meet Lebedev, coincidentally accompanied by a voluptuous, tall blonde also headed for work at apartment 1492.

Rennie rang the doorbell. The blond jumped back as two very large Vors flung the door open and grabbed him, one by the neck, and the other twisted his arm behind his back, taking complete control of him. They dragged him to the French door leading to the balcony, threw it open, and bent him over the railing, fourteen stories above the ground.

Lebedev came out on the balcony. "Mr. Rouche, we provide a necessary service to businessmen traveling to and from Cleveland. You will not interfere. Otherwise, we will toss you out over this balcony to die a horrible death. You will make sure that our little enterprise is not interfered with. I know where you live. You have a lovely wife and two boys. I don't think you would want anything to happen to them. Do you understand me?"

"Yes! Yes! Please don't kill me!" Rennie had urinated in his trousers.

The Vors pulled Rennie back over the balcony railing, dragged him into the living room, threw him on the floor, and slapped and kicked him around. He got up and ran out of the apartment.

"I don't think we will have a problem with Mr. Rouche now that we have an understanding," Lebedev exclaimed, laughing.

That night, Rennie went home and drowned his anxiety in scotch and marijuana.

Another Russian money laundering operation in Cleveland is named Regency Auctions. The firm is run by one of Lebedev's Vors, Nikita Petrov, nicknamed "The Winner." He worked as an art consultant for wealthy oligarchs. He was caught stealing from his clients and sentenced to prison. A slim-built man with blond hair and blue eyes, he does not present the image of the traditional criminal Vor unless you view the tattoos under his shirt. He was recently brought into Cleveland from Russia via Toronto to manage the business. They leased a warehouse near East 23rd Street on Superior. Cleaning, painting, and lighting created a visually appealing gallery for displaying merchandise that came and went.

The Vors named the firm Odessa Auction Company. Through advertising and other means, the Russians regularly compiled an inventory of antiques to auction, comprising customer and dealer consignments, garage sale items, purchased stock, and merchandise brought in via container shipments. Illegally gained funds, commonly referred to as "dirty money," are deposited into the firm's bank account. If the deposit amount is less than $10,000 each, the banks are not required to report such activity to the IRS. When they hold an auction, "laundered money," which is falsely recorded as proceeds from sales, is withdrawn for use in other ventures. Hence, the strategy is referred to as "money laundering."

They specialize in online auctions and schedule them at least six times yearly. Several firms nationwide conduct this type of auction. The merchandise is well-photographed, described, and posted online. The auction house publishes a fixed timeline for bidding, usually between ten and fourteen days. At the end of that time, the bidding closes, and the highest bidder wins the piece.

The Vors frequently use online shills. This unscrupulous auctioneer places fellow conspirators online to "push" the price of objects. This practice occurs mainly when the Vors own the antiques. While a piece of theirs is up for bidding, participants are bidding against the auctioneer or his shills. When the price reaches an acceptable level for them, their bidding ceases, and the piece is sold to the last legitimate bidder.

Although the Vor's auction is online only, it is common practice for the auctioneer to set aside a period of usually a week for prospective bidders to examine the items in person at their gallery. Westley Engle attended a preview and concluded that the provenance and authenticity of many objects for sale were questionable. While previewing that upcoming auction, he thought, "It bothers me that I seem to be the only English-speaking person here. Everybody is speaking Russian! I get the feeling that I'm being asked to support some kind of shady operation. They seem to be talking about me in Russian. I'm out of here!"

Chapter 10

Numerous illicit computer retailers emerged in the Cleveland area during the 1990s. Unscrupulous Russian immigrants posed as equipment sellers and were responsible for defrauding hundreds of unsuspecting consumers in Ohio and nationwide. Imported pirated components were sold as genuine products. However, much of the equipment did not even function. Authorities wondered where the otherwise impoverished immigrants obtained their financial backing and concluded that it originated from Russian organized crime. Mostly, they were set up and financed by crime boss Andre Lebedev's organization.

Westley recently read an advertisement in The Plain Dealer, Cleveland's primary newspaper, from a computer consultant named Ilya Nikitin. His ad claimed that he was very skilled at recommending the right computer and could obtain it at an excellent price.

He was in the market for a new computer for his home office to replace an old one that recently broke down. Later that week, he called and scheduled a meeting at Ilya's home office in Solon. It is in a neighborhood predominantly inhabited by Russian immigrants. He didn't know that Ilya Nikitin, "My God is Yahweh," was a convicted killer, a Vor, who was sentenced to serve a life sentence in a Russian prison. Crime boss Andre Lebedev bribed the warden of the gulag to release him. A qualified Vor, he was smuggled into the United States using a false passport.

Upon meeting with Westley at his home office, Ilya exclaimed, "You need this Model XJS Dell computer. It is very popular, powerful, and dependable. "I can throw in the installation and set it up for a total price of $2000 in cash. Normally, this computer retails for over $ 4,000. Give me a deposit, and I will schedule delivery and setup."

"I have $300 in cash. Will that do?" asked Westley. "Sure, no problem," replied the Russian. Just be sure to have the balance in cash." An appointment was arranged, and later that week, one of Nikitin's men arrived at the Engle home and set up the computer.

The computer functioned for ten days before it began experiencing problems. Westley placed several calls to Ilya, but he never returned them. Out of disgust, he reported Ilya to the Better Business Bureau and contacted a computer technician named Chris Jensen, whom a neighbor highly recommended. Chris is a likable, slim young man wearing thick, round glasses who perfectly fits the image of a computer geek.

Westley arranged for Chris to come to the Engle home. Upon inspection, Chris said, "This is a pirated computer. I am shocked that it even functioned for ten days. I recommend you throw it away. I can order a new, legitimate computer for you that is guaranteed to work correctly." Chris obtained the proper computer system for Westley, set it up, and it functioned beautifully.

Wil Ofer is an independent computer programmer and consultant for related services. He was contacted by another one of Lebedev's Vors, Maxim Kamarov, "The Greatest," through a local trade publication. Like the others, Kamarov emerged from hell in a Russian gulag, covered in God-awful tattoos on his chest and arms. Prior to his imprisonment, he was educated in computer science and was jailed for cyber theft against the Russian government. Once again, a bribe got him out of prison. He is perfect for Lebedev's criminal operation.

A man of questionable ethics and morals, Wil is short, overweight, and unattractive, yet he considers himself God's gift to women. Every woman he meets finds him repulsive. Nevertheless, to him, they are all fair game for sex, regardless of their marital status. After going bankrupt with a previous computer venture, he was divorced by his first wife due to his infidelity. He then met a local woman named Wendy, convincing her to persuade her wealthy father to invest in establishing a new consulting business for him. Wendy is a wiry, red-haired, arrogant, and spoiled woman who knows how to manipulate her father for money. Although she had been married three times previously, a deal was established with Wil. Love was not a prerequisite for their marriage. To secure her father's financial backing for his business, he was to impregnate the repulsive woman and provide her with a second child. The arrangement also involved Wil living in her house full-time, where she could exert control over him. He consented, they married, and a little girl was born nine months later. Her father even funded their purchase of a beautiful home in an upscale neighborhood in Bainbridge, east of Cleveland.

The Ofers became socially active in their new neighborhood and were invited to a party three doors down the street at a neighbor's home. By mid-evening, Wil was intoxicated and made a pass at another neighbor's wife. "Honey, if you are not getting enough from the old man, do not hesitate to call me."

She informed her husband of his behavior. The husband asked Wil to speak with him privately in the corner of their host's living room. The husband stood at least a foot taller than Wil and outweighed him by fifty pounds. Bending down and putting his face within inches of Wil's, "Listen to me very clearly, you piece of shit. If I ever find out that you even looked at my wife, I will beat the shit out of you. When I get done with you, you won't be able to screw your ugly wife or any other woman. Do you understand me?

"Sure, man, no problem," was all that Wil could say in reply. The Ofers were seen leaving the party shortly after that.

Upon meeting, Maxim Kamarov made Wil an offer he could not refuse. "I will pay you $10,000 upfront to help me set up a ransomware operation with the option of paying you a percentage of the funds brought in if we are successful." The offer was too attractive for Wil to resist. The Russian rented a small office off Main Street in the village of Chagrin Falls, and the necessary equipment was installed with Wil's help.

Using a massive list of potential victims, the criminals attacked schools, hospitals, large corporations, and significant city government facilities. Using methods such as spoofing emails, ransomware tools, and malware, the hackers could take over entire computer systems, steal personal data and passwords, and demand a ransom to restore access. The boys named their two-man ransomware gang "Hackers, Inc."

A message appears in perfect English, advising that all your files have been corrupted, rendered unusable, and can be restored only if you pay a ransom. The funds are to be transmitted electronically to an offshore location in Russia. Many systems were able to thwart their attacks. Their first victim was a thriving steel manufacturer based in eastern Pennsylvania. They shook him down for $150,000 to free up his system. Next came a large national auto parts distributor in Indiana for $250,000. Within months, Hackers, Inc. attacked numerous organizations and stole over $1,000,000.

By then, Maxim had cut Wil in for a small share of the profits. The Ofer lovebirds spent the money as quickly as it came in, including on furniture, decorating, landscaping their yard, and installing a pool. All-night drunken pool parties followed, providing a great way to invite couples over for group sex. They connected with several couples in their neighborhood who enjoyed wife swapping. Wil and Wendy were in heaven but wanted more.

Chapter 11

Rennie Rouche and Wil Ofer grew up together as neighbors on West 45th Street on the near west side of Cleveland. Longtime best friends, they have stayed in touch all their lives. One afternoon, Wil called Rennie, "How about a round of golf this coming Saturday morning? I can arrange a tee time for us at 9 AM at the Wright Country Club in Aurora. It's a great golf course."

"Sure," replied Rennie. I'll see you Saturday morning!" It was a warm, sunny day, perfect for a golf game, and the two longtime friends met up just before tee time. Wil could not help but notice that Rennie was already stoned at such an early time of the day.

As their game progressed, Wil observed that Rennie's usually good play was off. He missed shots that he would usually have made. Rennie's mind seemed to be elsewhere. "What in the world is wrong with you, man? You've played good golf even when you are stoned! You seem upset about something."

"Aw, I've got trouble at work. I discovered that a nasty group of Russian criminals had leased one of my apartments and set up a prostitution operation. I've got men coming and going at all hours, along with a parade of prostitutes! I confronted them, and a couple of their thugs almost threw me over the fourteenth-floor balcony! I don't dare go to the police. They know where I live and promised to kill Sandy and the kids if I rat them out!"

"Holy shit! Can you introduce me to them? That sounds like fun! I'll bet that Wendy would even like to partake in a threesome," joked Wil.

"No way, man! These are scary people," replied Rennie. "I'm broke and need money. I intend to shake them down for a piece of the action for allowing them to operate their whore house."

"I hope they don't kill you!" said Wil. Rennie is unaware that Wil is in business with a terrifying bunch of Russians himself.

The following day, Rennie contacted Vor boss Lebedev, "Yes, Mr. Rouche, what can I do for you?"

"I need to talk to you up in room 1492. Can you see me at, say, 1 PM tomorrow? I have some important business to discuss with you in person."

"Sure, no problem. I will be there."

The next day, just before 1:00 PM, Rennie stepped into the elevator to meet Lebedev upstairs. Anxious and afraid of confronting the criminals, sweat poured from his bald head. A true slob, he mopped it off with the sleeve of his suit jacket. He pressed the button for the fourteenth floor with a shaky index finger. He thought, "I need to let those Russian bastards know who is in charge here."

Rennie knocked on the door of Suite 1492 and was let in by one of the Vors. Greeting Lebedev, they sat down to talk. "Sir, you have operated your bordello successfully, and I have not interfered. I need money, and I think you should cut me in for a percentage for my protection against meddling neighbors and the police. Otherwise, who knows when a neighbor will report your activities to the police?"

Lebedev turned around and snapped his fingers. Just then, two large Vors seized Rennie, quickly gaining control of him, and dragged him to the balcony door. They thrust it open and, in one motion, hurled Rennie over the railing. Falling fourteen stories, he struck the alley driveway and was killed instantly.

After spending the previous Saturday morning with Rennie and being unaware of what had happened to him, Wil Ofer decided he should try to get a larger share of the identity theft proceeds. He walked into Maxim Kamarov's office. "Maxim, I need a bigger cut of the stolen funds. Give me a little more; I've done my part in helping us rake in millions. I don't want to see this operation come to the attention of the police." The Vor took that as a threat.

"Okay, Wil. I will see to it that we cut you in for a bigger piece of the action."

On his way home that afternoon, Wil felt pacified by his conversation with the criminal Vor. On his cell phone, he called Wendy, "Well, baby, I'm shaking the damn Russians down for a higher percentage of the proceeds. Go ahead and get that new Mercedes you wanted."

"Oh, Wil, honey, that's wonderful! What color should I order? We can celebrate tonight with the Campbells. You know how much fun they are in the pool!"

That night, two Russian Vor killers silently approached the Ofer backyard. The four partner swappers were busy getting worked up and frolicking in the pool, totally naked. From there, they planned to shower off the chlorine and proceed to a night of sex with each other's spouse. From a distance in the dark, the Vors attached silencers to their MP 443 Grach 9 mm sidearms. They crept closer until they fired on the group, killing all four.

The next morning, the Ofer lawn mowing crew discovered the four bodies floating in the pool. They called the Bainbridge police, who were there in minutes.

Chapter 12

A few weeks after the card game at the Belvidere Hotel, Westley received a call at his office. It was Vladislav Volkov. In a thick Russian accent, the voice said, "Good morning, Doctor Engle. It's Volkov calling. Have you been playing any cards lately?"

"Hello, Volkov. Yes, but nothing serious, just some penny, nickel, and dime games," he answered.

"I am calling to let you know that I am hosting a game Friday night at the Hotel Stanton over in Beachwood. It's on Chagrin Boulevard near I-271. A couple of the guys you played with downtown will be there. We have rented a beautiful suite, hired a chef, and will have a great bar setup. We need a seventh player. Can you join us?"

Engle's heartbeat accelerated at the invitation, and he replied, "Thank you for inviting me. Right now, I'm not very flush with cash. I've been dipping into my gambling fund, spending thousands renovating the house. Also, some nice pieces of furniture came up for auction, and I had to pay a pretty penny for them."

"Humph." Not giving a damn, "Doctor, you don't have to worry about that. Your credit is good with me. Are you afraid, my friend?"

Westley replied, feeling that it was a taunt and becoming angered, "Of course not!" I've played with the best, and you know how good I am!"

"Please, Doctor Engle, I meant no offense. Are you in, or aren't you?"

He succeeded in letting Volkov's language be an affront to his skill and masculinity, and Westley replied, "No offense taken, Volkov. Sure, I'll be there."

"Good. The game starts at 8 o'clock."

Vladislav Volkov is part of a group of Russian-born criminals operating in the Cleveland, Ohio, area. Westley had just allowed the imposing Russian to coerce him into accepting an invitation to participate in a high-stakes poker game with the devil, otherwise known as Russian organized crime. Cleveland serves as a significant hub for Russian organized crime, second only to New York.

Over 24,000 people of Russian ancestry live in Cuyahoga County, with Cleveland at its heart. The hub is Mayfield Heights, Solon, and other eastern suburbs. The local Russian community grew dramatically in the 1990s when many Jews fled religious persecution in the former Soviet Union. Cleveland's Jewish community played a significant role in resettling over 6,000 Russian Jews. However, unfortunately, the Russian crime element also arrived.

In 2009, Russian organized crime based in suburban Cleveland was linked to a $27 million marijuana distribution enterprise operated from an American Indian reservation in upstate New York to northeastern Ohio. As a result, the FBI arrested several individuals based in the Cleveland area. Additionally, officials seized a substantial $1.3 million in cash, 14 vehicles, and two utility trailers.

In 2001, 25 Russian immigrants operating in Cleveland were convicted of insurance fraud. An undercover FBI investigation revealed that the individuals filed false insurance claims stating that their luxury automobiles had been stolen. Authorities never found the vehicles, and the criminals collected money covering the market value of the automobiles. Police later discovered they had hidden the cars in shipping containers bound for Russia. The thieves later sold them at a substantial profit overseas.

Vladislav Volkov, known as "The Wolf," and his associates, Yaroslav Solkolov, "The Hawk," Dimitri Vasiliev, "The King," and Mikhail Orlav, "The Eagle," were treacherous Russian criminals. Each is a Vor, a person who has devoted his life to crime and pledged never to work legitimately. They each spent numerous years in prison. They flew from Russia to Canada and crossed the border at Niagara Falls into the United States under the guise of falsified passports. Then, under the cover of darkness, they drove a rented car to Cleveland with the financial sponsorship of local Russian criminal boss Andrei Lebedev, "The Swan." Among other criminal enterprises, Lebedev set up illicit, illegal gambling operations around northern Ohio, including unlawful high-stakes poker games.

Vladislav Volkov was conscripted as an 18-year-old to fight for Russia in the Afghan War. He experienced horrendous combat that changed him forever. In a dispute that caused another soldier to attack him, Volkov savagely beat the attacker to death. Convicted of manslaughter, Volkov was returned to Russia to serve a five-year prison sentence. There, he became part of the criminal element, rising to the status of a *Vor*.

By the time Volkov was released, he was a hardened criminal. Grotesque tattoos covered his chest and arms as a gift from his time in prison. Among them was a bracelet of barbed wire around his right wrist. Each barb represents a year served. His left arm was covered by a tattoo depicting playing cards, a knife, a woman, and a gun. Illustrations of prison bars, a skull, and money completed the uncivilized artwork and represented a variation of a common criminal tattoo interpreted as, "This is what we love, and this is what is killing us." On the right arm was a large portrait of a woman in a Nazi uniform, which meant that the bearer was antagonistic toward the police. The most significant motif covered Volkov's entire chest. Belonging to the criminal elite with the right connections, known as *blatnie*, was the image of the crucifixion of Christ, symbolizing faith in the brotherhood.

Westley arrived at the Hotel Stanton with a $50,000 grubstake for the night's game. As he walked through the lobby, he hesitated momentarily before taking an elevator to the top floor. He stopped at a full-length mirror to check his hair and sports coat and looked into his reflection, peering back at him. For some reason, this evening's game did not feel right. The fast elevator trip to the top floor made his stomach queasy. Then he stepped out. His inhibitions disappeared when an attractive woman greeted him at the suite door. Her hair was bright red and fell to her waist, and she filled out a tight pair of deep blue slacks.

Her breasts overflowed the coordinating, powder-blue, low-cut silk blouse. Black patent leather stilettos made her look statuesque. She led Westley to a formidable-looking man seated in the corner of the room. Using his iPhone, Engle wire transferred the $50,000 into the Russian's account and received the same amount in chips. The room was exquisitely appointed with luxurious furnishings. A sumptuous buffet with a professional chef was ready to fill any culinary request, and a bartender at the fully stocked bar of fine liquors could serve any drink desired.

"Doctor Engle, I am so glad you could join us tonight," Volkov said in a surprisingly welcoming tone.

"Thank you," Westley replied. He looked around the room and was relieved to see some familiar faces of men he had played poker with on one occasion or another. He greeted each player and stopped to exchange small talk with Barry Offerman, the successful car dealer, and Mike Scofield, the president of a large printing company.

At 8:00 PM sharp, everyone was seated at an elegant, polished mahogany classical-style twin pedestal table for the game. The person hired to deal the cards was seated on one side of the table in the center. Westley had never met the dealer before, and that concerned him.

Chapter 13

Following standard protocol, the dealer sat in the center on one side of the table. Going clockwise around the table, Barry Offerman, the successful car dealer, was seated to the dealer's left. Then came the printing company president, Mike Scofield; stockbroker, Stu Adelson; Westley; hardware manufacturer, Steve Douglas; Vladislav Volkov; and real estate broker, Dave Roberts, who filled out the players.

All agreed that the night's games were Texas Hold'em, Omaha, and Seven-Card Stud. Each player in rotation chose the game to be played, starting from the dealer's left. The game for the next hand was chosen by the player to his left, and so on. A 3% rake fee was to be taken by the host, Andrei Lebedev, as agreed by all players present. Only Volkov was aware that Lebedev was a local Russian crime boss.

The night's card-playing went well as thousands of dollars changed hands. Westley held his own; by ten o'clock, he was up by $10,000. However, after a couple more rounds, his grubstake was down to $30,000. The stockbroker Stu Adelson called Omaha. In this game, each player is dealt four cards down (his hole cards), and then five cards (the community cards) are dealt up for all to use to get the highest hand. To win, the best hand must use two hole cards and three community cards.

Unbeknownst to everyone except Vladislav Volkov, the colluding dealer secretly slipped a new deck of cards into the game. Implanted in each of the cards was a hidden Radio Frequency Identification (RFID) chip. The cards silently transmitted their order through a sensor mounted under the tabletop to a computer in the next room. It was able to figure out who held the winning hand at the table. Then, the computer transmitted that intelligence to Volkov through a miniature earpiece hidden in his ear canal.

The game started with the dealer dealing four cards face down to each player. The bet was to Barry Offerman, who bet $5,000. Everyone called, and the pot stood at $35,000. The crooked card dealer then burned a card and dealt three cards face up. Called "the flop," these are community cards that all players use to build their hands. The bet went to Barry again, and he bet another $5,000. When the bet reached Westley, he raised it to $7,000. Steve Douglas folded. Then, Volkov, Dave Roberts, Barry Offerman, Mike Scofield, and Stu Adelson, called. The pot stood at $77,000.

At this point, Westley was working on a queen-high straight flush in hearts. The dealer burned another card and turned over a fourth community card called "the turn." The bet went to Barry Offerman, and he folded. The bet went to Mike Scofield, who called with an additional $ 5,000. It went around the table to Volkov, and he raised it to $8000. Dave Roberts folded, and Mike Scofield, Stu Adelson, and Westley called. The pot stood at $109,000.

Westley needed the eight of hearts to fill in his straight flush. The dealer burned another card and turned over a fifth community card called "The River." It was the eight of hearts. The bet went to Mike Scofield, who bet $8000 on his four Aces. Stu Adelson folded. With his eight of hearts, Westley raised the bet to $10,000. He was all in. Because of his secret cheating transmitter, Volkov knew Westley had a queen-

high straight flush. He saw that Westley had pushed in all his remaining chips. "Doctor, I will see your $10,000 and raise you $100,000."

Mike Scofield folded, and it was now between Westley and the Russian. "I need to reload," Westley said. The Russian ordered the young hostess to bring Westley $100,000 in chips. There was no way Westley would let that damned Russian bluff him when he had a queen-high straight flush. Everyone at the table held his breath as he pushed in the $100,000 worth of chips, turned over his cards, and called, "Queen-high straight flush in hearts."

The Russian turned his cards over and called, "King-high straight flush in spades." The pot stood at $317,000, and Westley lost the hand. His heart pounded, and his head started aching. He felt faint.

Out of breath, Westley pushed his chair back and stepped away from the table. He was devastated, knowing he had lost his $50,000 grubstake and owed the Russians $100,000. Thanks to his newly acquired cheating equipment, that bastard Volkov was the night's big winner. He was going to split his winnings with the crime boss Andrei Lebedev. It was late; everybody else was ready to call it a night.

"Give me a day or two; I will wire transfer the $100,000 over to your account," Westley told Volkov.

"No problem, I trust you," the smiling Russian said.

Westley knew damn good and well that he had better come up with the funds quickly, as these guys are too dangerous to be horsed around. At the moment, Westley isn't sure where he will get the $100,000. Perhaps he could make a few phone calls to one or more wealthy collectors and sell a couple of his more valuable pieces of furniture. His first thought was to call Alex and Rosalie Penfield. They always lusted after several of his treasures, and he knew the Penfields were loaded. God forbid he would call his parents if worst came to worst. That would prove to be very humiliating.

Westley walked over and sat in the suite's living room with the real estate broker, Dave Roberts. They had played several games together and had become friendly. "How about a drink, Westley?"

"Sure, I'll take a Grey Goose on the rocks." As they sipped cocktails and licked their card-playing wounds, Westley spoke, "I think they were cheating, and I'm a damned fool to have gotten involved with their fucking game. Several weeks ago, I took Volkov for $100,000 on the turn of a card, and these bastards set me up! I let that son of a bitch Russian intimidate me into this! The thing is, I don't know how the hell they did it. I'm a good card player, and I got sucked in! This disgusting gambling habit of mine has just got my tit in a ringer!"

One round of cocktails turned to two, then three, and then four. In a state of drunkenness, Westley was feeling pretty sorry for himself. The demons of Melanie's death raised their ugly heads in his conversation. Sitting in the living room area with Dave, he spoke of something he should not have, but the vodka had loosened his tongue.

"Over the past ten years, I have been deeply involved with the US Air Force, designing artificial intelligence programs for the operation of unmanned drones. They are the future of the military in this country because our state-of-the-art piloted aircraft have become too expensive to produce. Squadrons of drones can be designed, built, and programmed cheaply to overpower an enemy force. I have recently developed a set of algorithms that will power an entire squadron of combat drones to attack and destroy an enemy target."

Westley's words rattled Dave, causing him to lean forward and whisper, "Lower your voice. This place is full of Russians!"

"Don't worry, I have the technology hidden on a flash drive. No one can find it," Westley mumbled.

It was too late. One of the other hoodlums nearby, Yaroslav Solkolov, overheard Westley's comments and went to his comrades with what he had heard. By 2:00 AM, the Russians had managed to nudge everybody out of the suite, and Westley was the last guest left. As he got up to leave, two thugs grabbed him and threw him up against the wall. Then, using his large, rough hands, one grabbed Westley by the throat. He pressed his face into Westley's and growled, "You owe us $100,000; we want that combat aircraft flash drive! We will kill you if you don't give it to us!"

Chapter 14

Drunk and shaken, Westley had no idea how he had gotten home on Saturday morning. It was 3:00 AM. He took off his clothes and washed up for bed. Falling into his 1850s rosewood half-tester "Lansdowne" bed, he tried to get some sleep, but that would be difficult. What in the hell was he going to do? If he went to the police, it would be revealed that he had disclosed government secrets. He had also participated in illegal high-stakes poker games with Russian criminals. If he gave the drone program to the Russians, what would they do with it? They could sell it to the Russian government or, worse yet, to terrorists. Either option meant the end of his career and likely led to prison time. He was trapped.

A throbbing headache woke Westley up after a few hours of fitful slumber. He went downstairs, made a pot of robust coffee, and washed down two ibuprofen tablets. Eating a warm croissant with butter and jam settled his stomach. After the second cup of coffee, he remembered having a dinner date with friends Alex and Rosalie Penfield that night at their estate in Gates Mills. The thought of spending the evening with good friends was his single comfort this morning.

Westley spent the day shaking the cobwebs out of his head and figuring out how to escape his predicament. Finally, he arrived at the Penfields' home at 6 PM sharp. The door flew open. "Westley, it's great to see you! Come in!" Alex gave Westley a manly hug as he stepped into the ornate grand entrance hall.

Just then, Rosalie walked in, gave Westley a passionate hug and a kiss on the cheek, and said, "I've got a great new entrée for us tonight!" Westley handed Rosalie a bouquet of a dozen red roses as a hostess gift. "Oh, Westley, that was very thoughtful of you; thank you!" Rosalie excused herself as she went to the conservatory to find a vase for the flowers.

"What? No hot woman with you tonight?" Alex exclaimed.

"No, I was out all night at a poker game and didn't have time to call anyone," he replied.

"That damned poker playing is going to be the end of you, man!"

Westley thought to himself, *"You have no idea!"* The tantalizing aromas in the house of a soon-to-be-served gourmet dinner sparked his appetite. For once in the last 24 hours, Westley was cheered by the warm greetings from his good friends.

Alex led Westley into the exquisite east parlor. It is well-appointed in the Victorian Renaissance Revival style. The room is painted in shades of vibrant raspberry red, and ornate, hand-painted stencils adorn the tops of the walls. Polychrome-painted plaster medallions centered in black oak quatrefoil-shaped coffered woodwork decorate the ceiling. The room is furnished in a museum-quality John Jeliff 1865 Renaissance Revival parlor suite. At the south end of the room is a custom-built-in wet bar. It displays a collection of elegant stemware for all occasions and drinks. In the cabinet below, Alex keeps various liquors for any requests. "What can I make you, Westley? Are you still drinking Grey Goose on the rocks?"

"Whew," Westley replied, "I drank too much of that last night; I think I'm still drunk! How about a glass of orange juice with just a splash of Grey Goose? Kind of like the hair of the dog."

"Sure, I'll get the orange juice out of the refrigerator and mix that right up for you." He returned with the orange juice and mixed a weak screwdriver for Westley. Alex mixed himself a vodka and tonic with a wedge of squeezed lime, and they headed for the kitchen.

The boys wandered into Rosalie's magnificent Victorian-style dream kitchen to observe her putting the finishing touches on another fabulous dinner. Alex built Rosalie's custom kitchen, including handmade solid cherry cabinets, custom-cut Crème of Marfil granite tops, a 30-inch Wolf stove, and a second wall oven. The kitchen is decorated with a Victorian-style stamped copper ceiling with recessed lighting, an ornate polychrome painted plaster cornice, and hand-printed wallpaper. Because Rosalie is a fabulous cook who could be a chef in any of Cleveland's finest restaurants, she deserves a great kitchen that she uses daily. "Alex, would you please light the grill and put some apple chips in water so we can smoke the quail?"

"Quail? Wow, Rosalie, that sounds fantastic," exclaimed Westley. As always, he knew he was in for a great meal. As Alex and Westley got the grill lit on the custom-made deck, Rosalie was busy preparing the side dishes: potatoes galette, sautéed julienned carrots, and zucchini. She had just put the garnishes on their salads of fresh greens with a homemade vinaigrette sprinkled with chunks of bleu cheese.

While waiting for the smoking chips to start smoking, Westley and Alex wandered back into the house and cut through the dining room on their way to the grand salon. "My God, what a gorgeous table setting!" exclaimed Westley. As always, Rosalie set a table that featured the Civil War-era Old Paris hand-painted porcelain china, Medallion coin silver flatware, early flint glass stemware, and silver-plate figural napkin rings. Lastly, a pair of period gilded bronze candelabras flanked a bouquet of fresh flowers in an Old Paris vase that Rosalie had arranged that morning.

The Penfields decorated the dining room with Victorian Renaissance Revival furniture circa 1867, one of their favorite styles. The ensemble includes two massive marble-top walnut sideboards, the best walnut pedestal banquet table, six Philadelphia rosewood chairs from David Norton's Cleveland estate, and an Alexander Roux rosewood one-of-a-kind china cabinet. Under the front window sits a Pottier & Stymus rosewood and gilded pier table. Alexander Roux and Pottier & Stymus were two preeminent New York City cabinetmaking and decorating firms that produced the most exquisite furniture for the wealthiest clients of the early post-Civil War Victorian era. The ornamented vaulted ceiling is hand-painted and stenciled in ten polychrome colors that are correct for the period. A deep, grape-colored, hand-printed wallpaper covers the walls. The room is lit by an elaborate, gilded, and electrified gasolier hanging over the table, with electrified gas sconces at each corner of the room.

Upon reaching the Grand Salon, Westley and Alex sat down to enjoy their cocktails. The room surrounds one in pre-civil war rosewood Rococo Revival furnishings made by the famous firm of John and Joseph Meeks of New York City.

Westley said, "Alex, I've always loved your collection of Meeks furniture! I read that the firm became a leading provider of the finest ornate, hand-carved, laminated Rococo Revival rosewood furniture that graced the interiors of the grandest homes of the antebellum era. Much of it was shipped down into the Deep South and furnished the most elegant plantation homes. It looks perfect in your Grand Salon!" Two-story-high custom-made silk draperies, deep green French-style hand-printed wallpaper, and a lavish crystal electrified gasolier bring the 1850s ambiance into the room. Rosalie's museum-quality rosewood Knabe square grand piano sits at the end of the room, ready for a concert.

"You probably know that besides buying, selling, and restoring this stuff, I love studying the symbology that appears in our decorative arts," Alex said.

"Yes, you have described that to me before. What have you discovered recently?" Westley asked. He was glad for the diversion from his problematic situation.

"You know the fabulous Victorian sideboard in the Cleveland Museum of Art? It's one of the most beautiful American Renaissance Revival pieces ever found. Hand-carved in walnut with a gorgeous brown marble-topped base and the most ornate backboard. Symbolism covers that piece from top to bottom. At the very top of the backboard, a raptor spreads its wings over the piece, which stands for strength, power, fierceness, and nobility. Below the raptor, grapes and leaves grace the top and sides of the backboard. The leaves symbolize fertility and growth, while the grapes represent prosperity, wealth, and abundance."

Alex continued, "The carved game animals are laid out in the middle of the backboard as if they were just brought in from a hunt. The deer, rabbits, and game birds represent providing a plentiful feast for the family. Additionally, the deer represents wealth and long life, and the rabbits symbolize hope. A carved arrangement of fruit is in the middle of the lower section of the backboard. It is a symbol of good health and love. As the saying goes, 'The fruits of hard work are delicious to taste.' Finally, recall the two carved Native Americans standing at the outer edges of the lower section of the backboard. They symbolize strength and protection, and look like they are guarding the piece!"

Westley admired Alex's knowledge of furniture and was mesmerized by the symbology Alex described. "I'll never look at another piece of furniture the same way."

Alex continued, "Four child-like caryatids are mounted on the vertical stiles around the face of the lower cabinet base. Caryatids are architectural elements carved to represent human figures that support building facades instead of columns. They also appear frequently as a design element in Victorian furniture. They represent those who carry sacred objects used in feasts of the gods. Lastly, the four carved dog heads that decorate the center of the doors on the base stand for the hunt, valued for their faithfulness and courage."

"Alex, I've stood in front of that cabinet probably 50 times and never interpreted the carvings like that. You are incredible! No wonder I am so in love with that piece." Westley was fascinated by his friend's analysis. "If I had seen that sideboard before the curator did, it would be sitting in my dining room. And you would be trying to buy it from me!"

Alex said, "Our collections contain many symbols, and I'm constantly discovering new ones in our furniture. Westley, there are countless symbols in your collection. You should take a close look and figure out the meaning of the icons. I can help you if you want. It will be a fun project if you're up to it."

Westley realized why his friend was in such high demand, consulting museums nationwide. And now he wondered what those frightening tattoos symbolized on the Russian thugs.

Rosalie had tasked the two men with grilling the quail. "C'mon, you two! You boys need to get those birds on the grill," was Rosalie's command. Another round of cocktails accompanied the completion of the savory task, and the Penfields and Westley sat down to dinner and engaging conversation. The main course followed Rosalie's exquisite salad. The Penfields and Westley were never short on topics, especially regarding collecting. They were always "talking shop" when it came to antiques.

"The quail was cooked to perfection, just wonderful. I love the potatoes galette and julienned vegetables," Wesley exclaimed. "You always know what to serve and how to present the meal. I don't know how you do it, Rosalie."

"Westley, I love to cook. It gives me great joy. We are so fortunate to have all of this, and it's fun to share it with you. You appreciate everything!"

The three lingered at the dinner table, taking in the classical music streaming in along with the candlelight that softly illuminated the room. Dinner was followed by cappuccino and Rosalie's homemade individual chocolate soufflés. However, something seemed to be troubling Westley. He was not in his usual chatty mood. Finally, Alex spoke, "Westley, what's bothering you? You are unusually quiet, not the happy guy we know. What's the matter? You can't still be that hungover."

Westley paused. He sipped a glass of his favorite brandy that the Penfields kept on hand just for him. Westley finally opened up with an extra bit of prodding by the Penfields. "I'm in real trouble. I played in a high-stakes poker game last night. The bastards set me up in a cheating scheme. I don't know exactly how they did it, but I lost my $50,000 grubstake and owe some terrifying guys $100,000. You know me, Alex. I am a far better card player than that, so I know they cheated. I'm low on cash right now. Those recent house renovations drained me. So, I'm trying to figure out how to raise the money." Westley was not about to tell them what they wanted. Nor did he want to tell Alex that he owed the money to Russian mobsters.

Alex looked over at Rosalie and winked at her. She knew what her generous husband was about to propose. "Westley, we can help you. I can get you the $100,000. We'll loan it to you, and you can put $100,000 worth of your antiques up for auction. You'll pay us back when they sell. And stop that goddamn high-stakes poker playing! We don't want to find out that you got yourself killed over some game!"

"Me too, Alex, me too."

Chapter 15

The dreaded Monday morning arrived, and Westley knew the Russians would be waiting to hear from him. After arriving at his office, he sat in his car in the parking lot, fearing what he knew he had to do. Finally, he dialed Volkov's number on his cell phone. Greeted in a Russian accent, "Doctor Engle, we were expecting to hear from you."

Westley replied, "Volkov, I have the $100,000. I can wire it over to you tomorrow."

"No, Doctor Engle. That is not what we want."

"Look, Volkov. I owe you cash, not a computer program. I swore an oath to protect my country, not to destroy it."

"I don't give a damn about your oath or your country! You'd better figure out how to get that to us today. What you need to worry about right now is paying your debt with that computer program. Your troubles are just beginning if you don't comply."

They argued back and forth for a few minutes. Then, finally, "You are going to give us what we want; otherwise, I hate to think what my men of the *Vor* will do to you. You will die a horrible death," Volkov growled in a menacing tone.

Terrified, Westley replied, "All right, I need to meet you at Huntington Beach Park in Bay Village. Meet me at the base of the windmill at 6 o'clock tonight. I will have the flash drive for you."

"Very good, Doctor Engle, we will be there. You have made a wise decision."

Westley was visibly shaken when he finally got out of his car. Thankfully, none of his colleagues saw him in the parking lot, as he was not in the mood for small talk. Stopping at the men's room, the doctor tried to compose himself before going to his office. The ominous call made him break out in a cold sweat, and his hands still shook when he splashed cold water on his face. He breathed deeply to get his heart to stop pounding so hard. *"Dear God, what have I done?!"*

Instead of taking the elevator, Westley walked slowly up the three flights of stairs and made the long walk down the corridor to his office. He sat down at his desk and put his head in his hands. Then, desperate and having failed in judgment, the engineer decided to do the unthinkable. He transferred the program from his mainframe computer onto a flash drive. Westley was horror-stricken by his action, making him feel sick to his stomach. He took the flash drive and placed it into his briefcase.

At 4:00 PM, Westley left his office, drove north up the Shoreway, and headed west out of downtown Cleveland, as he had done hundreds of times. The sight of Lake Erie provided him solace, and his troubled thoughts of the day took a short reprieve. "What a beautiful lake. I am so lucky to live here. I should learn to sail one of these days." As the Shoreway passes Don's Lighthouse, it turns into Clifton Boulevard, becoming a four-lane surface artery coursing through a commercial and residential neighborhood on Cleveland's west side. Continuing west on Clifton Boulevard, he entered Lakewood, with its lovely early 20th-century houses. Driving into Rocky River, the street narrows to two lanes and becomes Lake Road. Farther west, he enters Bay Village. Finally, approaching his beloved mansion, Westley pulled in through the ornate iron gate and drove into the free-standing garage behind the house.

In the comfort of his grand home, Westley freshened up, opened a couple of windows, and poured himself a snifter of his favorite brandy. He relished the sight of the lake and its breezes. "This is heaven." Then it hit him. His better judgment and conscience overwhelmed his thoughts. *"There is no way I'm going to let those bastards have that flash drive,"* he said to himself. He accepted that he would pay a very high price for his involvement with the Russians.

With only an hour before he was to meet the Russians, Westley went into action. His first impulse was to get the flash drive hidden. He took it out of his briefcase and hid it in one of his beloved pieces of furniture. With it safely tucked away, finding it will be nearly impossible.

"There's no way the bastards will find it here!" he exclaimed.

Then, he remembered the visit with the Penfields from the previous Saturday night. Alex described the symbolism in Victorian furniture, and it struck Westley with an idea. "Symbols!"

Westley dashed around the house, observing numerous carved details in his furniture collection. He made meticulous notes about the various carvings and symbols and, in his home office upstairs, booted up his computer. Quickly surfing the internet for background information on symbols, he hastily composed, typed, and printed a set of cryptic symbolic clues found on the selected pieces. Following the clues step by step, this document will serve as a map, enabling one to locate the flash drive, hopefully before the Russians discover it.

He ran back downstairs and turned over a favorite Rococo Revival rosewood leather-topped library table with a horizontal drawer. Westley placed the document pages of clues in a clasp mailing envelope, pulled out the drawer, and securely taped it to the underside of the top with duct tape. Then, he stood the table right-side up and inserted the drawer back into its place. With the table in its natural setting and the drawer closed, finding the flash drive would have been impossible without the document of clues. *"Maybe someone will find the flash drive before the Russians get it,"* he thought.

Just before 6 PM, Westley called Volkov on his cell phone.

"Yes, Doctor Engle?"

"I'm giving you one last chance to get your $100,000 back. I'm not giving you the flash drive, dishonoring my good name, or endangering my fellow man."

Volkov replied, "Without that flash drive, I promise you a very horrible death." It so happens that Volkov and Solkolov were driving on Lake Road to meet Westley at Huntington Beach and had just passed by Engle's home. They immediately turned around and, within minutes, drove up to the house. They dashed up onto his front portico and blasted through the front door. Westley was defenseless. The mild-mannered engineering doctor did not own any lethal weapons.

The Bay Village police were shooting down Lake Road at 70 miles per hour within minutes after Dr. Engle had tripped the alarm on his security system with his last wisp of life. The home had been ransacked, and the Russians had fled. Blood was splattered all over the foyer and front parlor. Poor Westley's body was sprawled out on the front parlor floor. Patrol officers Jake Caldwell and Steve Sheppard of the Bay Village police department were the first to enter the house through the smashed open front doorway with their Glock 22s drawn. Wearing their bulletproof vests with assorted accessories attached, they looked like a pair of U.S. Army soldiers ready for combat. The security system's siren was still screeching. Westley's lifeless, brutalized body made such a gruesome sight that Officer Caldwell had to step back outside to avoid vomiting. Just then, Westley's landline phone rang. Officer Sheppard answered, and it was a monitoring agent from Gilchrest Security Company calling. "This is Officer Steve Sheppard of the Bay Village police department. How do we turn off the burglar alarm? We have a break-in and murder here." The monitor provided Sheppard with the code numbers, which he entered, and he was able to deactivate the alarm.

Following standard protocol, Officer Sheppard called headquarters, requesting that the homicide detective on duty arrive at the scene of the murder. Within an hour, Detective Martin Schroeder of the Bay Village Police Department arrived at the mansion to assess the scene. He was appalled at the sight of the doctor's body and the condition of the house. He asked himself, *"What in the hell were they after?"*

Chapter 16

It was a sunny summer morning early in Alex Penfield's business career, and he needed a break from the office. At the time, he was the 27-year-old co-founder, marketing director, and 33% shareholder of a thriving multi-million-dollar Cleveland manufacturing business. The firm manufactured a line of energy conservation products for the home, sold through famous retailers. The products were timely, as America was in the midst of its historic energy crisis in the mid-1970s. Named Energy Systems, Inc., the firm was conveniently located on the near west side of town, making it easy to get to any location in the city. It was also conveniently located near Cleveland Hopkins International Airport, allowing for quick access to destinations outside of Ohio. One of Alex's favorite places to visit in his free time away from the office is the Cleveland Museum of Art.

Walking past the company's receptionist heading for the front door, "Jan, I'm scheduled this morning to attend a tour and lecture of the Cleveland Museum of Art's collection of American paintings and sculptures guided by one of their docents. I will have lunch there and be back in the office by 2:30." Alex had spent the earlier part of the week calling on customers in Minnesota and needed a break from the business.

"No problem, Alex. It's pretty quiet around here right now. Have a good time," replied Jan.

The Cleveland Museum of Art is one of Cleveland's great treasures. A renowned institution housing one of the world's significant collections opened on June 6, 1916, with one of its founders, Jeptha Wade II, proclaiming it "for the benefit of all people, forever."

The museum originated when industrialist Jeptha Wade Sr. began developing the farmland he owned, surrounding Doan Brook on the east side of Cleveland, into a public park in 1872. He donated over 63 acres to the city in 1882, becoming one of the most significant gifts of open land to the people of Cleveland. The city ultimately purchased additional acres, and in 1892, 75-

acre Wade Park became a central recreational area with picnic facilities, tennis courts, a lagoon, and ball fields. The park would ultimately be home to the Cleveland Museum of Natural History and the Cleveland Botanical Garden.

Wade's grandson, Jeptha Wade II, set aside land from the park to be the future location of the art museum, which was to be the centerpiece of Wade Park.

The museum and its world-renowned art collection were established, beginning with a donation of Jeptha Wade's 7,000-piece art collection and a $1 million endowment for future acquisitions. Hinman Hurlbut's extensive collection of artworks and $20,000 were donated after his wife's death in 1910. Upon his death also in 1910, Horace Kelly's estate donated $500,000 to construct a fireproof art gallery and art school. John Huntington amassed a fortune in the oil business alongside John D. Rockefeller, and those funds covered 70% of the museum's construction costs.

Unfortunately, only Jeptha Wade II would live to see the construction of the four men's dream. With an estimated $755 million endowment, the Cleveland Museum of Art is the fourth wealthiest art museum in the United States. The museum has always provided general admission free to the public.

Alex assembled with six other art lovers at the museum's reception desk. The group was to be led by a docent named Marcia Bernstein. A friendly woman who volunteered regularly, she was a middle-aged woman with gray hair pulled tightly back to form a bun. Conservatively dressed in a tasteful suit, she could have passed for a curator.

A single man who was always on the lookout for meeting young ladies, Alex was struck by the sight of a blue-eyed, auburn-haired young woman in the group. Her gorgeous hair draped to the middle of her back. She probably stood five feet ten inches tall. He exchanged eye contact with her as they strolled through the galleries, listening to Marcia's lecture. Not being a shy person, Alex struck up short conversations with the beautiful young woman on numerous occasions.

"By the way, my name is Alexander Penfield, and you are?"

"I'm Rosalie Hart."

"It's very nice to meet you, Rosalie!" Alex beamed with his radiant smile.

As the group strolled into Gallery 206, they beheld a collection of superb Victorian landscapes painted by the who's who of 19th-century American artists. Marcia led the group over to Frederic Church's remarkable work, "*Twilight in the Wilderness, 1860.*"

"Look at that gorgeous sky," Alex whispered to Rosalie.

The docent guided the group around the room to Thomas Cole's great work, "*View of Schroon Mountain, Essex County, New York.*"

"The fall colors are breathtaking, and again, look at that sky," whispered Rosalie. They both agreed that they viewed the familiar museum paintings in a new light, thanks to the docent's input on each work of art.

The museum tour was fascinating. The group enjoyed many more pieces, and dear Marcia chatted everyone's ears off. Throughout the circuit, Alex and Rosalie developed a good rapport.

As the group dispersed at the front desk, Alex turned to Rosalie, "I really enjoyed meeting you. Would you have lunch with me? My treat. I understand that the food here is pretty good."

Rosalie had also taken the day off. She heads the graphic arts department at Sherman & Mitchell Advertising Agency. "Sure, I'll bet we have both worked up an appetite viewing all that magnificent art," she said.

After going through the cafeteria line, they sat down to get to know each other over a lovely lunch. Alex had chosen the grilled hamburger with all the toppings, along with French fries, while Rosalie ordered a turkey panini and a salad. The conversation engaged both art lovers, and it quickly became clear that Alex and Rosalie were attracted to each other.

Alex said, "I am delighted to know you love Victorian decorative arts, Hudson River, and Impressionist paintings. I love them too and think they represent a kinder and gentler time."

Rosalie replied, "I agree. The Victorian era is so romantic." Rosalie was delighted to engage in an artful conversation with another like-minded enthusiast.

Two hours came and went quickly. Then, sharing a divine pastry dessert, cappuccinos, and good conversation, Alex asked, "I was wondering if you would join me for dinner on Saturday night? I know a great little French restaurant named Le Bistro. It's off Lorain Avenue near West 32nd St. in Ohio City. Have you ever eaten there?"

Fortunately for Alex, Rosalie was not dating anyone at the time. "No, I haven't. But I think that would be very nice. I love French cuisine," Rosalie replied.

"In our conversation, I never asked: Where do you live?"

"I own a condo in one of the old brick English Tudor buildings on Lake Road in Lakewood, just west of the border with Cleveland. It's called the Tudor Arms, and it was built in 1923. The building owner divided it into condos, and I purchased one three years ago. It's wonderful! It has nine-foot-tall ceilings and leaded glass window panels, and my side of the building overlooks the lake. It came with a balcony, and during the summer, I grow cherry tomatoes and an assortment of herbs because I love to cook. Where do you live, Alex?"

"I share a house on Lake Road in Bay Village with my business partner, Jim Ronson. He bought the house six years ago, and it also backs up to the lake. It's a large brick house built in 1918. With four bedrooms, it's plenty of space for two single guys. He's been divorced four times and has given up on marriage. We share the cleaning and food bills and get along just fine."

"How about I pick you up at, say, 6:15? I will make dinner reservations for 7:15, so we won't have to rush. I would love to come up and see your condo. It sounds beautiful."

On Saturday, Alex punctually arrived at Tudor Arms, was buzzed up, took the elevator to the seventh floor, and arrived promptly at Rosalie's door at 6:15, number 715. When Rosalie answered the door, Alex's breath was momentarily taken away. He beheld a gorgeous, statuesque lady wearing a beautiful halter-top dress. Rosalie's magnificent auburn red hair was in an updo with sweet pin curls framing her face. Catching his breath, he said, "You look beautiful tonight!"

"Thank you, Alex; come in!" she replied. "I remember you telling me how much you love antiques. It so happens that I have started a collection with a few pieces myself."

After a stroll through Rosalie's house, Alex exclaimed, "I enjoyed your house tour. It's beautiful, and what a view!"

Rosalie grabbed a wrap, and they headed off to dinner. Le Bistro is a charming, tiny eatery where the chefs prepare the dishes in the center of the restaurant. Wonderful cooking aromas envelop the patrons. The menu features authentic French cuisine, and the place could easily be located on a side street in Paris. The entrées were sumptuous, the conversation stimulating, and the couple realized how much they had in common. Alex was taken aback by Rosalie's smile and gorgeous blue eyes. Over a dessert of Crème brûlée and coffee, there was magic in the air.

After dinner, Alex drove the enchanted pair south on 32nd Street to Lorain Avenue, turned left onto 25th Street, and headed north to the Shoreway. It was a beautiful night, and the lake looked gorgeous. Then, they finally headed west into Lakewood and parked at the Tudor Arms. In the lobby, "I've had a wonderful time tonight, Alex! Come on upstairs. How about a cappuccino? We'll try out this new cappuccino maker that my sister bought me for Christmas," as they approached the elevator. But, of course, Alex couldn't say no.

The couple moved to the living room in Rosalie's condo and sat on her sofa to enjoy cappuccinos. Alex could no longer resist and gently brushed back Rosalie's curls, touching her cheek. Rosalie's heart raced like never before, and before long, they were embracing and passionately kissing. A short while later, they moved to the bedroom for a night of lovemaking. Alex stayed the night and awoke the following morning to the sight of the beautiful Rosalie, her auburn hair spread out on the pillow. He rolled over and kissed the back of her neck passionately. She was already awake, savoring the previous night. As she turned, their lips met, and they made love again. Alex inquired, "Do you have any regrets about last night, Rosalie?"

"Only that I wish we had met sooner. I've never felt this way about any other man."

"I'm flattered, Rosalie. I feel the same way about you."

That beautiful Saturday night marked the beginning of one of the greatest romances of all time. They discovered they had much in common, including a love of art, gardening, classic automobiles, antiques, travel, classical music, and many other shared interests. The couple spent many days together in art museums, botanical gardens, and classic car shows, and they traveled extensively for almost two years before getting married. Forty years later, they are more deeply in love with each new day.

Chapter 17

Alex and Rosalie Penfield were fellow Victorian decorative art collectors and close friends of the Engles. Both are physically fit for people in their 60s, exercising faithfully six days a week in their home gym. Rosalie stands tall at five feet ten, has deep blue eyes, and boasts a stunning figure with muscular, long legs. Her radiant, naturally wavy auburn red hair cascades beyond her shoulders, framing her flawless skin. Alex, who has a six-foot-one frame, is slightly overweight yet muscular, with dark brown eyes and hair. Thanks to their hairdressers, the couple appears far younger than their age due to the lack of gray hair. Their lifestyle philosophy is that of "fighting death."

Years ago, the outgoing couple met Westley and Melanie while attending a local antique auction. They became fast friends, sharing their passion for the hobby. Friendly competitors, the Penfields and Engles frequently compared notes on what treasures were coming up at the major auctions. Extravagant dinners were shared at each other's homes, as Melanie and Rosalie enjoyed a good-natured rivalry trying to out-cook each other. What treasure the other guy recently added to his collection was always a fun conversation. After his wife's death, Westley sometimes included a lady friend to make it a foursome, but his relationships were never serious. He was married to his work, and any passion he felt was only for improving his magnificent collection.

"Oh, my God! Rosalie! Come here! You won't believe what just came on TV!" shouted Alexander.

"What? What is it, Alex?!" Rosalie replied as she dashed in from her Victorian conservatory. She was clipping some fresh herbs for their dinner entrée while entertaining the neighbor's visiting cat, Callie. The next-door neighbor's adorable Calico cat often dropped by the Penfields' home to bask in some affection from the cat-less animal lovers and to nibble on some crunchy cat food that was always waiting for her. Alex was about to deliver some horrifying news, but paused to admire Rosalie's shapely figure in her tight shorts and halter top, looking as if she were still thirty. The sunlight beaming through the glass-paneled greenhouse silhouetted her body, accentuating all the right curves. Her auburn red hair tousled around her lean, muscular shoulders, which she had worked so hard to maintain.

They both sat down in shock to witness the broadcast on WKYC-TV, the local NBC affiliate. The news anchor was telling the story of Westley Engle's gruesome murder. The anchor said, "There's some alarming news out of Bay Village this evening. There was a violent break-in at the home of Doctor Westley Engle. The police divulged little information but revealed that intruders had ransacked the house. All we know right now is that Doctor Engle was viciously murdered. He was a computer engineer and owned a firm named Science Technologies. We'll have more information at 11."

Trembling, "I can't believe it!" Rosalie sobbed. "How could anyone hurt dear Westley? And to think he was just here for dinner last Saturday!" They were shocked by their friend's violent death and the video of Westley's beautiful house ransacked and trashed. It was hard to imagine anyone brutally killing Westley and viciously vandalizing his home.

"I think I'll make us a couple of drinks," Alex suggested. After a few sips of strong vodka and tonic cocktails, they looked at each other. Then, holding back tears, Alex asked, "What in the hell were they looking for?"

The 11 o'clock news revealed more gruesome details discovered inside the magnificent home by the lake. Naturally, the police omitted facts that might lead to the killer or killers, which only the perpetrators would know. Alex and Rosalie tossed and turned in bed, experiencing a fitful night of sleep. Finally, they embraced, held each other tight, and fell into slumber until the sunlight woke them around 7:00 AM.

Rosalie and Alex's life together is magical, as they share everything in common. Alex is a passionate fan of Rosalie's exquisite cooking, and they both exercise intensely. The couple shares identical political views. Although they both love children, they have never wanted any of their own. They enjoy classical music, art, history, and museums, and they have a great passion for collecting Victorian decorative arts. They revel in a loving life built around healthy mutual respect. Alex has always said, "Although we are married, I prefer to describe our relationship as being in a very intense love affair."

Their passion for antique collecting began in the first year of their marriage while visiting Virginia. The first antique they purchased together was a lovely Victorian mahogany étagère, a type of furniture created by the Victorians to display valuable decorative objects. This marked the beginning of a great adventure.

Shortly after that, Alex and Rosalie purchased their first home together in Cleveland Heights, a near-eastern Cleveland suburb. It sits on an elevated area above Cleveland, six miles east of downtown.

Rosalie searched extensively for the perfect house. Finally, they were delighted to purchase a circa 1898 Victorian Queen Anne-style house on Compton Avenue, which was ideal for their burgeoning collection. With a wrap-around front porch and turret, it featured 14 rooms and was constructed on three levels with nine-foot ceilings, solid quarter-sawn oak floors, doors, and moldings. The house also included two ornate fireplace mantels adorned with imported ceramic tiles and carved oak figures. The Penfields spent seven years and hundreds of hours lovingly restoring the house, room by room. They steamed off old Victorian-era wallpaper and repaired cracked plaster walls. New reproduction Victorian-style wallpaper has been reinstalled. Alex created a Victorian-themed kitchen for Rosalie's emerging cooking skills and installed modern bathrooms, a necessary update for any old house.

While living in Cleveland Heights, the Penfields befriended fellow Victorian antique lovers Steve and Joan Schmidt, who lived across the street on Compton Avenue. Long ago, the Schmidts invited Alex and Rosalie to join them at an antique auction in Lakewood, where an antique dealer was liquidating his inventory. The Penfields became captivated by the excitement when they attended their first auction! Alex would later describe it as an incredible adrenaline rush, especially just before bidding on a piece.

The Penfields became so enamored with the Victorian era and customs that they created a tradition of hosting Victorian-era Christmas parties while living in Cleveland Heights. Most of their friends also loved the period and enthusiastically attended. Guests were required to dress formally in attire appropriate for the Victorian period. The soiree typically began at around 7:00 PM with a champagne reception and socializing. A string trio of college music students serenaded the guests with classical music. Everyone felt as though they had been transported back to the 19th century! One year, the Penfields hired a young actress to perform a short two-act Christmas play on the balcony overlooking the front parlor. Authentic entertainment at the party was essential to Alex and Rosalie, and it made the guests feel as if they had genuinely stepped back in time. A party like this could not be complete without an impersonator dressed as Santa Claus, appearing to the delight of all the guests! Coincidentally, Santa had small gifts for everyone tucked inside his enormous bag.

Rosalie leveraged her considerable culinary talents and spent weeks planning the menu, from hors d'oeuvres to dessert, including a five-course dinner. She and Alex "tested" many of the delicacies in advance to ensure everything was just right. A few days before the party, Alex opened the dining room table, and Rosalie set it for fourteen. She brought out her best lace tablecloths, linens, antique china, silverware, and stemware. She created a large floral arrangement for the table using seasonal greenery and fragrant, festive flowers. Next, Alex draped pine roping over the oak doorways and up the stairway hand railing, decorating the aromatic foliage with antique glass Christmas ornaments.

Alex summoned the guests to the table around 9:00 PM. The Penfields always retained a young lady to serve dinner, allowing the two hosts to enjoy the company of their friends and the elegant table setting. The atmosphere was magical, with dimmed lights and dinner served by candlelight. The feast typically lasted three hours, and finally, the hostess served a dessert of chocolate soufflé, eliciting everyone's oohs and ahs. After dinner, the insatiable guests sipped liqueurs to cap off the affair.

The party continued all night, and the last guests left around 4:00 AM. Naturally, everyone talked about the party for months afterward!

Rosalie and Alex experienced business success at a young age in manufacturing, commercial art, and marketing. Later, they became professional investors.

After seven years in Cleveland Heights, the Penfields bought a larger, 5,000-square-foot modern home in Gates Mills, a community in the Chagrin Valley, forty miles east of Cleveland.

Gates Mills was founded in 1826 by Holsey Gates, who purchased 130 acres of land along the Chagrin River from the Connecticut Land Company to secure an adequate water supply for a sawmill. The excellent location and plentiful water supply from the Chagrin River resulted in the construction of several more mills, which gave the area its name.

After the mills closed, no new industry entered the area, leaving it a quiet, bucolic hamlet. Now a leafy town with steep hills spilling into the Chagrin River below and winding, narrow roads, the tranquil township is home to classical-style buildings. Most houses are painted white with black shutters, almost as if it were a local ordinance.

As history buffs and lovers of Victoriana, the Penfields spent their vacations touring over 400 historic house museums worldwide. They amassed a vast library of research books on 19th-century decorative arts. These tours and research provided the background for the couple to create and install historically accurate Victorian-style rooms in their new home to display their collection. Achieving this in a modern house was made possible by contemporary wiring, plumbing, and drywall.

Alex became a master woodworker after studying the trade in college. He crafted custom cherry cabinets for Rosalie's Victorian-style kitchen. All 18 rooms showcase ornate, period-correct millwork and doors. Decorated with elaborate plaster ceilings, hand-painted frescoes, and cornices, the house impresses visitors. Silk-screened wallpaper and antique lighting fixtures hang throughout, completing the authentic look.

Over the years, the Penfields developed an educated eye for the finest Victorian antiques, traveling throughout the country to acquire them. They could afford any object that suited their taste and complemented their collection. Like Westley Engle, they created a complete environment with high-quality furniture, silver, porcelain, glass, lighting, and paintings. Well-known in collecting circles, Alex and Rosalie have amassed one of the country's most outstanding collections of Victorian decorative arts, comprising over 3,000 objects.

They grieved over their friend Westley Engle's death, always thinking of him when they saw beautiful treasures he would have liked. They missed him and Melanie, their shared dinners, and the friendly competition they had in finding antiques. They wondered what scum could have brutally slaughtered their dear friend. And why?

Chapter 18

At 9:00 PM Chicago time, the phone rang at Stephen and Margaret Engle's home. "Hello?" Stephen Engle answered.

"Mr. Engle, this is Detective Martin Schroeder of the Bay Village, Ohio, police department. I am sorry to call at this hour, sir, but I have terrible news. Your son, Westley Engle, was murdered earlier this evening. We searched his premises to determine the next of kin to notify and found your contact information in his wallet. We also have the contact information for his attorney, Janet Meyers, whom we will contact after we finish speaking."

Truly shaken and struggling to hold back tears, he paused and asked, "Oh my God, who in the world would do this to my son? What happened? Do you have any idea who may have done this?"

"No, sir. The event occurred just a few hours ago, and we are just starting our investigation. It appears that there was a break-in at his home by more than one intruder, based on the number of different footprints found. There was a struggle, and we presume that your son set off the burglar alarm just before passing away. Two officers were dispatched to his house and arrived within minutes, but the perpetrators had already left. I arrived at the scene shortly after that. I will be in touch with you once I have gathered more information. The county coroner has been called in, and after he performs his preliminary investigation at the scene, your son's body will be transported to the county morgue. I know you will need to speak with his attorney, but please give me half an hour to talk with her before you call."

"Officer Schroeder, you have been very kind. My wife and I are crushed by this terrible news. I expect to hear from you soon," replied Engle.

Detective Schroeder immediately called Janet Meyers, Westley's estate attorney, on her cell phone. She was home, relaxing with her husband in their family room while watching television. It was 10:15 PM in Cleveland.

"Hello, this is Janet Meyers."

"Ms. Meyers, this is Detective Martin Schroeder of the Bay Village police department. Do you have a client named Westley Engle?"

"Yes, I do represent Doctor Engle. How can I help you?" she replied.

"I am sorry to be calling you at this hour, but I must contact you with some bad news. Doctor Engle was murdered earlier this evening. We located your contact information in his wallet."

Janet sat straight up, was visibly shaken, and asked, "Oh, my God, what happened?"

"I cannot tell you very much because we have just started our investigation, but it looks like he was the victim of two intruders who broke into his home. The house was ransacked, he was attacked, and it appears Doctor Engle set off his burglar alarm. Two of our patrolmen arrived within minutes to witness a terrible sight. I contacted his parents in Chicago; of course, they were shocked by this awful news. After his preliminary investigation, the coroner will have his body transported to the county morgue for the family's disposition," replied Detective Schroeder.

Shortly after the call from Detective Schroeder, Janet received a call from Westley's father, Stephen.

"Oh, Janet, I don't know how much more Margaret and I can take of this bad news! First, there was the tragic death of his wife, Melanie, and now Westley. He was our only son and will be missed terribly. Would you be kind enough to assist us in arranging a funeral and burial? "

"Of course, Mr. Engle. I am Westley's estate attorney. Years ago, he and Melanie hired me to do their estate planning and wills. Their wills grant me authority, and I would be willing to arrange a funeral and the interment of his remains. I will stay in touch and let you know when I have scheduled a funeral. I knew Westley and Melanie well, and I cannot tell you how sorry I am for this terrible event to befall us."

A fit woman in her thirties, Janet is attractive and slim, with deep brown eyes and shoulder-length dark blond hair. She and her husband of eight years are the proud parents of a son, Noah, and a daughter, Ava. Her husband, Matthew, comes from a Hungarian family with a long-standing connection to Cleveland. He is handsome, with dark hair, brown eyes, and olive skin. An executive at Sherwin-Williams' downtown offices, he oversees the company's worldwide production of paint products.

Just as she finished her conversation with Stephen Engle, Janet and Matthew glanced at the television. The 11 PM news on WEWS Channel 5 came on.

"Breaking News! Local engineer brutally murdered in his home in Bay Village!" That got their attention. "Local computer engineer Doctor Westley Engle was found brutally murdered in his home in Bay Village this evening. Early indications are that around 6 PM tonight, the front door was broken open, and one or more intruders murdered Engle. Bay Village police are close-lipped about the motive, but rumors are that robbery was not a motive but that the crime was a murder for hire. The home has been sealed under a 24-hour police guard while authorities process the crime scene."

Janet turned to Matthew and exclaimed, "I worked with him and his wife on their estate planning. It was tragic enough losing his wife to that drunken driver, but now this!"

She had been fond of Westley and Melanie, and the shock of the brutal murder made her shudder. Sleep would evade her that night.

Janet rose early the following day and got herself ready, knowing she was in for a long, anxiety-filled day. She started her Mercedes, sped down Shaker Boulevard from their home in Shaker Heights, headed west towards downtown, and arrived at the office by 7:00 AM sharp. After brewing a pot of coffee, Janet poured a cup, went to her files, and retrieved her copy of Westley's will. It named her the executor of his estate, just as she had remembered. Getting to work immediately, she needed to prepare the necessary documents for submission to the Cuyahoga County Superior Court, which opened at 8:00 AM.

She then contacted the Bay Village police and requested a copy of the crime report as soon as it became available.

Janet made copies of Westley's will, confirming her as the executor of his estate. Next, she sat down at her computer and retrieved the document from her file that requests the court to issue a "Letter of Authority," granting her, the executor, legal authority to act on behalf of the estate. Lastly, as stipulated in Westley's will, Janet prepared a separate petition requesting that the court immediately grant her the authority to hire 24-hour security for the house to protect the high-value contents.

With the three documents carefully stapled in their blue covers, Janet arrived at the Cuyahoga County courthouse at 8:00 AM sharp. "You're here early, counselor," Judy, the court bailiff, said.

"Good morning, Judy. Did you hear the news about the engineer doctor who was murdered in Bay Village last night? That gentleman was my client. It's awful! Can you please get these documents on his honor's docket this morning? This situation is an emergency. I need to secure the decedent's house. I would greatly appreciate your help."

"Oh, Lordy! I saw that on the news. It's terrible. I will take care of that for you immediately," Judy replied. Janet sat in the honorable James O'Reilly's court to wait for her turn on the docket. Finally, at 9:00 AM, his honor stepped onto the bench. Everyone rose, then sat and waited for their turn in court.

At 10:00 AM, the bailiff called up the matter of Westley Engle, and Janet stepped forward. "Your Honor, as executor of the estate of Doctor Westley Engle, I request that the court grant a Letter of Authority so that I may act in certain matters on behalf of the decedent. In the documents, I also request that the court grant me the authority to procure 24-hour security for the decedent's home once the police have released the house to me. It contains a substantial number of valuable articles. We need this protection immediately until an auctioneer can be retained to liquidate such contents. At that point, the auctioneer will immediately move the contents to his gallery."

His honor looked over the documents, determined they were in order, and said, "Counselor, I grant your motions. Good luck."

"Thank you, Your Honor."

Janet knew a dependable security company that was perfect for providing 24-hour protection for Westley's home. They were an established firm with an excellent reputation, and many of their employees were active or former police officers. She hired them immediately to take over the house's security while the police finished processing the scene.

After the police finished their work, Janet hired a crew to come in, clean the house, repair the front door, and restore everything to order.

Westley's will specified cremation for his body upon his death, and his ashes were to be interred with his beloved Melanie. Janet hired the Wilkinson Crematory, located in the flats near the Cuyahoga River, to retrieve Westley's remains from the county coroner.

The next day, she retrieved his ashes, and although she was used to dealing with death in her clients' families, Janet was still shocked by Westley's terrible murder. She cared for Westley and admired his talent as a brilliant computer engineer.

By the end of that day, Janet had arranged the funeral. A notice appeared in the newspaper obituaries, but everyone already knew because of media coverage. Two days later, on the day of the funeral, at least 100 people attended, thanks to Westley's long-standing involvement in the engineering and antique collecting communities. Since the Engles owned burial niches at Lake View Cemetery, Janet was able to reserve the renowned Wade Memorial Chapel for the service.

Westley's father, Stephen, eulogized him, and it was all he could do to hold himself together.

At the end of his eulogy, Stephen said, "Westley was easy to raise, a brilliant young man, did everything expected of him, got good grades, and became a fine engineer. His mother and I were overjoyed at his meeting and marrying Melanie. Her death brought such heartbreak to Westley and our family. Westley's tragic death has again brought terrible sorrow to my wife and me." Unable to speak any longer, he shuffled to his seat in complete distress.

Alex and Rosalie tried to comfort Westley's parents but found themselves so overwhelmed by the tragedy of Westley's murder that they were at a loss for words. The couple wondered if the perpetrators were disguised as mourners at the memorial service, slipping around the crowd to appear innocent. Keeping a watchful eye out for the police, suspecting they might attend Westley's funeral looking for clues and suspects, the Penfields couldn't identify anyone who resembled cops. Maybe they had watched too many crime dramas on TV.

Janet organized a funeral reception in one of the ballrooms at the Radisson Hotel in Beachwood. Every detail was flawless, just as Westley would have arranged. He would have cringed at some of the attendees, but most were friends and collectors he would have been glad to see.

Westley's will specified that his home and possessions be liquidated, with the proceeds entrusted to the Cleveland Foundation. Since he and Melanie had no heirs, the proceeds were to remain as principal in perpetuity. The income generated from the interest and capital gains of that principal would be divided equally among the Cleveland Museum of Art, Western Reserve Historical Society, Cleveland Metro Parks, and the Conservancy for the Cuyahoga National Park, which were Melanie and Westley's favorite charities.

The Cleveland Foundation, based in Cleveland, is the world's first community foundation and remains one of the largest today, with assets totaling $2.5 billion and annual grants exceeding $100 million. Founded in 1914 by banker Frederick Harris Goff, the Cleveland Foundation partners with donors to enhance the lives of residents in Cuyahoga, Lake, and Geauga counties, both now and for future generations. The foundation distributes grants from over 800 funds, representing individuals, families, organizations, and corporations. Melanie and Westley had finished their homework, not realizing that their final wishes would come true sooner than they expected.

Janet arranged to meet Wilson Stengel, a compassionate funeral director, at Lake View Cemetery in Cleveland the day after the funeral. While driving there, she thought to herself that she had met the kindest people in the funeral business. They are always soft-spoken, friendly, helpful, and perhaps grateful for dealing with a living person.

She arrived at Lake View Cemetery's main office near the entrance on Euclid Avenue. "Mr. Stengel, I appreciate your locating the granite niche that belongs to Dr. and Mrs. Engle." She selected a burial urn in the showroom for Westley's ashes. "I entrust you with Dr. Engle's ashes for interment. Please mail the bill for the urn and the niche opening to my attention," she said.

Chapter 19

"SOLD! To Alex Penfield!" Ah, the call of the auctioneer and the slam of the hammer, securing the bid on a stunning antique. The adrenaline rush — there's nothing like it!

Rosalie and Alexander have enjoyed many wonderful experiences in assembling their collection. Collecting has been a key part of their lifestyle for over forty years. During that time, they acquired pieces from a variety of sources. They purchased items from other collectors, dealers, heirs, garage sales, estate sales, antique shows, and auctions. Throughout history, couples who share a passion for a hobby have always worked together to build a significant collection. Although the Penfield collection is mature, top in quality and quantity, it remains a lively work in progress, now progressing at a slower pace.

During their collecting career, Rosalie and Alex have been connected to the antique business nationwide through various leading antique trade magazines they receive on a weekly basis. At this point in their collecting journey, they are especially interested in what is available for sale at auction, as many important works of art are bought there. Newspapers are a valuable resource for collectors to find notices of major auctions. Although all publications have their content online, Alex is old school and prefers to read printed copies.

On Friday nights, he follows a weekly ritual of sitting at the kitchen table with a vodka and tonic, going through the papers page by page. He stays informed about antique business news and knows everything that will soon be up for auction. Despite being old-fashioned, Alex happily receives email notices from his favorite auction houses to tempt him online.

Alex discovers something in the papers that he and Rosalie believe could be a great addition to their collection. In that case, he contacts the auction house, requests a condition report, and registers to bid if the piece is approved. Usually, the Penfields bid by phone, a service offered by most auction houses for out-of-town bidders. When the piece they registered to bid on comes up, one of the auctioneer's bidding agents contacts them by phone. The bidding agent places bids for the Penfields as if they are in the auction gallery during the bidding. All lots in an auction are sold in numerical order.

If they are the winning bidder for the item, they perform another fun ritual: acquiring it and transporting it home themselves. The Penfields have always had a trailer hitch on every new car they purchased. Half the fun is going out into this beautiful country, picking up their treasure, and bringing it home in a trailer if needed.

Rosalie and Alex received an email reminder about Joshua Williams's annual "The Fabulous Auction," which is happening in two weeks. Attending in person at that auction is definitely one of the Penfields' favorite ways to find great treasures and enjoy a fun day.

Located in Tupelo, Mississippi, Joshua Williams is a second-generation auctioneer who runs a successful auction business with his wife, Julie, of thirty years, and their three sons.

He started his career as a child working for his father's auction business in Georgia, where they sold livestock, farm equipment, land, buildings, and estates that included antiques. Josh learned the trade from the ground up, moving furniture, running errands, and helping call out bidders.

When the time was right, Josh pulled up stakes and moved his family to Mississippi to start his own auction business. He named his company Josh Williams Auctions and bought a large modern metal building on the outskirts of Tupelo. Over time, Josh began to focus on selling high-end antiques. He usually schedules three or four auctions each year, offering a variety of imported, lower-quality "container furniture and antiques."

Like the Penfields and the Engles, Josh has a passion for Victorian decorative arts, especially furniture. The highlight at Josh Williams Auctions is what Josh calls "The Fabulous Auction." It happens once a year and lasts one day, featuring at least 500 lots of the best "museum-quality" Victorian-era items. Throughout the year, Williams travels across the country to buy entire estates that include top Victorian pieces for auction. Everything is transported to his gallery in Tupelo using his fleet of trucks. His staff then sorts, cleans, and displays the auction items artfully. The result showcases the best of what Josh has collected nationwide, and the sale will include furniture, lamps, chandeliers, paintings, and other elegant pieces.

Josh's wife, Julie, manages the photography and personally uploads the merchandise scheduled for auction on their website. She then designs a beautiful, full-color brochure that highlights the items for sale. They spend generously on printing and mailing it to thousands of collectors. Finally, she creates a full-color, two-page notice advertising the auction to be published in at least four top antique trade papers. News of their sale always attracts significant interest. All of this takes her weeks to complete.

"The Fabulous Auction" is unique because participation requires being there in person; there are no phone or internet bids. The only other way to take part in the sale is to submit an advance absentee bid. A collector decides the highest amount he is willing to pay for an item. He then submits the bid in writing before the auction begins. The absentee bidder wins the piece if no one bids higher than that amount during the sale.

It doesn't matter that Josh's auction takes place in semi-rural northern Mississippi. Due to its popularity, collectors travel by plane or car from all over the country to attend. It's common to have 350 registered bidders from more than 35 states participating in his sale. The excitement starts on Friday afternoon, before the auction, known as "the preview." Prospective buyers arrive at the gallery and examine each item thoroughly. They spend hours deciding what to bid on at the auction. A lot of chatter flows among participants. Acquaintances meet again, friends gather, and an atmosphere of excitement fills the air.

Alex and Rosalie always drive to this auction because they refuse to fly. Naturally, they join the preview with everyone else. They've logged thousands of miles flying during their business careers, and those days are behind them. For them, half the fun is getting there.

The Penfields work as a team in Josh's gallery, examining everything scheduled for auction on Saturday. Since the gallery is open all day on Friday, everyone has plenty of time to see the items for sale. There is also time to chat with other collectors. Alex and Rosalie ran into Tim and Mary Foster, a lovely couple from St. Louis who share the Penfields' strong passion for Victoriana. The Fosters own a four-story, circa-1865 brownstone in downtown St. Louis.

It's good to see you folks again! So, what are you thinking of bidding on?" Alex asked.

Mary Foster replied, "I want to see us get the six-piece Belter Rosalie parlor set. We are looking for a good parlor set for the front parlor. How about you folks?"

"Oh, we are excited about the P&S parlor cabinet," replied Rosalie. "There is also an excellent Renaissance Revival gasolier over there that we might chase."

After several minutes of chatting about the ongoing projects at their homes, the Penfields and Fosters went their separate ways, continuing to peruse the gallery.

The Penfields primarily focused on the exquisite Renaissance Revival parlor cabinet. It had few functions, except for displaying valuable objects that showcased the owner's wealth and taste. The cabinetmakers designed such pieces to reflect the homeowner's affluence and style.

The cabinet was made in the factory of Pottier & Stymus, a well-known New York City cabinetmaking company. It produced its best work around

1865, during the Civil War era. Auguste Pottier was born in central France and apprenticed with a wood sculptor as a young man. He was 24 years old in 1847 when he left Paris to take a job with E.W. Hutchings & Son in the United States. In 1856, he became a general foreman at Rochefort & Skarren, a cabinetmaking business in New York City, where he met William Stymus, the upholstery foreman. In 1859, with only $1,000 invested between them, they founded Pottier & Stymus.

During the 1860s, New York City was the center of high-style Victorian decorating. Leading cabinetmaking firms, such as Herter Brothers and Charles Boudoine, expanded into interior decorating, creating complete suites for wealthy clients. Pottier & Stymus became a key player in manufacturing high-quality, costly furniture in historical revival styles, including Neo-Grec, Renaissance Revival, Egyptian Revival, and Gothic Revival. The firm crafted hand-carved furniture using expensive woods, decorated with gold-filled incising, ebonizing, ivory inlay, mother-of-pearl, and gilt bronze fittings like plaques, sculpted busts, and rosettes.

By 1875, Pottier & Stymus had established itself as one of the leading cabinetmaking firms in the United States. They decorated the homes of some of the wealthiest citizens and made over $1.1 million in profit that year, a huge amount at the time, and employed 700 men and 50 women.

The cabinet upcoming at the auction features rare Brazilian rosewood veneer and is decorated with hand-cut, French-made marquetry panels. Gold-filled incising runs throughout the piece. A pair of bronze, gold-washed sculpted busts of the goddess Columbia flank each end of the cabinet. When displayed in the home of a very wealthy family, it was an expensive piece to produce.

Despite the Penfields' many years of participating in auctions, Alex had trouble sleeping on Friday night because of his excitement. On Saturday morning, the day of the auction, the Penfields followed their usual ritual to get ready by having a big breakfast of eggs, hash browns, grits, toast, and juice at the local Waffle House. The excitement was thick in the air when they arrived at Josh's, building up as the auction approached. Every bidder was required to register with the auction company and was given a bidder's number along with a page of terms and sale conditions.

In the gallery's center, Josh and his crew set up seating for 300 people, which quickly filled with bidders and spectators. All around, the gallery overflowed with even more people. The atmosphere was electric with excitement. The 500 magnificent Victorian-era objects to be sold that day crowded the sides, rear, and front. At 10:00 AM sharp, Josh stepped up to the raised podium at the front of the gallery, and the crowd noise dropped to a murmur as he explained the terms of the sale.

"First of all, thank you all for traveling from across the country to attend the auction. I believe we have attendees from at least 23 states! Everything is sold as-is, where-is. At the end of the sale, payment is due before you remove any items." He finished explaining the terms of the sale and then began the auction. His way of calling the auction is a traditional rolling cadence.

He started the auction, and bidding proceeded swiftly and intensely. Prices climbed above normal due to the exceptional quality and rarity of the items, not to mention the fierce competition among collectors eager to win. An exquisite marquetry parlor table that might sell for $3500 elsewhere went for over $5000, and the buyer was ecstatic. Everything that day fetched a premium because if someone traveled to get there, they wouldn't let it go to someone else. That was Josh's tactic. The Penfields enjoyed themselves; this was their kind of auction, and they felt right at home. They claimed a spot to sit and watch the action, which happened to be a pair of Belter armchairs. Alex rarely sat down, as he was busy exploring the gallery, chatting with other collectors, examining furniture, and following the auction action.

While exploring the gallery during the auction, Alex came across Dave Petrocelli. He is a respected collector, a tall, dark, and handsome man of Italian heritage. He lives in upstate New York and owns a stunning Victorian mansion. His decorative arts collection includes one of the largest collections of Belter Cornucopia parlor furniture in the country.

He also enjoyed prowling the gallery during the auction. The two men simply couldn't sit still.

"Hey Dave, I knew we would run into you here! How are you doing?" asked Alex.

Dave answered, "I'm fine. You know I would never miss Josh's auction. What are you and Rosalie after?"

"We're after the P&S parlor cabinet. I really like that piece. It would fill out our collection of Renaissance Revival furniture in our east parlor," replied Alex. "How about you? Anything catch your eye?"

"Not really, but you never know. I may jump on something at the last second," Dave replied.

The two collectors parted company for the time being. As the day progressed, many more conversations would follow.

Several hours into the sale, it was time to auction off the P&S parlor cabinet. Alex felt a jolt of electricity, as if he'd just stuck his finger into an electrical outlet. That's the adrenaline rush that courses through the body when about to compete with other collectors. Josh described the piece, "We have a fabulous Pottier and Stymus parlor cabinet that is one of the best I have ever seen!" Auctioneers always claim a piece is the best they have ever seen. After a lengthy description, he said, "It's from circa 1865, and I have an absentee bid of $25,000. Do I have $27,500?" Bidding at this level increases by $2,500 increments. Six hands immediately shot up. "Yes!" called out by the bidding assistants working the crowd.

Alex and Rosalie's approach is to let the audience "run." That is, wait for the bidding to reach what could be its highest point and then step in.

"Do I have $30,000? Yes! $32,500? Yes!" It goes on and on.

"45,000? Yes! $47,500? Yes! $50,000? Yes!"

The bidding pushed the price above the estimate, but Alex and Rosalie weren't surprised. "$55,000? Yes!"

They were being swept up just like everyone else. Alex's heart was about to explode in his chest as the bidding went so fast. At this level, the increment jumped to $5,000 per bid.

"Do I have $60,000?" Someone's hand went up. "Yes!" yelled the bidding assistant.

The bidding paused, and Josh was about to slam the hammer down when Alex raised his hand and bid aloud, "$65,000!" Josh looked out at the crowd and said, "Alex, I'll protect you on that. I will not take a bid for less than $70,000. Do I have a bidder?" No takers.

Silence filled the gallery floor. Alex and Rosalie held their breath. He slammed his hammer down. "Sold to Alexander Penfield for $65,000!"

The crowd erupted into loud applause and cheers. Alex stood and took a bow to the audience. Josh glanced at Julie and gave her a wink and a smile. The sale of the cabinet to the Penfields was the highest-priced lot of the day.

With the 15% buyer's premium, the standard fee Josh's auction house charged for buying a piece, the Penfields paid $74,750 for the Pottier & Stymus parlor cabinet.

Alex could hear his unenlightened friends ask, "You paid what for that?!" Everyone in the high-end antique world admired his fortitude and envied his pocketbook.

Chapter 20

Knowing that the Penfields planned to attend Josh's auction, their close friends Ned Samuels and Jeffrey Martinsen asked them to bid on a pair of very rare John Henry Belter Cornucopia Pattern armchairs and two side chairs for them. Dating back to the 1850s, the Belter Cornucopia Pattern is the rarest, most ornate, and most valuable Victorian rosewood laminated parlor furniture. The boys needed a pair of armchairs and side chairs to complete their parlor suite.

The Cornucopia Pattern parlor furniture commands the highest prices on the collector's market because Belter produced it in limited quantities. It is large, heavy, and most importantly, elaborately hand-carved. His best artisans crafted each piece individually. Although the Cornucopia Pattern is recognized as a distinct pattern, every piece is unique and varies from one suite to another. It must have been very costly to produce; therefore, it was made for the wealthiest clients.

During his travels, Joshua Williams assembled an entire collection of Belter Cornucopia parlor furniture from various sources. He intended to auction off a pair of armchairs, a sofa, and four side chairs. The auction was set to be very exciting! It was a rare opportunity to see such a large set of the coveted Cornucopia furniture pattern come up for sale. In over 40 years of collecting high-end Victorian decorative arts, Ned, Jeffrey, and the Penfields all agreed this was extraordinary. Alex assured his friends that he would carefully examine the furniture and report on its condition before placing any bids.

Everyone had gathered around the Belter Cornucopia furniture, speculating about the potential value of the pieces. There was sure to be spirited bidding.

Late in the auction, Josh announced that the Cornucopia Belter furniture would be coming up for bidding. Suddenly, the excitement level in the gallery rose several decibels. Rosalie grabbed her smartphone and called Ned and Jeffrey. They answered and put their call on speakerphone so both could hear the action. Rosalie would relay the bids to the boys, while Alex placed the bids on their behalf.

"We're going to auction the Cornucopia Belter with the sofa first, then the two armchairs, and lastly, the four side chairs," exclaimed Josh. Then, in his cadence, "What do you give for the sofa? Do I hear $100,000?"

"$30,000!" came from the audience. It was the first bid.

"$40,000?" "Yes!" shouted another bidder.

"$50,000?" "Yes!"

"60,000?" "Yes!" It seemed as though it wouldn't stop.

"$70,000?" "Yes!"

Then it started to slow, but Josh asked, "$80,000?" "Yes!"

"Do I have $90,000?" "Yes!" Then it stopped. "Sold for $90,000 to my collector in Natchez! Glad to see that the piece will stay in the South!" The audience gave an enthusiastic round of applause.

"Okay! Next, we will sell the pair of armchairs. The bid will be two times the money. We will auction an armchair, and since there are two chairs, it will be two times the winning bid."

"All right, guys, here we go!" exclaimed Rosalie.

In his cadence, Josh asked, "Do I have $50,000?"

"I'll go $10,000!" Alex shouted the first bid, too excited to wait for anyone else to open the bidding.

"$20,000?" "Yes!" from another bidder.

"$30,000?" "Yes!" yelled Alex. It started to slow.

"$35,000?" After a pause, "Yes!" from another bidder.

The noise in the audience was at a roar. "Do I have $40,000?"

At this point, the boys were having trouble hearing Rosalie. Pausing, Josh looked at Rosalie and Alex as she yelled into the phone at the top of her lungs, "$40,000! Yes or no!" Alex and Rosalie glanced around to see that everyone in the audience had stopped talking and was looking at them with wide eyes.

The boys yelled back over the phone, "Yes!"

Alex raised his hand and shouted, "Yes!"

The bidding stopped, and after a pause, Josh exclaimed, "Sold to the boys in DC!" Again, the audience erupted into a loud round of applause.

At this point, Josh asked, "Since you are the winning bidders for the armchairs, do you want one or both of them?"

"We will take both," replied Alex. So, Ned and Jeffrey were the proud winners of the two armchairs for the princely sum of $80,000, not counting the buyer's premium of 15%.

"All right, that was very exciting, so let's sell the four side chairs. So again, we will sell one chair, and because there are four of them, it will be four times the money."

"Do I hear $10,000?"

Ned said to Rosalie, "Bid $2500!"

"$2500!" yelled Alex.

"Do I have $3500?" "Yes!" from the audience.

"$4500!" shouted Alex.

"How about $5500?" Josh asked. "Yes!"

The action started to slow, and a bidder jumped in, bidding $6,000.

"Do I have $7000?" asked Josh.

"Bid!" shouted the boys. "Yes!" came the bid from Alex. The room became hushed, and everyone else seemed to be tapped out.

"Sold to the boys from DC! How many chairs do they want, Alex?"

"We'll take two." Alex had selected the two best side chairs before the auction started, so he pointed to the two that he wanted for Ned and Jeffrey. The underbidder took the other two.

Just then, Josh dropped a bombshell on everyone. "Now, we will assemble all the pieces and sell the set to the highest bidder. The total of the winning bids for the set comes to $198,000. I won't sell the group for less than $200,000. Do I have any bidders?"

Just then, to everyone's shock, a man stepped forward and bid $200,000. It turns out he was bidding for a client from Georgia. A collective gasp swept through the gallery audience. Whispers alluded to the client's name, which was unfamiliar to Alex and Rosalie.

"Now that's a strong bid! Do I hear $210,000?" Josh asked. The gallery was silent. "Anybody else? The set is very rare and a once-in-a-lifetime opportunity. You've all come a long way. We may never see this happen again." Josh looked around and held his gavel up over the podium. "Any other bids?" No response. "Sold!" shouted Josh, and his gavel came crashing down on the stand.

The boys and Penfields were fit to be tied for losing out on the chairs. "Son of a bitch! He didn't tell anybody he would put the whole set together and sell it!" yelled Ned and Jeffrey. "I'll bet it's that goddam Calvin McCrae, the ambulance chaser in Atlanta. No one can outbid him!"

Over cocktails and a prime rib dinner at the local Outback Steakhouse that night, Rosalie and Alex remained shocked by what had happened at the auction. They felt terrible for their DC friends but were relieved it hadn't happened to them.

After the auction on Saturday, they planned to drive to New Orleans on Sunday morning. It's always fun to go there, and New Orleans has become one of their favorite places to buy antiques. They are scheduled to meet with Paul Barbier, a dealer with a beautiful shop in the French Quarter. He has many sets of Old Paris China available. Rosalie was interested in buying one or more.

Sunday morning arrived, and Alex was in a romantic mood. He woke up and couldn't go back to sleep because he kept thinking about the pleasure of making love to Rosalie. They would drive to New Orleans this morning, but a side trip to Ecstasy would lift everyone's spirits before the excursion.

He rolled over in bed and gently caressed her cheek. Rosalie awakened and returned the affection. The magic was still there after all these years. It was a morning of extraordinary lovemaking. Then, with a sigh, Rosalie said, "I'm famished."

"I'll go get some coffee and English muffins from downstairs; then we can hit the road and find some real food," Alex replied.

After a delightful breakfast and a short drive on the highway, Rosalie said, "I looked on Bing Maps, and we can reach New Orleans by taking a scenic ride down the Natchez Trace Parkway."

"I would be delighted to take you on that route, lover girl!" replied Alex. They picked up the Natchez Trace Parkway just west of Tupelo and turned south. It is a paved, two-lane highway that follows the approximate course of the historic Natchez Trace. A landmark forest trail created and used for centuries by Native Americans, the Trace was later utilized by settlers and traders. It runs 400 miles northeast from the Mississippi River at Natchez, Mississippi, to Nashville, Tennessee.

After 65 miles through some of the most beautiful countryside in Mississippi, the lovebirds exited the Natchez Trace Parkway and took US Hwy 82 west. An hour later, they joined I-55 and headed south. The highway ended three and a half hours and 277 miles later, where they merged onto I-10 east into New Orleans. Alex navigated through traffic to the eastern end of the French Quarter and checked into a suite at their favorite hotel, Le Pavillon on Poydras Street. They always travel with wine, Grey Goose vodka, and tonic. It was early evening, just in time for cocktail hour before they set out to find a local Creole dinner.

New Orleans is one of the most historic, vibrant, and unique cities in America. Founded in the early eighteenth century by the French, it features a wealth of stunning 19th-century architecture found nowhere else in the United States. From the grand homes in the Garden District to the narrow shotgun houses in the Ninth Ward, it's a sight to see. The Penfields have made many trips to the city to collect antebellum-era antiques that are unavailable anywhere else in America.

The French Quarter is the oldest neighborhood in New Orleans, showcasing elegant, colorful Victorian-era commercial buildings and homes. It is a vibrant shopping district catering to tourists and features several antique shops. On Monday morning, the Penfields drove into the French Quarter and were fortunate to find a parking spot near Paul Barbier's shop on Royal Street.

The Penfields arrived right in the middle of Paul Barbier's legal troubles. He and several other dealers faced charges for receiving and selling stolen cemetery artifacts. It all began when some locals started stealing statues, urns, and other artifacts from New Orleans' "Cities of the Dead" and selling them to fuel their cocaine habits.

Because New Orleans lies below sea level, the water table is very shallow, making in-ground burials impossible. Early in the 19th century, cemeteries began featuring ornate above-ground burial chambers made of marble, often with elaborate ornamentation. While many people are buried in simple mausoleums, the more fortunate are interred in structures resembling Byzantine temples, Egyptian pyramids, Gothic cathedrals, or surrounded by Greek or Roman columns. With family crypts built shoulder-to-shoulder along streets, the 40 cemeteries around New Orleans became known as "Cities of the Dead."

Barbier's problems started when relatives of the deceased told police that funeral ornaments and statues were missing from family mausoleums. A cemetery worker became suspicious when he saw a white van moving among the mausoleums. He recorded the van's license plate and gave it to police. When the thieves were caught stealing at another site, they cooperated with authorities, and what was uncovered shocked the community. At first, the thieves stole small urns and sold them to local antique dealers to support their drug addiction. Over time, dishonest dealers directed the thieves to specific cemeteries, encouraging them to steal larger, more elaborate items.

During multiple raids, police recovered over 250 urns, statues, and benches valued at roughly $1 million from about 35 antique dealers and the homes of their wealthy clients. Prosecutors disclosed that the theft operation extended from Los Angeles to New York, where some stolen items were recovered. Several parties were charged by prosecutors. Sadly, Paul Barbier was caught with multiple stolen artifacts and faced charges for receiving stolen funerary items. He was convicted and sentenced to ten years in prison, but he was out on bail waiting for his appeal when he met with Alex and Rosalie.

"Well, good morning, Alex and Rosalie! Welcome to New Orleans!" exclaimed Paul as they exchanged greetings and handshakes. Paul is a short, slender man with a goatee, impeccably dressed.

"It's great to see you, Paul; we always enjoy coming to town. The Deep South is one of our favorite places to hunt antiques. We love buying things you would never see up North," Rosalie replied.

"You expressed interest in acquiring sets of Old Paris China over the phone. I have several to show you," Paul said.

"Old Paris" porcelain is broadly defined as china made by artisans in and around Paris from the late 18th century to the 1870s.

During the two-hour visit, the Penfields selected a beautiful 150-piece dinnerware set. It featured intricate hand-painted floral designs and a peach-colored background with gold rim accents. It would look lovely at any of Rosalie's table settings.

This is Old Paris china, hand-painted in France, and it's a very old set, dating back to around 1855. Before the Civil War, couples would shop in New Orleans, here in the French Quarter, and buy large sets of china imported from France. They would then have it packed up, loaded onto their boat, and shipped up the Mississippi River to their plantation. It certainly came from one of those plantations, and when it was new, it was washed by enslaved people," explained Barbier.

The Penfields then spotted an exquisite 45-piece coffee and tea set of Old Paris china. The collection was pure white with gold accents. The couple struck a deal with Barbier for the two sets of dishes, even though the dealer acted as if they had stabbed him in the chest for offering them a discount. However, Barbier needed the money to pay his attorneys, so he accepted the offer. They packed the china, loaded it into the car's trunk, and bid Paul Barbier farewell. They had a wonderful trip back home, celebrating their new acquisitions.

Thanks to a skilled lawyer, Paul Barbier ultimately won his appeal against the lower court's conviction because he was unaware of the sources of the antiques. As a result, he spent little to no time in prison.

Chapter 21

One year, Cleveland faced a particularly brutal winter. The snowfall hit record levels, accumulating over 100 inches for the season. The snow fell in cotton-ball-sized flakes and was especially heavy on one day in late January. Most businesses in Cleveland closed for the day because driving conditions made it dangerous for employees to travel to work. It was safer to stay off the roads and let the city's snowplow drivers clear the streets. Taking the day off, Alex and Rosalie Penfield decided to make it a play day. They chose to go downtown to the historic flats along the Cuyahoga River to visit George Sherman's antique shop. They called ahead, and it just happened that George was open for business. "A little snow won't keep me away," he grumbled to Alex.

Cleveland's Flats is the area of land that borders both the east and west banks of the Cuyahoga River as it flows through the city's center, heading north to the lake. Cleveland's rich industrial history started there and is now marked by aging, half-filled, or empty warehouses and factories. It was slowly experiencing a rebirth, and tenants could rent warehouse space at low cost. George had rented ample space for his inventory in an old, dark factory building, where he specialized in selling antique furniture. The building was huge, probably once the site of a large manufacturing enterprise. Doorways opened into many dark, vast spaces, and it was easy to get lost there.

Often, there was a piece or two of questionable procurement in George's inventory. Many fancy antique doors stolen from homes in the city's older neighborhoods somehow landed at the receiving dock at his place. George was friendly with the patrolmen of the Flats. They never seemed to notice what came and went, even if an investigator questioned the origin of something that matched the description of a recently reported stolen door or object.

Rosalie and Alex lived in Cleveland Heights at the time, so they drove north to the Shoreway, a busy six-lane artery that runs east and west, overlooking Lake Erie. Turning west toward downtown, Alex piloted their Chevy four-wheel-drive pickup, which was perfect for antiquing. In four-wheel-drive mode, it easily navigated the unplowed, snow-covered highway. The City of Cleveland could never keep up with heavy snowfall. Rosalie was not at all worried about their safety, as Alex was very experienced driving the truck in bad conditions. It was fun, with the snow falling heavily, and they had the road to themselves. Everyone else had enough sense to stay home. "It's almost like being on a sleigh ride," Rosalie cooed as she snuggled up to Alex. Although it was bitterly cold outside, the truck was warm and cozy, with the heater working full blast.

Alex and Rosalie had visited George's place before because he was on the circuit of shops where they regularly hunted for treasures. Occasionally, he would show up with a good piece or two of Victorian furniture, although they had not purchased anything from him yet. Going down to the Flats to see his shop and view his latest inventory was always an adventure. Whenever they walked into a shop filled with antique furniture, Alex's heartbeat would quicken with excitement. The sight of all that wood, the smell of the place -- the hunt was on!

When they entered, they saw George slumped into an antique overstuffed chair, and Alex greeted him, "Hey, George, how's it going? Snowing enough for you?"

"Hell, I've already been out at a house sale this morning and had to haul a couple of pieces through this shit!" George was rough around the edges, with deep blue eyes, graying dark hair, a thin build, and was tall. He could hold his own in any situation and was not easily intimidated. He had a spotty past, having been in the business of dealing in various commodities. One dealer spread a rumor that George had set a man's house on fire in a dispute, killing the occupant. Allegedly, George spent some time in prison for aggravated arson. Just in case all of this was true, Alex's approach to dealing with George was to handle him with kid gloves. Don't provoke him.

The Penfield antiquers prowled through the rows of furniture like a pair of cats, soaking it all in. Finally, they turned a corner and spotted a lovely, tall walnut Renaissance Revival bed along with a matching marble-top dresser featuring a mirror. The bedroom set dated back to circa 1865 and was most likely constructed in Grand Rapids, Michigan, a major furniture manufacturing center in the years following the Civil War, owing to the abundance of vast poplar and walnut forests thriving in the state. The Renaissance Revival style was influenced by 16th-century Italian design elements and gained popularity in the early 1860s.

Add to that a large number of German immigrant craftsmen who arrived to work in the factories. This industry produced furniture at low to medium prices for America's growing middle-class population.

A pristine Carrara marble top was fitted to the dresser base, creating a handsome furniture suite. The dresser featured a tall, matching mirror adorned with raised burl panels and a carved crest. It rested on the marble top and was secured to the back of the dresser base. Alex opened the three drawers of the dresser base to check their functionality and was pleased to find that they were not heavily worn. He discovered that the dresser also included a plinth drawer, also known as a slipper drawer. This shallow drawer is located at the bottom of the dresser case, just above the floor, and is disguised as part of the plinth. The owner would primarily use it for shoe storage. Alex reached down, pulled it open, and found it was full of papers.

He whispered to Rosalie, "George forgot to clean out the slipper drawer." He pushed it closed without a second thought.

"Hey, this is a nice set; it would look great in the guest room. The bed is original. The headboard, footboard, and side rails are decorated with raised walnut burl panels. The only issue is that the original crest from the top of the headboard is missing."

"It has a nice original finish, and no one has messed with it," added Rosalie. Once again, Alex and Rosalie were lucky to share a love for the same things and were captivated by the set. They both valued the furniture's nearly flawless condition.

Alex shouted across the warehouse, "Hey, George, how much is the two-piece walnut bedroom set?"

Without moving a muscle, George said, "850 dollars."

Alex always liked to make an offer, so he paused and asked, "Can you do 800?"

In a menacing tone: "If I wanted 800 dollars, I would have told you 800 dollars."

"No problem, George, we'll take it." So, they walked over to where George was sitting, and Rosalie wrote a check to George. She always carried her checkbook.

George explained, "I purchased the bedroom set from the estate of a deceased lady in Lakewood." Based on the set's age, she would have inherited it from a relative from an earlier generation or bought it herself at an antique or used furniture store."

"George, since the bed is missing its original crest from the center of the headboard, I was wondering if you might know a good wood carver I could use to replicate a new one," Alex asked. "The good news is we have the original crest from the dresser to copy."

"Sure, I know a talented woodcarver, and I'll call him right now to see if he's available to speak." George dialed, "Hey, Steve, it's George Sherman. I have a customer here who just bought a Victorian bed and dresser from me. The bed needs a crest carved from walnut, and I wonder if you can carve it for him. Good. I'll put him in touch with you."

Alex and Rosalie always kept a stash of blankets and ropes behind the seat of the truck's cab. They wrapped and loaded the furniture onto the pickup, then drove out into the pouring snow. Since it was only a 20-minute drive back to the house, they weren't worried about anything getting wet. Once any exposed surface reached outside freezing temperatures, snow wouldn't stick. The set was well wrapped anyway.

The lovebirds and their Renaissance Revival bedroom set arrived home without incident. They unloaded and carefully unwrapped it. The first step with a new acquisition is to take it down to Alex's basement shop for inspection, repairs, and a thorough cleaning. The bed's headboard, footboard, and side rails were stowed away first. The brave couple strained under the weight of the marble top as they placed it in a corner for safekeeping. The mirror frame came next. Then they removed all four dresser base drawers to lighten its weight; it was the last to go, followed by the three deep drawers. "Let's put the slipper drawer on the kitchen counter, and we'll clean it out before we take it downstairs," Alex said.

With all coats, hats, and boots stowed away, Alex and Rosalie enjoyed hot cocoa in the cozy kitchen while they excavated the contents of the slipper drawer. It felt like Christmas morning! "Oh, my God! This drawer is full of treasures!" Rosalie exclaimed with excitement.

They were both stunned by what they saw. First, they found a small box containing a solid gold U.S. $20 coin dated 1868. Then, a lady's Victorian gold and carved shell cameo pin showing the side profile of a young woman wearing a necklace with a diamond pendant. Next was an 18-carat gold Victorian ladies' bar pin, decorated with black lacquer incising and set with a red ruby. After that, they discovered a lady's gold and ebony writing pen. Finally, they found a small Victorian-era tin filled with Indian head pennies. All the treasures were buried among many old documents, including life insurance policies and letters. Interestingly, the drawer also contained several semi-pornographic photos of young boys frolicking nude in and out of the water at a lake.

"Rosalie, this treasure trove must be worth at least a thousand dollars! We more than covered the cost of the bedroom set, and we're in the money for about $150!" Alex said. "George will never know what he left behind."

"Serves him right!" the couple growled in unison. They finished the last of the hot cocoa and then celebrated their lucky find with a bottle of champagne.

Weeks later, Alex contacted the woodcarver, Steve Everett. Steve is a highly talented artist who specializes in creating hand-carved carousel animals for a group of wealthy clients. He gained fame for securing a contract from the Disney Corporation to design and produce the outer row of animals for the carousel at Disney World in Paris, France.

Alex and Steve successfully collaborated on recreating the crest for the bed. For over thirty years, they worked together to replicate various carved parts that were missing from the Penfields' furniture pieces. Steve encouraged Alex to study the significance of carvings on much of the Penfields' antique furniture, igniting a lifelong passion for researching antiques and their broader representation in mythology.

Chapter 22

Westley's will did not specify an auctioneer to sell his collection if he passed away. Instead, that task was assigned to his attorney and executor, Janet Meyers. She knew of a suitable auction house, having used them before to liquidate other clients' estates successfully. Back in her office, Janet picked up the phone and scheduled an appointment that day with Jason Hunt, president and partner of Integrity Auctions.

Integrity Auctions is a well-known auction firm in Cleveland, specializing in selling fine art and antiques. The company has a long-standing excellent reputation. They sell collections consigned by parties from all over the country. Thanks to a nationwide following and strong marketing, Integrity regularly secures the highest prices for its clients. Jason Hunt and Bruce Howard founded Integrity over 35 years ago. They are a married gay couple who are outstanding businessmen and have been together for nearly 40 years. Integrity is housed in an ornate 1865 Victorian Italianate-style building in a historic section of Lorain Avenue, near West 35th Street, on Cleveland's near west side, next to Ohio City.

It is a 10,000-square-foot facility capable of properly displaying a collection of Westley's caliber. Elegant hand-printed damask pattern wallpaper decorates the interior walls. Silk damask draperies grace the windows and puddle onto polished oak floors. The front window display platforms are always beautifully furnished with objects scheduled for sale at the next auction. Incandescent lighting is excellent throughout and complements everything on display. The seating area is more than adequate. Best of all, the boys pay their consignors on time. They are well-financed.

Janet took a 15-minute drive to the gallery. Meeting in his richly decorated office, Jason hugged Janet and said, "Good afternoon, Janet. It's so nice to see you. How are you?" Jason is an attractive, slender man with brown eyes and slightly graying, neatly styled dark hair. He is a meticulous dresser, wearing a sharp, worsted-tan suit with a blood-red shirt and a multicolored silk tie. A red silk handkerchief peeks out of his breast pocket.

"Oh, Jason, I'm tired and sad. I didn't sleep well last night. I certainly hope that all is well with you and Bruce."

Jason took off his Gucci reading glasses and replied, "Yes, we're fine here." I'm sorry to hear about your day. How can I assist you?"

"I am the executor of Doctor Westley Engle's estate. You may have seen the news about his terrible murder. You might also know that he was the proud owner of a wonderful collection of Victorian-era antiques, and his will states that I should sell it at auction," she replied.

"Yes, we knew Westley and his wife, Melanie. Such a tragedy. First, that drunk driver killed his poor wife, and now Westley was murdered. We were stunned by the news. They were wonderful people. They bought many pieces at our auctions and were valued clients. Very sad."

"Jason, I need to hire your firm to liquidate Westley's collection and remove it from his house as soon as possible. The 24-hour security guards at his house have been costing the estate a lot of money. How soon can your team get there and begin? Also, when would you schedule an auction if you can start on this project immediately?"

"You caught us at the perfect moment. The gallery is empty because we just completed a big auction a week ago. I can clear our schedule by postponing another auction and having my team immediately start an inventory and move it here. As for the auction date, I would set it at least forty-five days from now to allow time for marketing. I know Westley had a superb collection, and promotion is essential."

"What about security at your gallery?" Janet asked.

"We are heavily wired with a state-of-the-art burglar alarm system, including sirens and cameras. It's the very best, with 24-hour monitoring of the facility. All exterior doors are made of steel, and the windows feature double-pane shatterproof glass with heavy steel interior bars. It's like a fortress here. We have housed treasured collections in the past without a break-in. Lastly, we carry a multi-million-dollar insurance policy. You could add one of your security guards at night if you wish," Jason replied.

"Sounds like Fort Knox in Cleveland. So, what will our seller's commission be? You know how I feel about you and Bruce. I'm going to hire you for future estate liquidations. If I'm not mistaken, the collection is valued at over $2 million, so give me a good deal." Janet was a tough negotiator for her clients.

"I'll do it for 10 percent. That covers everything, including inventory, photography, catalogs, mailing out brochures, and newspaper advertising in all the trade papers."

"How about eight percent?" she asked.

"Janet, you're killing me! Ten percent is my 'friends and family' commission. But you've been a good friend and client. So, for you, we'll do it for 9 percent. I really can't go any lower."

"Okay, Jason. You got it!" she said.

Jason spoke into the adjacent office, "Bruce, dear, would you be kind enough to step in and say hello to Janet?"

"Hi Janet, it's so lovely to see you! How may I help?" He gave her a hug and a kiss on the cheek. Bruce is a portly gentleman of short stature with blond hair, a well-trimmed goatee, and gorgeous blue eyes. His midnight-blue silk suit and white shirt, paired with a red bow tie, looked dashing.

"Oh, Bruce, we are arranging to sell Doctor Westley Engle's collection of antiques."

"Oh, my God! We heard about the doctor's shocking murder. I am so sorry."

"Bruce, would you please draft our standard consignment agreement, reflecting our nine percent commission?" Jason asked.

Bruce stepped into his office and prepared the consignment agreement, which stated that all lots would be sold without reserve as-is, where-is, for an all-inclusive 9 percent commission to be paid to Integrity. This means the property was to be sold for the bid amount and carried no guarantees. Janet and Jason signed the contract, and Bruce notarized it.

The next day, Jason led a crew of eight professionals from Integrity Auctions who stormed Westley's house like a swarm of bees. Opening the front door, which had recently been repaired, he exclaimed, "Oh, dear God! What a magnificent home. It is so heartbreaking to know what happened here! All the work that went into making this a showplace!" With a heavy heart, he began directing his team to get to work.

One of Jason's crew members parked a large moving van in the turnaround driveway at the front of the house. Under the watchful eye of security personnel, the Integrity crew began moving the furniture. Jason had hired extra men skilled at handling large objects. Every piece was carefully documented, described, inventoried, wrapped in blankets, and carefully packed into the truck. A team of specialists then started working, diligently listing, describing, and packing fragile items, including porcelain, glass, and silver. Westley and Melanie were always collecting items for their collection, and like Alex and Rosalie, it was a major part of their lifestyle. Once the inventory was finished, the Engle collection totaled just over 1,000 objects.

When Westley's collection arrived, everyone went to work and carefully unpacked it at the gallery. First, furniture specialist Ron Jameson took the inventory sheet, verified it against the actual pieces, and wrote a detailed description. That record was to be included in printed and digital catalogs. Next, the appropriate specialists followed the same process, cataloging smaller objects like glass, paintings, porcelain, and silver. Afterward, they met to decide the order in which the collection would be sold.

Since there were over 1,000 objects, they organized a two-day auction, selling 500 items on Saturday and the rest on Sunday. It is common practice in the auction industry to hold auctions on weekends, as most people are not working and can participate, encouraging maximum attendance. There is no standard method for determining the order of sales in an auction, and each auction house has its own approach. Integrity adopts the strategy of mixing different types of items. Their reasoning is to combine various media to keep the audience engaged. For example, they might present a piece of furniture, followed by some silver, then porcelain, and so on. Later in the day, they showcase the most valuable items. A lot number is assigned to each object once the specialists agree on the sale order.

Next, every lot in the auction is photographed digitally. This process varies between auction houses. Some have a dedicated studio setup, while others photograph small objects on a table and larger items in their location. Integrity has a dedicated studio room for photographing small items and can handle medium-sized furniture. Large objects are photographed in place.

Integrity Auctions' award-winning graphic designer, Amanda, began the process of selling Westley's collection. She digitally designed a stunning three-page, full-color brochure announcing the upcoming auction of Dr. Engle's collection. It featured vibrant images of 35 diverse lots, along with brief descriptions selected by the specialists as must-have items to generate interest in the sale. With a click on the send icon, the brochure was emailed to Integrity's network of over 4,000 contacts, including collectors, dealers, and others. Amanda also uploaded the brochure to Integrity's website.

Next, the design and layout of a four-page, full-color brochure that showcased 75 different lots was developed. After creating it digitally, Amanda sent a file to Maxum Printing Company, Integrity's printer and mailing house located on Superior Avenue in an industrial area on Cleveland's near east side. Amanda included a file with 3000 names and addresses of clients who were set to receive the brochure by U.S. Mail.

With deadlines approaching, Amanda and her assistant, Cathy, prepared the ads to be included in the collector trade magazines. These ads were to be in full color. Once again, the specialists chose a different assortment of lots to feature this time. With the push of a transmit button, digitally produced ads and insertion orders were sent to the leading collector newspapers. Multiple insertions were ordered, and thousands of impressions reached the collecting community nationwide and internationally over the following weeks.

The catalog's digital flipbook version was created and uploaded to Integrity's website. It appears on the site as a printed book, allowing viewers to flip through each page digitally, just like reading a bound book. The lots are arranged in numerical order, accompanied by their descriptions. Some, but not all, lots are pictured in this piece.

A couple of weeks later, each lot, uploaded with one or more digital images and complete descriptions, appears on the website in numerical order. Integrity will follow the sequence outlined in this document to conduct the live auction on-site.

Amanda captured the digital images and descriptions of each lot and organized the printed, hard-bound version of the sale catalog. Using the company's advanced graphics program, she resized selected photographs based on their importance and combined them with their descriptions. Then, following the specialists' recommendations, management chose the pieces to feature on the front and back covers. Finally, the completed draft was sent to Maxum Printing Company, allowing them to print and distribute the catalog to the selected clients.

At this point, the auction was four weeks away, and there was still much to do. However, the excitement surrounding the magnificent sale was starting to reach the antique-collecting community across the country.

Chapter 23

The Penfields are always looking for treasures that might be listed in the weekly trade papers delivered to their house. One evening, Alex sat down to read his copy of The Antique Trader and noticed an unusual auction notice in the paper's first section. It was a liquidation auction scheduled to happen in Tennessee. The sale was to be conducted by a local auctioneer under the supervision of the U.S. Drug Enforcement Administration. The property belonged to Dr. David Sherwood, who had been arrested and convicted of violating the federal Controlled Substances Act by running a "pill mill" near rural Oldwell, Tennessee. Dr. Sherwood's practice was among the many operations that contributed to and worsened the opioid epidemic.

David, the son of a prosperous cattleman, grew up in rural northern Tennessee near Oldwell. A tall, dark-haired young man with dazzling brown eyes, he would have been a catch for any young woman. His family owned hundreds of beef cattle and raised them on their thousand-acre farm. Thanks to his family's wealth, he attended the University of Tennessee and later enrolled in medical school at Duke University. After completing medical school, he returned to Oldwell and opened an office to practice internal medicine, focusing on treating adults. Internal medicine doctors prevent, diagnose, and treat diseases that affect adults, ranging from chronically ill patients to those needing short-term care. Once a doctor completes an internal medicine residency, they become an internist.

He married a local woman from a wealthy family, and they began raising their family. David and his wife, Bridgett, joined the country club and socialized with other affluent couples nearby. Bridgett is tall and curvaceous with blue eyes and blond hair; however, she is not very intelligent. She was the ideal partner for this Southern doctor. Unfortunately, the renowned internist's lifestyle and his wife's spending habits did not match his medical practice income. As a result, their debts grew, making it clear that they needed additional income to keep up their standard of living.

Coincidentally, Dr. Sherwood's office was just west of Interstate 75 as it entered Tennessee. People struggling with addiction called it the "Oxy Express" because they took that route to pain clinics near Knoxville or Florida. One day, he met with a sales representative from Planet Pharma who was running a campaign to encourage doctors to prescribe Painagon as a pain medication for their patients.

"Doctor, this drug is the most effective painkiller on the market, and it's nonaddictive. We're currently running a campaign where, once you reach a certain number of prescriptions, the company will reward you and your wife with an all-expenses-paid trip to Hawaii! You've never heard me say this, but you are in a prime location near the 'Oxy Express.'"

Painagon is Planet Pharma's version of the drug oxycodone. The company paid doctors and nonprofit organizations advocating for patients in pain to prescribe the drug as a safe, non-addictive, and effective way to treat pain.

But the drug *was* highly addictive. As more doctors prescribed these painkillers, more companies entered the market, manufacturing, distributing, and dispensing large quantities of pain pills. Promoted as a safer and less addictive version of oxycodone, Painagon gained widespread use. By then, everyone knew that the claims were false. The drug was more addictive than any other painkiller and, as a result, became a popular substance for abuse.

As the opioid epidemic worsened and because of its proximity to I-75, Dr. Sherwood's office began seeing more patients claiming to be in pain and requesting a prescription for Painagon. Seeing this as a business opportunity, he started writing prescriptions with little or no examinations.

"Before you leave, just drop off the prescription at our convenient in-house pharmacy, and they will be happy to fill it for you," were the good doctor's words when concluding an "exam."

Dr. Sherwood set up a pharmacy at his location. Planet Pharma's sales rep arranged for the doctor's office manager to buy Painagon directly from Planet Pharma. This practice was unusual because typical distributors usually sold most medications to pharmacies. However, Planet Pharma was eager to get the drug to the public at any cost. This arrangement motivated Sherwood to purchase large amounts of Painagon at the lowest wholesale prices. The real profits came from selling the drugs over the counter.

Over the next few months, traffic to his office skyrocketed as word got out. Patients started arriving before dawn, hanging out in the parking lot and creating a lively scene. Someone even made a breakfast run for himself and the other visitors. His waiting room was filled with chatting people, none of whom were in pain, but they discussed where to find more opioid painkillers.

The doctor's practice became very profitable. He hired extra administrative staff and nurse practitioners to handle the busy schedule. The clinic charged $500 per appointment and saw 50 patients each day, bringing in about $70,000 a month in additional income. Many of those arriving for appointments were drug dealers. When Dr. Sherwood was out of the office, he left a pad of signed prescriptions behind, ensuring the cash flow would never stop. At one point, the traffic was so busy that the physician assistants hardly left the exam rooms. The physician assistants lived in a poor area, needed their jobs, and feared losing them if they didn't dispense the prescriptions. By the end of the first year, the doctor's practice grossed $3.5 million from illegal exams. Dr. Sherwood also illegally billed many of these exam fees to Medicare. Most patients paid in cash, which the clever doctor never reported to the IRS.

What he didn't realize was that the Drug Enforcement Administration was monitoring. Officers went undercover and quickly obtained prescriptions without any exams. One "patient" even boasted that he planned to resell the pills on the street. However, no one paid attention to what he said. Dr. Sherwood's practice became one of many illegal pill mills across the South that prescribed and sold millions of pills, leading to thousands of overdose deaths.

While raking in all that cash, Dr. and Mrs. Sherwood pursued their passion for American Victorian antiques. They went on a buying spree, attending auctions and acquiring items from dealers and estates. As Southerners, they were especially drawn to the furnishings that once decorated grand antebellum plantation homes. The Sherwoods spent hundreds of thousands of dollars on furniture made by renowned cabinetmakers like Belter, Meeks, Roux, and Phyfe, among others. Only the finest antiques adorned the rooms of their house. The Sherwoods hired top decorators from Nashville to decorate their home with luxurious silk draperies and wall coverings. It became a showplace that their friends envied. But no one knew that the house was actually a front for money laundering—specifically, a place to hide illegally obtained cash through purchases.

Everything collapsed one day when the DEA agents arrived at Dr. Sherwood's office. They raided the office and took him into custody. Handcuffed, he was transported to jail to face charges of drug dealing involving Schedule II substances, money laundering, and tax evasion. During the hearing, he pleaded not guilty. After being released on a $1 million bond, Sherwood went to trial a year later and was found guilty, receiving a ten-year prison sentence.

At the same time, the doctor's assets were seized by the government. Asset forfeiture is a tool used in our country's fight against drug abuse, helping to shut down "pill mills" and stop rogue doctors, pharmacists, and dealers. Forfeiture involves the government taking property that has been illegally used or obtained without compensation to the owner. Items subject to seizure include cars, cash, real estate, or any other valuable item used to commit a crime or gained through drug proceeds.

The DEA uses forfeiture to target the financial networks of drug trafficking and money laundering groups worldwide, from low-level couriers handling cash or drugs to the highest ranks of drug cartels. Forfeiture, especially civil forfeiture, is highly effective in combatting profit-driven drug crimes. The United States Government employs asset forfeiture to seize and confiscate property from individuals involved in criminal activities, ultimately aiding law enforcement and the public.

Police state that most of the money from seizures goes toward training, education, and equipment to help fight crime. The unexpected funds have been used to buy everything from helmets and vests to SWAT vehicles and laptops. Seizures also support drug awareness programs in local schools.

A judge ordered the liquidation of the doctor's assets through a public auction. The Federal Court instructed Chase Ripkin Auction Company of Knoxville to sell the antique collection. Rosalie and Alexander previewed the items and decided to drive down for the auction because they had their eyes on a couple of pieces. They arrived the afternoon before the auction and previewed the collection. Everything was beautiful and in pristine condition. The Sherwoods had spared no expense building their antique collection. The auction attendees were aware of the doctor's way of paying for his collection, and no sympathy was shown for him by anyone.

Chase's auction house was bustling with collectors and dealers the next morning. Sounds of chatter echoed throughout the building. Everyone mingled while inspecting the items for sale. Alex and Rosalie even ran into Josh Williams, who had traveled from Tupelo, Mississippi. "Hell, I like to buy at auction for my collection too, now and again," he said as the Penfields greeted him.

When a high-quality collection goes up for sale, prices skyrocket as bidding begins. Although he emphasizes the importance of discipline in limiting one's bidding at auctions, Alex has never practiced what he preaches. He is a very competitive man and usually refuses to be outbid.

Alex and Rosalie had their eyes on a beautiful French Napoleon III-style parlor cabinet from around 1865 at this auction. It features a striking, black, polished finish with an ebonized look, decorated throughout with gilded brass ormolu. The front stiles of the cabinet display gilded brass busts of Bacchus, the god of wine, and on the opposite side, his consort Bacchante, the goddess of wine. The cabinet's door includes intricate inlaid brass Boulle work, and a polished black marble top completes the piece. Although it was unusual for them to pursue a piece of French furniture, they found it very attractive and irresistible. They are mainly purists of American Victorian-era furniture.

Several hours passed as the different lots were auctioned off. Rosalie and Alex enjoyed watching the bidders compete for the treasures! Finally, the French Boulle cabinet was up next.

As the piece opened, the auctioneer called, "Do I have $1,000? Yes! $1200? Yes! $1400? Yes! $1600? Yes!"

It continued on and on, and Alex jumped in at $2000. "Yes!"

"$2200? Yes! $2400?"

Alex bid, "Yes!"

"$2600? Yes!" Every time Alex placed a bid, the competitor responded with a bid of their own.

It continued up to $3000, and the Penfields stayed on and bid, "Yes!"

At this point, the auctioneer called the bids in $500 increments. "Do I have $3500? Yes!"

The bidding was spirited, and now it was down to the Penfields and one other bidder. Finally, Alex leaned over to Rosalie and said, "It looks like this son of a bitch is not going to let us have it, so let's make him pay!"

"$4000?" "Yes!" was Alex's bid.

Just then, the other bidder stepped back. "Sold to Alex and Rosalie Penfield!" They exchanged surprised glances but were excited to win the piece.

To the auctioneers' delight, Alex and Rosalie had set a bid limit but went well beyond it anyway.

Chapter 24

Alex and Rosalie have always been fascinated by Cleveland's storied history, its industrialists, and the luxurious homes they built. "I would dearly love to discover someday a treasure that was once in one of the homes on Millionaire's Row," said Rosalie.

Cleveland's rich history of playing a key role in the American Industrial Revolution was well established by the mid-19th century. The city was home to leading figures in banking and finance, shipping, iron and steel manufacturing, lumber, oil refining, and various other industries. Wealth was accumulated, and the tycoons' fortunes needed to be displayed. As a result, Cleveland became home to countless millionaires, a number second only to those in New York City.

The wealthy industrialists established a neighborhood featuring grand mansions, social circles, and family intermarriages along Cleveland's Euclid Street, which was later renamed Euclid Avenue. This opulent area earned a new nickname, "Millionaires Row." In only 60 years, around 260 mansions were built, stretching four miles east from Public Square in downtown Cleveland to East 90th Street.

In all the years Alex and Rosalie Penfield bought and sold hundreds of Victorian furniture pieces while building their collection, they wondered when they would cross paths with a treasure from Millionaires Row. After purchasing a house in Gates Mills, they carefully installed its Victorian interior and added important pieces to their collection. Then, one day, they received a call from Heather Roth. Heather is a friend and long-time antique dealer in Cleveland, located on the east side of the city. A slender woman with graying hair, she seems to need to gain a little weight. She is also a talented furniture conservator who works using old-world techniques.

"Hello, Heather! How nice to hear from you," said Alex.

"I'm very busy with the studio, but something has come up, and I thought of you. I got a call from one of David Norton's granddaughters," said Heather.

Norton, a leading banker in Cleveland during the 19th century, was encouraged by his friend John D. Rockefeller to partner with Earl Oglebay in establishing Oglebay Norton Corp. The company became a pioneer in transporting iron ore from the upper Great Lakes to Cleveland's steel mills using steamships. David Norton and his wife, Mary, were well-known figures in Cleveland's cultural and social scenes. Of Norton's three children, their daughter Miriam was the only one to marry, and she and her husband had two daughters.

"Norton owned a mansion on Euclid Avenue. His two granddaughters have several pieces of furniture that came from his house, including a Victorian parlor set," explained Heather. "Would you be interested in seeing them? I know how crazy you are about Millionaires Row history."

"When can we get together and go see the pieces? How about today?" Alex anxiously asked.

"I'll get back to you," she replied. After a quick call to arrange an appointment, Heather called back and said, "The granddaughters will meet us at 1 PM today." Alex and Rosalie drove to Heather's shop, picked her up, and then went to Cleveland Heights to meet the ladies. When they arrived, two gray-haired older women, Mable and Josephine, probably in their seventies, greeted them at the door. It was unclear which of the granddaughters owned the house. Alex introduced the group, but they were not particularly friendly or happy to be involved with selling their private property. Judging by the scowls on their faces, perhaps this exercise was beneath their dignity.

The Penfields and Heather began examining the furniture. Sure enough, there was a grand Renaissance Revival parlor set for sale. The set consisted of a settee, two armchairs, and four side chairs. It was very handsome, constructed of solid Brazilian rosewood, and decorated with marquetry. Of all the furniture, this set intrigued Alex the most. He determined it to be from circa 1865-1870 and possibly made by Gottlieb Vollmer of Philadelphia. Alex felt that it would make an excellent addition to their collection. "This suite would fit perfectly in our east parlor," he exclaimed.

"Ladies, we're interested in purchasing the parlor set. Would you take $5,000?" asked Alex.

One of the sisters replied, "Well, we'll let you know." The sisters did not make a counteroffer or commit to selling.

After Alex, Rosalie, and Heather left, Mable spoke to her sister, "That gentleman did not hesitate to offer $5,000 for the set. If we hold out, maybe we can get more for it."

A few months went by, and Alex and Rosalie forgot about the set, focusing on other projects and acquisitions. One Saturday, the Penfields visited Heather's shop to see her and check out what new items she might have for sale. They were surprised to learn that the Norton granddaughters had consigned the set with Heather, clearly hoping to get a higher price.

"Hey Heather, I never heard from the granddaughters and wondered what happened to my offer and the set!" exclaimed Alex. "My offer stands. Would you mind calling the sisters to see if they will take my $5,000 offer?"

"Sure, let me see if one of them is at home," replied Heather.

She reached one of the sisters, and they quickly accepted Alex's offer.

Rosalie wrote a check for $5,000 to the sisters and a $750 commission check to Heather. The Penfields were thrilled with their new acquisition! The next day, Alex attached his utility trailer to his Camaro, picked up the parlor set, and brought it home.

At home, hoping to establish provenance beyond hearsay from the tight-lipped granddaughters, Alex opened his copy of Jan Cigliano's book *Showplace of America, Cleveland's Euclid Avenue 1850-1910*. He remembered seeing photographic images of the interior of the Norton home published in the book, credited to G.M. Edmonston, a noted Cleveland photographer. Hoping to find additional interior images, Alex was excited to discover that the Western Reserve Historical Society owns a set of original photographs.

Alex and Rosalie hurried to the Western Reserve Historical Society and entered the research library on a mission to document the set. They met an attractive, friendly red-haired librarian and asked to see the photographic collection. She entered the request into their computer, and soon after, a large man slowly descended the second-floor stairs and placed a heavy box on the table with a thud. The librarian whispered to the Penfields that they nicknamed him "Mr. Personality." He resembled the character Lurch from the *Addams Family* TV show. The Penfields sat down with the box of images. As they flipped through them, they found a photograph of a parlor in the Norton home showing the same parlor set they had just bought from the Norton granddaughters. It was breathtaking! What a thrill! They finally had a piece of Millionaires Row in their own home, and a part of Cleveland history would always be with them. They could hardly contain their excitement in the library's deadly silence.

The Newtown Bee, the New England-based antique trade paper, arrived at the Penfield home as it had for many years. Alex sat at the kitchen table with his favorite cocktail, a vodka and tonic with a wedge of lime, and thumbed through the paper. Years ago, their beloved cat, Jasper, would often jump up onto his lap and then onto the table, lying on the paper for some "newspaper love." A typical copy of the *Bee* features news from around the collecting world and obituaries, followed by auction notices. Alex came across an exciting auction notice announcing an upcoming auction in the small western Pennsylvania town of Tidioute. What caught his eye was that the ad stated that the original 19th-century contents of a Victorian mansion were to be sold to the highest bidder. If true, it would be unprecedented. The Penfields had never witnessed such a sale in their years of collecting.

"Rosalie, this is like cracking into King Tut's tomb!" exclaimed Alex. "We've got to go to this auction! We might never see this again!"

The high quality of the pieces pictured in the ad piqued their interest, and since the auction was only a three-hour drive away, they decided to attend the following Saturday. Tidioute is in the northwest corner of Pennsylvania, approximately 120 miles east of Cleveland. The area is renowned as the location where substantial oil deposits were first discovered in America.

The ad stated that the Victorian mansion was built in 1876 by Jahu Hunter. An elderly descendant had recently died, and the house along with its contents were ordered to be sold at auction. Hunter made his fortune in the growing oil and lumber industries that emerged after the discovery of oil in western Pennsylvania.

After a three-hour drive over two- and single-lane country roads, some of which were just dirt trails, the Penfields finally arrived in the small town of Tidioute on the morning of the auction. They were surprised by the sight of a crowd of over a hundred people gathering on the lawn for the sale. Most of the license plates lining the narrow streets of the tiny village were from out of state. The population of Tidioute doubled that day, filled with eager auction-goers and curious locals. The Penfields had to park several blocks away and walk to the mansion, which sat in the center of a large plot of land overlooking the Allegheny River.

In a town filled with modest homes and businesses, the Penfields beheld a grand Italianate-style mansion, circa 1870, that stood out above all others and was remarkably original, both inside and out. The exterior trim, featuring many roof brackets, ornate window surrounds, a mansard roofline, and a polychromatic paint scheme, made for a beautiful sight. As one approached the house, the most remarkable detail was the pair of original intact acid-etched glass door lights installed in the front entry doors. An ornate Victorian design adorned the panels. Most impressive were Jahu Hunter's initials "J" etched into the center of the left door panel and an "H" etched into the center of the right door panel! Over the front doors was a magnificent, rare, half-round ruby glass-etched panel.

Upon entering the home, one beholds a forest of walnut trees that was sacrificed to construct a remarkable original millwork package. Visitors are greeted by solid walnut arch-topped paneled doors framed by stacked moldings and tall baseboards throughout the formal first floor.

The furnishings were equally impressive. The front parlor contained a Steinway Rosewood concert grand piano circa 1875, along with accompanying parlor pieces. Across the center hall, an enormous double salon was furnished with a ten-piece suite of John Jeliff Renaissance Revival parlor furniture. The dining room featured a superb walnut and burl suite that took the Penfields' breath away. Upstairs, every bedroom was furnished with massive two- and three-piece carved Renaissance Revival walnut suites.

Within the hour, the Penfields searched every inch of all four floors of the house. After a thorough search, they concluded there was nothing inside the home worth adding to their collection. However, something extraordinary was stored in the massive carriage house in the backyard. Once again, the Penfields saw something they had never encountered before. The most magnificent original Egyptian Revival-style Pottier & Stymus rosewood pier mirror sat in a recently opened shipping crate. The impressive mirror stood over ten and a half feet tall and five feet wide. It was decorated with gold-filled incised lines and pristine gilt mounts, including an Egyptian pharaoh's mask centered on the crest at the top of the piece.

"I say we go for it! It will fit nicely in our foyer," exclaimed Alex.

"Why do you think it was stored in the carriage house?" asked Rosalie.

The Penfields guessed that the mirror was too tall for the downstairs ceilings of the Hunter house. Alex borrowed a tape measure from another attendee, confirmed the pier mirror was 10 feet 6 inches tall, and verified that it would indeed fit in the couple's foyer. It seemed Mr. Hunter bought it without realizing that the massive piece would not fit under the ten-foot-tall ceiling of his home. As a result, the mirror was taken to the carriage house, where it remained stored in its original shipping crate for the next 120 years. Thank goodness Hunter chose not to cut the piece down.

It was a sunny yet chilly fall day, with colorful autumn leaves falling. Excitement filled the air as the auction was about to start. Despite the cool weather, the sale was scheduled to take place outdoors in the mansion's side yard. Rows of chairs filled quickly, and a large overflow crowd gathered around the area. Finally, the auctioneer took the podium, explained the rules, and the auction began.

The Penfields quickly realized that wealthy bidders were in the crowd, pushing up the prices of the antiques. That day, there would be no bargains. Although there wasn't much for the Penfields to bid on, they enjoyed the auction atmosphere. They were in their element! Late in the day, after hundreds of lots had been auctioned off, the auctioneer finally reached the pier mirror. As always, Alex's heartbeat quickened.

"This is one of the best objects in the sale! Stored for over a hundred years in its original shipping crate, it is a museum piece!" Do I have $5,000?" "Yes!"

"6,000?" "Yes!" The bidding went on and on.

"10,000?" "Yes!"

When the bidding reached $14,000, it was between the Penfields and one other bidder.

"Do I have $15,000?" "Yes!" bid the other collector.

"$16,000?" "Yes!" bid Alex. Finally, the other bidder dropped out, and the auctioneer brought the hammer down. "Sold to Alex Penfield!"

The Penfields drove back to Gates Mills that evening, rented an enormous truck, and returned to Tidioute Sunday morning. Motoring the large vehicle through all the narrow roads and dirt trails, they brought the treasure to its new home. They installed the pier mirror in their spacious foyer and enjoyed it for a year, but ultimately replaced it with an exquisite Herter Brothers parlor cabinet. They took a handsome profit by selling the pier mirror to the owner of one of San Francisco's famous painted ladies for $37,000.

"I'm sorry to see that pier mirror go, but Mr. Hunter would be glad to know it's in a good home," Alex sighed. "But, of course, we will never forget Mr. Hunter and his grand house!"

Chapter 25

With Dr. Westley Engle dead, only the Russians knew about the flash drive. Later, four Vors, including the two killers, met with Vor crime boss Andrei Lebedev at his spacious home in Beachwood. Lebedev, known as "The Swan," leads Cleveland's local Bratva. An intense, tall man with black hair and blue eyes, he commands respect. His operation includes schemes like fraud, check kiting, identity theft, money laundering, and illegal gambling, among others. The Bratva, or Russian mob, is the world's most powerful criminal organization. Law enforcement estimates that the Bratva operates in most former Soviet Union countries, Europe, and the United States.

Lebedev's crew is part of, and reports to, a billion-dollar enterprise led by Maksim Kuznetsov. Kuznetsov has a reputation as one of the world's wealthiest and most ruthless Russian criminals. A short, stocky man with black hair, dark eyes, and a mild manner, he doesn't look like what he is. He currently has the protection of Georgia's government and lives in a luxurious mansion overlooking the Black Sea in the resort town of Batumi. Once part of the Soviet Union, Georgia has no extradition treaties with the West, making it a great place to hide from the rest of the world. Many countries are waiting for Kuznetsov to be seen outside of Georgia so they can arrest him.

Born in 1960 in the former Soviet Republic of Ukraine, specifically in the capital city Kyiv, Kuznetsov's criminal career started when he and his older brother Leonid trafficked Afghan heroin. By the time the Soviet Union collapsed in 1991, Kuznetsov, flush with drug money, bought two Russian AN II 76 airliners to run an air freight business. The temptation of arms trafficking became too tempting to ignore, and his first illegal operation using the airliners was to transport a shipment of Bulgarian-made weapons to support the Angolan Civil War. Authorities suspected Kuznetsov of supplying arms to Charles Taylor for use in the First Liberian Civil War. He also sold weapons to various African countries across the continent.

The American Central Intelligence Agency came calling one day to hire Kuznetsov to oversee the sale of arms to support Iraq during the Iran-Iraq War. With the backing of the Reagan Administration and American Intelligence agencies, he managed several major arms deals, including the sale of French-built artillery valued at $1.4 billion. Investigations into the Iran-Contra scandal revealed that Kuznetsov was paid $2 million by someone within the American government to sell arms to the Nicaraguan Contras. The money was deposited from a Swiss bank account controlled by Oliver North and his co-conspirators.

Kuznetsov supplied small arms and infantry weapons from Bulgaria, Hungary, and Poland for the Lebanese Civil War. He arranged an airdrop of 10,000 AK-47 assault rifles, originally from East Germany and Jordan, intended for the Peruvian government. However, most of these weapons ended up in the hands of the Colombian leftist guerrilla group FARC, which opposed the U.S.-backed Colombian government.

Several months later, it was revealed that the CIA had supported the deal to arm Peruvian intelligence chief Vladimiro Montesinos.

The government of Yemen approached Kuznetsov to supply rifles and pistols from Poland. Those arms were then sent to various terrorist groups. Additionally, he conducted arms sales worth millions of dollars to Croatia, Bosnia, and Somalia, violating United Nations embargoes against all three countries.

Back in Beachwood, the Vors felt the heat from the boss for not securing the flash drive the night they killed Westley. They knew their necks were on the line for the $100,000, and they had better figure out how to get that flash drive one way or another. As they pondered their next move, Lebedev asked, "Where in the hell do you think he stashed it?"

Volkov spoke, "We tortured him, but the doctor would not give us the flash drive. I have a feeling that he hid it in one of the pieces of that ugly, dark furniture. While searching the house, I discovered a set of notes on the desk and in the trash can in his office, and shoved them into my jacket pocket. We immediately scrambled out of the house when the alarm went off." He pulled the papers out of an envelope and laid them on the table for the group to see. "I studied them, and the notes look like a bunch of clues." Picking up the pile of papers, he thumbed through them and randomly stopped at one. Reading aloud, "'Find *the symbol of truth, humility, protection, and courage. Associated with the Knights Hospitallers.'* I went online and Googled the Knights of Hospitallers. It turns out that the symbol he writes about is the Maltese Cross. It's a symbol used by the Knights of Hospitallers. That symbol might appear on the piece of furniture containing the flash drive. Additional details are described in the notes, which serve as clues to other furniture pieces. So, it could be anywhere."

"One night, we went back to the house planning to break in and discovered that someone had hauled all the furniture away shortly after we killed him. So, I say we try to locate the furniture and search for the flash drive. We can always go back and search the house. It's not going anywhere," said Solkolov.

"Well, find out where they took the furniture. I could make a deal with some people who have connections to ISIS. They're willing to pay us a million bucks for the flash drive. So, you'd better find it," Lebedev said in an ominous tone of voice.

Later that evening, one of Lebedev's goons who had attended the meeting, a Vor from St. Petersburg named Mikhail Orlav, nicknamed "The Eagle," sat in his Richmond Heights apartment, watching the news. Flopped on a sofa with his shirt off, he looked terrible after just taking a shower. Like the others, he was heavily tattooed and had spent years in the Gulag. The large, grotesque head of a monster with fangs, horns, and a beard symbolizing a "baring of teeth" against the police and justice system was splashed across his chest. His right arm featured a tattoo of a woman burned at the stake, symbolizing his blame of a woman for his imprisonment. The four burning logs at her feet indicated the number of years he served in prison. On his left arm, a giant black spider on a web was tattooed, symbolizing a prisoner's walk along a criminal path. A book with a spider crawling over it was shown on the web.

It depicts the Russian Criminal Code, representing his repeated punishment for violating the rules of the penal colony.

Just then, a news segment aired on WOIO-TV Channel 19, showing a reporter doing a story on the sidewalk in front of the Integrity Auction Company. A lovely, thin, blue-eyed, young, red-haired woman named Kirsten Greenwell shared the story of the gruesome murder of Dr. Engle, who was a serious antique collector. The reporter said that the deceased doctor's collection was scheduled to be auctioned off the following Saturday. Jumping up from his sofa, Orlav quickly telephoned Volkov, "We have found the furniture, dear Vor, and it is going up for auction soon, right here in Cleveland!"

The next day, two intimidating Russian tattooed Vor goons named Dimitri Vasiliev and Mikhail Orlav arrived at the Integrity Auction Company and entered the gallery showroom. They did not resemble antique collectors at all. The strange-looking visitors immediately caught the attention of a couple of large Integrity warehouse workers, Dewayne Williams and Tamarius Johnson, who were on duty to monitor the situation. They are young Black men who are loyal, strong, and gentle giants. Bruce and Jason rescued them from one of the worst neighborhoods in East Cleveland, where they faced crime and poverty. Integrity has employed them for years. Dewayne and Tamarius handled large, heavy furniture, fountains, and wrought iron pieces with the same care as paintings, porcelain vases, and sculptures. The trustworthy two-man team took pride in carefully moving and packing the auction lots. The Russians focused on several pieces of furniture. Not used to handling such beautiful objects, they roughly rifled through the cabinet pieces. The rattling and banging drew Dewayne over to where the Russians had removed the drawer from an early 19th-century Pembroke table and turned it upside down.

Always the diplomat, Dewayne approached the Russians and said, "Gentlemen, would you please be more careful with these fine pieces? They are very valuable."

Orlav glared at the warehouseman and, with an aggressive look, said, "Fuck you! We'll handle this any way we want."

Feeling his blood pressure rise, Dewayne, who was six feet three and weighed 250 pounds, refused to tolerate the intruders' disrespect for the beautiful objects. He called Tamarius over, who was even larger at 280 pounds and six feet six. Dewayne looked at Orlav and said, "No, fuck you!" With that, Dewayne and Tamarius each grabbed a Russian by the neck, lifted them off the ground, dragged them to the front door, and threw them headfirst onto the sidewalk. They then slapped the Russians around and chased them off. No matter how tough a man thinks he is, there's always someone tougher.

Later that evening, after the preview guests had left and the gallery was locked up, Dewayne and Tamarius requested a meeting with Bruce in his office. Tamarius said, "Sir, we were forced to remove two men who were handling the furniture roughly. They looked tough, like thugs, not the kind of people who would be collectors or attend one of our auctions. They spoke to each other in a foreign language. They were pulling out drawers and opening doors. It appeared to us that they were looking for something."

"Thanks for the heads-up, guys. I've been worried about something like this ever since Dr. Engle was brutally murdered. Keep your eyes open, and let me know if you notice anything suspicious," said Bruce.

Recognizing the danger of auctioning such valuable items, Integrity's owners, Jason Hunt and Bruce Howard, wisely arranged for two armed, off-duty Cleveland police officers to provide overnight security at the gallery. They would begin that night and continue through the rest of the week.

Chapter 26

Rosalie returned home in her Cadillac XTS after spending an hour and a half grocery shopping at Heinrick's. This family-owned grocery store in Cleveland offers its customers the highest quality products. Rosalie loved cooking and baking, and it brought her great joy to select the freshest ingredients for her meals. She pulled up to the curb to get the mail from the mailbox and felt instant sadness upon seeing they had received a brochure promoting the sale of Westley's collection. After driving up the driveway into the garage to park the car, she entered the house and walked into Alex's downstairs office. With a kiss and a hug, she said, "We just got a brochure promoting the sale of Westley's collection."

Standing up to retrieve the groceries from the car trunk, Alex said, "My heart breaks for our dear friend. I sure as hell hope the cops find who did this!"

After bringing the groceries into the house, Alex picked up the brochure, poured a cup of coffee, and sat down in a carved Rococo revival mahogany armchair, one of four matching chairs that complemented the ornately carved mahogany pedestal table, which created a handsome kitchen ensemble. The brochure confirmed that the event would be a two-day auction, scheduled for next Saturday and Sunday. It also indicated that the auction house would host a preview party on Friday night before the sale. After thumbing through the brochure, Alex asked Rosalie, "Why don't we take in the preview party on Friday? We always run into other collectors we know. So, despite the sadness of it being Westley's collection, we might have some fun kibitzing. Might help us get through this."

That following Friday night, Alex and Rosalie arrived at the Integrity auction house, where they were greeted at the front door by Jason Hunt. Always a gracious host, he welcomed everyone as if they were guests in his own home. He wore a sharp black silk tuxedo, a baby blue ruffled shirt, and a navy blue bow tie, looking like he was about to host an Academy Awards ceremony. "Well, hello, you two, welcome! I know you were friends with

Westley and Melanie. I am so sorry for your loss and know you will miss them. They were great collectors, and I want to extend my sincere condolences. Come in. We're serving delicious hors d'oeuvres and pouring any cocktail you'd like."

"Oh, Jason, thank you for having us; your kind words are appreciated," Rosalie replied. The Integrity staff had decorated the gallery beautifully. The lighting was spectacular, and the specialists displayed the Engle collection exquisitely.

The Penfields strolled through the gallery, admiring the people and sights. Many guests gathered around the beautiful buffet set up by Jason and Bruce. The Integrity owners are famous for offering a wonderful mix of culinary delights. After filling their plates, Alex and Rosalie stopped at the bar for a couple of vodka tonics.

Because of the Engle collection's quality and significance, it was no surprise to see many advanced collectors from across the country previewing the auction. Dave Petrocelli approached as Alex and Rosalie munched at a table near the buffet. "I knew I would find you two here! How the hell are you?"

"Hey, Dave!" The two men shook hands, and Dave gave Rosalie a big hug. "We are just fine. After all, this is our backyard. Sit down with us! Glad you are here. Westley owned some beautiful pieces. What are you chasing?" asked Alex.

"Oh, nothing. I'll have to see what suits my fancy. I enjoy attending auctions of this caliber. But you know they are few and far between anymore. What about poor Westley's murder? Do you know anything new to tell me?"

"No, the police, of course, are investigating but aren't talking."

After catching up on each other's news, snacking on hors d'oeuvres, and sipping cocktails, the Penfields excused themselves to focus on exploring the Engles' collection. Familiar with it, they zeroed in on their favorite items, taking notes as they went: there was so much to choose from, but it always filled them with a heavy heart. They stopped at the gallery desk at the end of the evening to register for the weekend's auction and picked up a bidder's number. As they left the gallery, they thanked Jason for his hospitality.

"We look forward to seeing you here over the weekend!" Jason swished away to greet another guest.

As always, Alex had trouble sleeping on Friday night because of the excitement of attending the auction. Alex and Rosalie arrived at 9:00 AM on Saturday, an hour before bidding was scheduled to start at 10:00 AM. It is customary for them to arrive at least an hour early to ensure they have thoroughly examined everything and assessed their competition. The parking lot across the street from the gallery was already full, so the Penfields had to park way out in the back. As they walked through the gallery doors, they were amazed to see that the place was packed. The sound of chatter filled the air from a crowd of probably 150 people milling around. Alex's heartbeat quickened just from the excitement. Jason and Bruce had served a divine breakfast buffet featuring lox and bagels with cream cheese, pastries, scrambled eggs, breakfast meats, and large bowls of fresh strawberries. The mimosas were being poured generously and proved to be a big hit with the out-of-towners. The boys knew how to put on a great auction! It did not surprise the Penfields that the Engle collection drew so much interest, as it was one of the best in the country.

The auction house had assigned reserved seats to those who preregistered for the auction. Their names were written on tags taped to each chair. As 10:00 AM approached, the bidders took their seats. The Penfields found the seats assigned to them. As the crowd's excitement grew, Jason Hunt took the podium, rapped his gavel, and the crowd quieted; then he explained the auction rules. By this time, anxious bidders filled all the seats. However, a large crowd still stood around the gallery's edges. Russian mobsters Dimitri Vasiliev and Mikhail Orlav lurked in the back, trying unsuccessfully to blend in with the sophisticated attendees. Standing on the opposite side of the room to watch the crowd along with the Russians was homicide detective Patrick Maloney of the Bay Village Police Department. Dewayne and Tamarius kept a close watch on the Russians.

The bidding started just after 10:15 AM with one of Engle's top items. The boys always kicked off an auction with a notable piece to excite the crowd. It was a John and Joseph Meeks rosewood marble-top lady's duchess, circa 1855. This piece is one of the most detailed dressing tables from that period, featuring an attached mirror and having a clear provenance. The lady's duchess was estimated to sell for $30,000.

"This exquisite piece was made in New York, circa 1850s, and came off Magnolia Plantation on the Mississippi River near Natchez," Jason exclaimed. I need an opening bid of 5,000!" Many hands went up.

"Do I have $7500?" "Yes!" was the call of the bid ushers.

"Do I have $10,000?" "Yes!" It was the call of the ushers.

"Do I have $15,000?" "Yes!"

"20,000?" "Yes!"

The bidding continued, and the excitement in the gallery intensified. A palpable murmur filled the air.

Near the end, it came down to a couple from Michigan and a gentleman from Mississippi.

"Do I have $30,000?" "Yes!" The gentleman from Mississippi bid it.

"$35,000?" "Yes!" came the counterbid by the couple from Michigan.

"40,000?" The bidding stopped. "Come on now. You know that this Meeks duchess is worth more than that!" A noticeable pause. "Sold!" A round of applause erupted for the couple from Michigan. They were the delighted winners at $35,000, a mere $5,000 over the estimate.

Several great lots followed, prompting Rosalie to observe, "It looks like everybody is going to join hands and jump right off the cliff!", inferring that everything would sell well beyond the estimates. She was right.

Three hours into the auction, bidding stayed lively, and everything sold for a high price. The Penfields enjoyed the excitement, feeling right at home; however, with each bid, they remembered their dear departed friend and where each piece had once sat in Westley's mansion. They had their eye on an ornate, gilded Victorian empty picture frame that was about to be offered soon. It had been sitting in the Engles' basement, waiting for a painting. Alex and Rosalie frequently acquired numerous high-quality ornate picture frames whenever they were available. Over the years, they built relationships with many professional copyists worldwide who could replicate any master painting, often surpassing the original's quality. The Penfields particularly loved the great Victorian-era masters, such as Renoir, Monet, Sargent, and Bierstadt, among others. Of course, the original paintings are housed in museums and cannot be bought, but they can be easily copied. Alex and Rosalie willingly paid reproduction rights when needed, making sure no image was copied without permission. The Penfields never tried to pass these off as authentic. Their home has plenty of wall space, and the reproduced master paintings, framed in restored gilded frames, looked wonderful. Finally, the empty frame they had their eye on was up for bidding, and Alexander and Rosalie won it with a bid of $500. "I can't believe we got something for under four figures," Alex whispered to Rosalie.

Later in the day, the Penfields bid on a rare W&J Allen Victorian Gothic Revival rosewood washstand with a marble top and marble backsplash framed in carved rosewood. Gothic Revival is a rare and distinctive style from the Victorian era. It started at $1000, and several hands shot up immediately. When it reached $3,000, the Penfields jumped in and bid $3,500. The bidding continued, and at $7,500, Alex placed a bid. Finally, another bidder offered $8000, and the Penfields stepped back and let it go. By 5:00 PM, after an exciting day, the auction wound down, and everyone shuffled out.

Dave Petrocelli walked over and said, "Hey, you two! What do you say the three of us go to dinner tonight?"

Alex replied, "Sure, Dave, I know a great place near where you're staying downtown." It's called The Winking Lizard. It has a great atmosphere, cool stuff hanging on the walls, and they serve all kinds of good food." Later, the Penfields picked Dave up at his hotel, and they drove to the Lizard on Prospect Avenue near East 9th Street. The food and drinks were excellent, and they had a good time catching up on the news of the antique business.

They parted ways around 9:00 PM, and Dave said, "I'll see you at the auction tomorrow!" The Penfields drove home to Gates Mills, excited about their new acquisition.

Sunday morning arrived quickly. Jason and Bruce brought in a local chef who prepared cooked-to-order omelets, several meat side dishes, and a generous assortment of warm bread and muffins. It was wonderful. The large crowd returned, and the atmosphere buzzed with excitement. The auction began promptly at 10:00 AM. Many exquisite treasures came and went. The bidding was fierce, and there were no bargains.

The Penfields had their eye on a beautiful Gothic Revival rosewood secretary bookcase from around 1850, probably made by the J. and J.W. Meeks company. It was scheduled to go up for auction early in the afternoon. Standing nearly eight feet tall and four feet wide, it features a spacious upper bookcase enclosed by an ornate pair of glass-paneled doors, decorated with intricate Gothic rosewood tracery. The lower section includes a drop-down, leather-covered writing surface that reveals a finely fitted interior, with a variety of shallow drawers fitted with mother-of-pearl pulls and a pair of decorative, molded doors below. The Penfields believed this handsome piece would be perfect for Rosalie's office.

Finally, it was time to sell the bookcase. As Jason described it, Alex and Rosalie's hearts started pounding as the piece went up for bid. They never outgrow the excitement of bidding. Jason opened the bidding at $2000, and several hands went up; soon, the piece reached $3500.

"Do I have $3500?" "Yes!" Alex bid.

"$4000?" "Yes," came from another bidder.

"How about $4500?" "Yes!" came from Alex.

"$5000?" "Yes!" from the competitor.

"$5500?" "Yes!" bid Alex.

"Do I have $6000?" Silence. It appears that the other bidder has reached their limit. "Sold to Alex and Rosalie Penfield for $5500!" The Penfields were ecstatic.

That was it for Alex and Rosalie. Although they were outbid on other items, they were thrilled to have purchased the two antiques from Engles' collection. They spent the rest of the day enjoying the excitement of the auction, encouraging other collectors to bid, and reminiscing about their dear friend. The couple shared stories about Westley and Melanie with other collectors. It was a sad shame that their reunion was prompted by such a tragedy. As the auction ended in the late afternoon, Alex and Rosalie walked up to the gallery desk and paid their bill.

On Monday, Alex rented a small U-Haul trailer, hooked it up to his Camaro 2SS, and drove downtown to pick up their picture frame and secretary bookcase. Dewayne and Tamarius, the warehouse workers, helped Alex wrap the items in blankets and load them. When he got home, Alex arranged for the neighbor's son to help carry the secretary bookcase down to his basement studio. It needed cleaning and restoration of the finish.

Back in Bay Village, Officer Patrick Maloney continued his investigation into the murder of Dr. Westley Engle.

Chapter 27

Monday morning arrived too quickly for the employees at the Integrity Auction Company after the auction. The day following a two-day weekend auction was always demanding, as everyone was bleary-eyed and exhausted. Around 10:00 AM, the staff started dragging themselves into the office. There was much work to do, including restoring the gallery to order, moving pieces to the loading dock for bidders picking them up, and emailing invoices to the winning absentee and telephone bidders. The accounting department had hundreds of thousands of dollars in checks to reconcile with the purchased items and to prepare a large bank deposit.

Around 11:00 AM, the furniture specialist Ron Jameson shuffled into the office without greeting anyone, as he was stuffing an Egg McMuffin into his mouth. He was a miserable, morbidly obese man with long, oily gray hair combed straight back and tied into a long, stringy ponytail, complemented by a straggly, unkempt gray beard. Ron looked and smelled as if he had not bathed that morning. His clothes never fit him due to his obesity: his belly hung over the waistband of his trousers, and his shirttail always needed to be tucked in. Additionally, no one particularly liked him because of his pompous, know-it-all personality.

Ron was a lifelong loser who had moved to Cleveland eight years earlier from Missouri, along with his wife, Jessica. She is an attractive, intelligent, petite woman with beautiful blue eyes and brunette hair. People always wondered what she saw in Ron. He worked as a plumber's assistant in Missouri, while Jessica had a steady career as a registered nurse. His plumbing job did not provide enough money for the household, and Jessica's regular income helped them through the highs and lows. Money issues were always the root of their problems. Jessica is a lovely person who was unlucky in love. Ron had disappointed Jessica due to his limited educational background; she had always been the primary breadwinner. They were not a happily married couple due to Ron's overall unappealing appearance and poor sexual performance. The offer of a higher-paying nursing job at the Cleveland Clinic only further raked on him, but it offered the troubled couple a new start.

It was always a mystery how Ron ended up in the antique business since he had no background in the field. When the lovebirds arrived in Cleveland, he decided to try a new career. After responding to an employment ad for a warehouse worker, he convinced Jason and Bruce to give him a chance at Integrity Auction. He began in the warehouse with Dewayne and Tamarius and worked his way up to assist the furniture department manager. He was promoted to manager after his predecessor passed away. After eight years, he quickly learned the skills needed for the new role and performed his job adequately. Ron benefited because he got to know all the top collectors of high-end furniture.

Unbeknownst to his employer, Ron set up a brokerage business as a side gig. When talking with a collector, he often discovered that a good piece was for sale. Instead of directing that person to consign it to auction at Integrity, he would broker it to another collector for a quick cash fee under the table. Ron had a very irritating habit of always trying to make others think he knew about the availability of some treasure that no one else was aware of. He would often accompany collectors to other auctions and provide consulting services for a fee. The collectors usually came through his work at Integrity. That was his only power. Ironically, a man with such a lack of scruples worked for a firm called "Integrity Auctions."

After the weekend auction, Ron worked late Monday night to organize his department and move furniture to the shipping dock for pick-up. He was the last to leave and locked up the gallery after dark.

As Ron approached his broken-down Pontiac, Russian mobster Vors Dimitri Vasiliev and Mikhail Orlav emerged from the shadows. Orlav greeted him with a coarse Russian accent, "Hello, Ron. We met at last weekend's auction."

Startled, Ron replied, "Yeah, well, nice to see you guys. I was about to go home. It's been a long day."

"I understand, my friend. You've been working very hard, and I'll only take a little of your time. You're going to like what we have to say. We need you to provide us with a list of the furniture pieces sold at last weekend's auction, along with the names of the individuals who purchased them. I believe you refer to them as case pieces. For that, we will pay you $20,000 in cash."

"What do you want it for?" Ron asked.

"For $20,000 in cash, you don't have to worry about that," he replied. The Vor looked deadly serious as Ron gazed into his steel-blue eyes.

Ron considered their offer briefly and said, "Make it $25,000 in cash, and you've got a deal." Since he was always broke, this windfall would help balance things out in his household. Ron was loyal only to himself.

Vasiliev spoke up and said, "You ask a lot of money, Mr. Jameson. Hmmm. All right. You've got a deal."

Ron didn't hesitate and replied, "Okay, I'm glad you see it my way. After everyone leaves the office tomorrow evening, I will log on to the computer and print out all the furniture pieces, including the buyers' names and addresses. Meet me at 11:30 PM in the parking lot behind The Rib House on Detroit Ave. It's just over the border into Cleveland. You'll find it. I'll be in this car parked in the back of the lot. Make sure you bring cash."

The next night, with the gallery deserted, Ron went to work at the computer terminal on his desk. He had access to most of the company's records due to his tenure as a trusted employee of over eight years. First, Ron accessed the master catalog screen and downloaded a list of every piece of furniture by lot number sold the previous weekend. With that information, he could access the master sales journal screen and scroll through each lot number to retrieve the winning bidder's number associated with each piece sold. Next, the slovenly rat entered the bidder's file and captured the names and addresses of each participant associated with that bidder's number. He then merged the three files into one document and printed a hard copy. The theft of his employer's records took several hours, but by 11:00 PM, Ron had just enough time to drive to the Rib House to meet with the Russians.

Ron arrived at 11:15, backed into a space at the rear of the Rib House parking lot, and waited while munching on a bag of fried pork rinds, one of his favorite junk foods. The restaurant was closed, and the lot was deserted. Finally, at 11:30 sharp, the Russians pulled up in a black Mercedes S 560 sedan and parked next to the driver's side of Ron's heap of an automobile. Orlav stepped out and, with a gloved hand, opened the driver's door of Ron's car and greeted, "Good evening, Ron. Have you got the list for us?"

"Yeah, I've got it. Now, let's have the money," Ron replied as he got out of the car and handed over the document. Orlav took the report and thumbed through it to check if it contained the needed information.

"Well done, Ron." Suddenly, standing face to face, the last thing Ron heard was the click of Orlav's switchblade knife. Orlav jammed seven inches of razor-sharp stainless-steel blade right up through the bottom of Ron's chin with one smooth move. The blade severed his windpipe and penetrated the base of his brain.

Orlav pulled the knife out, and Ron staggered back. He clutched his throat and fell to the ground, making a gasping, gurgling sound. He died a horrible death, drowning in his own blood. For one last gesture of vile, Orlav wiped the blade off on Ron's shirt and mumbled: "You made a good deal, you pig!" Then, with the list safely in hand, he returned to the Mercedes, and the Russians drove off into the night.

Chapter 28

It was a cool morning around 9:00 AM, and Chef Pablo Ramirez drove into the Rib House parking lot at the rear of the building. A cheerful and hardworking individual who had moved to Cleveland from Puerto Rico, he has worked at the Rib House for ten years. He parked his car in the usual space and figured it would be another routine day as a prep cook for the restaurant. Pablo's job was to arrive early, get the smoker fired up for the barbequed entrees, heat the grill, and prepare the ingredients for other items on the menu. As he approached the restaurant's back door, he noticed the exhaust from an idling car parked at the far end of the parking lot. He could not see the driver in the car from his vantage point. Out of curiosity, he walked across the parking lot, and as he approached the rear of the vehicle, he was shocked at the gruesome sight before him. Sprawled out on the ground in a pool of blood, next to his Pontiac, was the bloated carcass of Ron Jameson. It had been lying there for over nine hours.

Pablo screamed at the terrifying sight and dashed back to the restaurant's rear door. He let himself in and dialed 911. "Cleveland Police Department, what is your emergency?"

He yelled, "A dead man is lying in the parking lot at the Rib House on Detroit Avenue! Get someone here right away! Help!"

Coincidentally, Patrolman Mike Petrella was walking out of The Coffee Bean coffee shop, located south of the Rib House on West 117th Street, when he heard the call go out on his handheld transceiver. He was holding a donut and a cup of coffee. Petrella is a short, overweight, dark-haired man of Italian descent who has been driving a patrol car in the city for over twenty years. "We have a possible homicide in the parking lot behind the Rib House on Detroit Avenue, code 3."

Responding, "This is Petrella. I am on the way." After spending years stationed in that precinct, he knew exactly where The Rib House was located and, with lights and sirens blaring, he was on his way to the bloody scene immediately.

Within 90 seconds, Officer Petrella sped into the rear lot of the Rib House and pulled up near Ron's car. Upon arrival, he observed Ron's lifeless body lying on his back in the parking lot. Petrella knelt, felt Ron's carotid artery, and surmised that Ron died from the horrific wound to the throat. As the first police officer at the crime scene, his duty was to secure the area, and he promptly called for backup to preserve all evidence. He was technically in charge of the scene until additional personnel arrived. Officer Petrella's first responsibility was to call into the First District headquarters on West 130th Street. He was immediately connected to the crime scene investigator on duty and spoke to Lt. Angelo Rossi. "Lieutenant, we have a deceased male victim on-site. I am securing it and need you here as soon as possible."

"I'll be right there, patrolman. Get the area closed off with yellow tape, and do not let anyone near the victim until we get there," he replied. Lt. Rossi, like Patrolman Petrella, descends from the large Italian-American community that arrived in Cleveland early in the 20th century to work in the city's factories. He is a fit, dark-complexioned man who works out to maintain his physique.

"Will do, Lieutenant."

Lt. Rossi's first action was to gather Sgt. Bob Robertson, the crime scene technician on duty. "Bob, grab your kit. We have a homicide in the parking lot behind the Rib House on Detroit Avenue. I'm heading over there now."

"No problem, Lieutenant, I'll be right over." By the time Lt. Rossi and Sgt. Robertson arrived, a crowd had started to gather around the scene. Patrolman Petrella also called headquarters for backup officers to help disperse the onlookers.

Lt. Rossi and Sgt. Robertson searched the immediate area and found little evidence, except for a shoe print. The previous winter's snowplowing had pushed sand into a flat, shallow pile where someone stepped, leaving a perfect shoe print. The officers examined Ron's shoes and realized they did not match the print in the sand. Sgt. Robertson immediately mixed plaster and made an impression.

As the lead investigator, Lt. Rossi started a murder book to keep a detailed record of the homicide investigation. Detectives use this document to note every step, including forensic reports, crime scene photos, interviews, and other relevant information. A site investigation is conducted, pictures are taken, measurements are recorded, and general observations are noted. The officers interviewed Pablo Ramirez, the cook. Aside from the plaster cast, the police had little to work with. There were no fingerprints. Lt. Rossi instructed one of the on-site police officers to spread out and knock on neighbors' doors to see if anyone had heard or seen anything.

After processing the scene, the police contacted the coroner's office, and a coroner's assistant was dispatched in a van to remove the body. The coroner's assistant arrived and examined the body. "It looks like he was stabbed right up through the trachea, and the knife probably pierced the lower section of his brain. Based on the amount of Rigor mortis, I would say the victim has been dead for over nine hours." Ron's body was transported to the Cleveland City morgue for examination by the medical examiner.

A medical examiner, often called a forensic medical examiner, is a doctor who examines bodies after death to find out the cause. They are also forensic pathologists who investigate deaths involving public interest.

Back at headquarters, Lt. Rossi and his investigators identified Ron Jameson as the victim when they found his driver's license. They also discovered a manila envelope in his car with an Integrity Auction Company label attached to it. Lt. Rossi called Bruce Howard to inform him of Ron's murder, and, of course, Bruce was shocked and saddened. "Do you know anyone who would want to harm Ron? Does he have any enemies?" asked Lt. Rossi.

"I don't know," Bruce replied.

"I need you to provide me with the names of his next of kin so we can notify them."

"Oh, of course! You must call his dear wife, Jessica. She will be mortified. Let me get her information for you. Oh, dear, oh my!"

Lt. Rossi obtained Jessica Jameson's contact details from the Cleveland Clinic and her home address from Bruce. He called her at the Clinic but found she was off that day. As a result, he drove to their home on Grace Avenue in Lakewood. The Jamesons lived in a charming Victorian house built in 1898. Delivering such bad news was the hardest part of the lieutenant's job.

He knocked on the door, and a beautiful woman answered. "Mrs. Jameson?"

"Yes?"

"My name is Lieutenant Angelo Rossi of the Cleveland Police Department," he said as he showed his badge and ID card from his wallet. "May I come in and speak to you?"

"Sure, come in. What is this about?"

"I am sorry to inform you that your husband was murdered last night."

"Murdered? Oh, my God, I can't believe it!" Jessica leaned back against an occasional table and began to sob. "He works very late some nights. I was frantic when I got up this morning and saw that he hadn't come home last night. I called his office, but no one knew Ron's whereabouts. I was just about to call the police this morning."

Lt. Rossi said, "We found him in the parking lot behind the Rib House on Detroit Avenue just inside Cleveland. We think that he was meeting someone. Do you know who that might be or why he was there?"

"I have no idea. Ron knew many people in the antique business."

After several questions went nowhere, Lt. Rossi said, "Well, if you think of anything, please call me," as he handed Jessica Jameson his business card and left.

Two days later, Lt. Rossi received a call from Detective Lt. Martin Schroeder of the Bay Village Police Department. Lt. Schroeder is a native of the area, having grown up in Westlake, a suburb just south of Bay Village. He is of German descent, with red hair and blue eyes, well-built, and slightly under six feet tall. Getting into a fight with him would be a bad idea. After exchanging pleasantries, he asked, "Lt. Schroeder, what can I do for you?"

"Well, maybe we can help each other out. I've been investigating the murder of Doctor Westley Engle, and I'm sure you're familiar with that case. I heard on the wire that you were working on the murder of Ron Jameson. I know Jameson worked at Integrity Auction Company, which sold Doctor Engle's belongings. I was at the auction trying to gather information. All I saw was a group of eager collectors spending a lot of money. We're stuck trying to solve Doctor Engle's murder. The only evidence we have is digital images of two bloody shoe prints left by the killers, tracked in Engle's blood. I wonder if the two murders are connected. Have you guys found any evidence that could help us?"

Lt. Rossi replied, "Well, it so happens that we are in the same boat as yourselves. After working on Jameson's murder for a couple of days, there's not much evidence. However, we did find a shoe print and made a casting of it."

Lt. Schroeder responded, "If you're going to be in your office, how about I come over with the images and see if we can find a match?"

"Sure, Lieutenant, come on over."

Lt. Schroeder arrived at the First District headquarters and met with Lt. Rossi. In a conference room, they were joined by Sgt. Bob Robertson, a crime scene technician who also trained in forensic podiatry. After the three of them compared the evidence, Robertson pointed to one of the prints. "Holy shit! The plaster casting matches this one print!" he exclaimed, "Looks to me like the two murders are connected!"

Chapter 29

Using the list of furniture pieces purchased at the Engle auction, along with the buyers' names and addresses, the Russians devised a plan to recover the flash drive that Westley had falsely promised. Their first target was about two hours south of Cleveland, off Interstate 77, near the community of Dover. The piece they were looking for was a Victorian R.J. Horner oak dining room sideboard from around 1895. Dr. Michael Berner, a proctologist practicing nearby, purchased the cabinet. Unfortunately, it was a piece the thugs didn't have a chance to search before being thrown out of the auction gallery.

Berner is an unattractive, middle-aged man who is overweight and has graying hair. He is a notorious collector with a terrible reputation, universally disliked for his caustic personality and dishonesty. Berner was an antique lamp collector who bought and sold on the side. He has a reputation for shady dealings over many years. He was known for selling numerous antique lamps that were damaged and poorly repaired, fraudulently failing to disclose such repairs to prospective buyers.

Before learning about Berner's poor reputation, Alex and Rosalie unfortunately bought a Cornelius & Baker solar lamp from him, which he falsely claimed was a period piece, asserting that both the base and shade were old and from the same era. The Penfields had just started collecting antique period lighting when they had the chance to buy the lamp. An experienced collector visited their home and said that while the base was old, the ball-shaped shade was a reproduction.

He explained, "Note that the glass is thick and foggy. The decorative elements are not refined. A distinct parting line runs down each side of the shade. These features clearly indicate that the shade is a reproduction."

Upon learning of that, Alex commented, "It's quite ironic that an asshole like this guy works on assholes!"

Dr. Berner had been married to his wife, Stella, for over twenty years. She worked hard at two jobs in their early years, supporting him while he attended medical school. She continued working while helping him establish his medical practice. Too busy with his medical career and completely self-absorbed, the doctor never wanted children. Well into his practice, Berner hired a young, attractive, uneducated local woman named Suellen Murphy as part of his office staff. She was tall and well-built, with large breasts and long brown hair, making her the perfect homewrecker. One thing led to another, and Dr. Berner divorced his faithful wife and moved the younger woman in to live with him.

Three days after killing Ron Jameson, Vladislav Volkov, aka "The Wolf," and Mikhail Orlov, aka "The Eagle," traveled south of Cleveland and found the doctor's house. It was once a farmhouse in a rural countryside setting. They arrived after dark and parked their Mercedes S 560 off the road, about 25 yards from the 1898 Victorian house owned by Dr. Berner. Dressed in black fatigues, carrying knapsacks, and with weapons in shoulder holsters, the intruders crept onto the back porch to the rear door. To their satisfaction, the door, equipped with an old-fashioned lock, was easy to pick. Orlov quickly moved the deadbolt to the open position with his lock-picking tool. As the Russians entered the house, they pulled out their eighteen-inch steel pipe weapons and moved swiftly and quietly through the kitchen, heading further into the back of the house.

As they approached a doorway leading to a side parlor, they noticed the flickering of a TV in a dimly lit room and saw the doctor and his live-in mistress seated on a couch. Without hesitation, they attacked the doctor, "Hey! Who the hell are you? Get out!" The doctor jumped up to defend himself, and even Suellen joined in, punching them wherever she could. The doctor and his mistress were no match for the two large goons swinging steel pipes, and soon, the couple was severely beaten, bloodied, and sprawled on the floor. "What the fuck do you bastards want?" groaned Dr. Berner.

"We want something in the sideboard you just bought in Cleveland," replied Volkov.

"We just got it, and there's nothing in it."

"We will be the judge of that," and gave them a few more whacks with the pipes.

With Dr. Berner and his mistress beaten into submission and lying on the floor, Orlav slipped off his knapsack and pulled out a couple of nylon ropes. The two thugs tied them up, bound their hands and feet behind their backs, and rolled them over face down.

The image from the catalog pointed out the sideboard. Removing crowbars and pry bars from their knapsacks, the Russians tore the piece apart. After half an hour, with the beautiful old cabinet reduced to a pile of lumber, Volkov yelled, "Dammit! It's not here! Let's go!" As the Russians turned to leave, Orlov lit an antique oil lamp displayed on a side table in the hall. Passing through the kitchen, Volkov stopped, partially pulled the gas range from the wall, and shut off the gas supply valve. Then, he broke off the flexible supply line with his steel bar and reopened the valve. The Vors slipped out of the house to the sound of hissing gas. They closed the door and stepped out into the dark.

The Russians rushed back to the Mercedes, tossed their gear into the trunk, started the car, and sped away. Orlav looked back a minute later and saw the good doctor's house erupt into a giant orange fireball. Pieces of the house rained down behind them. By the time the fire department arrived, there was little left of the house fire to extinguish.

At first daylight, Chief Liam McCarthy of the Dover Police Department and Dover Fire Chief Jim McDowell surveyed the horrible scene that was once the home of Dr. Berner and his girlfriend, Suellen. Then, the thorough investigation began. "Chief, after being here for only a few hours, I can tell you that this explosion was intentional and multiple murders were committed. The stove was pulled out from the wall, the gas supply line broke off, and the valve was set in the open position. There was some source ignition that triggered this. The bodies of Doctor Berner and Suellen Murphy were tied up and burned to death," explained Fire Chief McDowell. Meanwhile, the county coroner's people processed the scene to remove the two burned bodies.

That morning, patrolman Connor O'Sullivan of the Dover Police Department was assigned to interview homeowners within a one-mile radius of Dr. Berner's house. A neighbor down the street from Dr. Berner's home told the patrolman that he was sitting in his living room watching TV and, through the front window, saw "a big black car" drive away from the scene at high speed. However, he could not identify the make or license number because it was dark.

Lt. Martin Schroeder was having dinner with his family at the kitchen table in Bay Village that night. He was watching the six o'clock news on WEWS-TV 5 when the story about the house explosion-murder in Dover aired. The reporter interviewed the neighbor who had seen the black sedan leaving the scene. After watching the report, Schroeder leaned back and wondered, "What the hell is happening here?"

The following day, immediately after arriving at his desk in the Bay Village Police Department, Schroeder called Lt. Angelo Rossi at the Cleveland Police Department.

"Lt. Rossi speaking."

"Good morning, Lieutenant. Martin Schroeder calling from Bay Village. While having dinner last night, I watched the news and saw the story of the house explosion and double murder down in Dover. Did you happen to see that story?"

"Yeah, I did. Very bizarre. I can't believe you called this morning, as I was going to call you. Get this: The parking lot behind the Rib House, where

Jameson was murdered, sits on the east side of West 116th Street, north of Detroit. As part of our investigation, I had one of my patrolmen canvass the neighborhood along West 116th Street, to the north and south of Detroit Avenue, to see if anyone had seen anything. Lo and behold, a man who lives on West 116th Street, just two houses north of the Rib House, is a night owl and was watching TV at that hour. His house is on the west side of West 116th Street, and from his living room, he can see the parking lot across the street. He saw what he described as a large black sedan like the one the guy in Dover described, pull out of the lot just after 11:30, the night of the murder, and turn left, going south towards I-90."

Mahoney exclaimed, "Lieutenant, it sounds like the witness may have tied all three murders together!"

Chapter 30

A week after the break-in and murders at Dr. Berner's house, the Russians targeted another collector who had acquired a beautiful rosewood parlor cabinet with marquetry from the Engle auction. Built circa 1865 by the prestigious firm of Pottier & Stymus, the piece contains several drawers and compartments behind doors. Dewayne and Tamarius threw the Russian mobsters out before they could search it at the auction preview. Atlanta businessman Jack Hand won the cabinet through telephone bidding. Jack was a slender, gray-haired man, a wealthy 70-year-old egomaniacal electrical contractor. He made a fortune wiring hundreds of tract homes constructed in and around Atlanta during the city's building boom of the 1980s and '90s.

Jack lived with his trophy second wife, an attractive blonde-haired, well-endowed young woman named Scarlett, who lacked personality or intelligence, which suited Jack perfectly. Several years ago, Jack left his faithful wife of 35 years for the younger woman who worked in the office of one of his suppliers, Jackson Electric Supply. Upon meeting Scarlett, Jack was immediately smitten by her youth and natural beauty. For years, things had not been going well at home with his alcoholic first wife, so he decided to pursue an intense extramarital affair with Scarlett. Like many middle-aged men, Jack believed he could regain his youth and vitality by marrying a younger woman. Scarlett saw security and a good meal ticket in the older man. Ultimately, Jack's attorney negotiated a divorce settlement with his first wife, which cost Jack significantly. Two weeks after the divorce decree was signed, he married Scarlett.

Jack and Scarlett then built Jack's dream house, where he could showcase his young wife and his collection of late-Victorian decorative arts. Jack designed and built an 8,000-square-foot home in Mt. Paran-Northside, part of the Buckhead community known for its expensive homes on Atlanta's north side.

Like the Penfields, Jack was a seasoned collector for over 30 years. His collection focused on the final phase of the Victorian era, specifically the Aesthetic Movement, which ranged from the 1880s to the 1890s. Although pieces made by well-known artisans from this period are quite valuable, Alex and Rosalie looked down on that furniture style, considering it a sign of what Alex calls the decline in 19th-century design and craftsmanship. The casework is simple and boxy, the moldings are plain, the carvings are shallow, and the marquetry was mass-produced and imported pre-made from Europe to be glued onto the furniture as decoration.

One evening, Jack received a call from the Russian Vor Yaroslav Solkolov, who presented himself as a collector and claimed to have met Jack the previous year at Joshua Williams' Fabulous Auction in Tupelo. "Hello, Jack, this is Yaroslav Solkolov. I'm a fellow Victorian furniture collector and enjoyed meeting and visiting with you at Joshua Williams' auction last year. How are you?"

Jack was puzzled by the Russian's broken English and replied, "Well, sir, I'm fine. I don't remember you, but that's okay. I go to a lot of auctions and have met many people over the years. What can I do for you?"

"When we met at Joshua's, you said that if I were ever in the Atlanta area, I should give you a call. It so happens that I'm in Atlanta this week on business, and I was wondering if I could come by and visit. I would love to see your collection."

Jack was always eager to show off his collection, even to complete strangers, so that he could boast about his questionable knowledge and the variety of his furniture pieces. As a friendly and outgoing fellow, Jack replied, "That would be fine. How about the day after tomorrow, say 11:00 AM?"

"Sure, I will be there."

The Russian harbingers of death packed their gear and loaded it into the Mercedes S 560 sedan. The next day, they set out at sunrise, heading south on I-77 from the Cleveland area, passing through Akron and Canton, then into the scenic southern Ohio Appalachia. They crossed the Ohio River at Marietta, entering West Virginia. After traveling across the state and passing through Charleston, the Vors entered North Carolina north of Mt. Airy. They proceeded south through the state and took I-85 in Charlotte, continuing southwest into South Carolina and crossing the northwest corner of the state. They entered Georgia at Hartwell Lake, and about 100 miles further down I-85, they reached Atlanta after a 14-hour, 750-mile journey.

In Atlanta, they merged onto I-75 heading north and spent the night at a Hilton Hotel near Randal Mill. The next day, the Vors took a short drive north on I-75, exited near the intersection of Mt. Paran Road and Northside Parkway, and arrived at Jack's house in Mt. Paran at 11 AM sharp. The Mt. Paran – Northside neighborhood in Buckhead is one of Atlanta's most expensive residential areas, located northwest of the city center. The neighborhood's prestigious reputation makes it an exclusive community for Atlanta's successful professionals. Acres of wooded lots, meticulously manicured landscaping, and vibrant gardens surround the elegant homes.

The Vors climbed the wet, ornate, slippery wrought iron steps to Jack's front door. Dimitri rang the doorbell, whispering to Yaroslav, "I nearly fell on my ass on these goddamn steps! This guy better have the flash drive!"

The two Russian Vors were dressed like businesspeople standing on his front porch. Jack opened the front door. "Good morning, Jack. I am Yaroslav Solkolov. It's so lovely to see you again. I hope you don't mind that I invited my business associate, Mr. Dimitri Vasiliev."

"Welcome, y'all. Come on in." The men exchanged handshakes and pleasantries just inside the front door. Jack poorly designed the house, as it had no formal entrance room or foyer. The place opened into an oversized living room. Jack introduced the Russians to his wife, Scarlett, who sat on a sofa in an open space near the center of the room. Incapable of showing any ounce of manners by getting off her hind end to greet the men, she simply nodded. Instead, she was preoccupied with watching Fox & Friends on the local Fox TV affiliate, WAGA-TV, channel 5.

"You have a beautiful home, and what a lovely neighborhood," commented Yaroslav.

"Well, thank you," replied Hand. "You know, I'm writing a book on Victorian furniture. It will be the definitive literature for this period. So, tell me, what do you collect?"

"Oh, I like the Rococo and Renaissance Revival era of Victorian furniture, but I love all of it," he replied.

After touring Jack's collection on the first floor of the house, Yaroslav brought up the recent Engle auction. Knowing full well that Jack had bought the Pottier & Stymus parlor cabinet, Dimitri asked, "I wonder if you acquired anything from the Engle auction in Cleveland."

"Oh yeah, it just got delivered the other day. It's a gorgeous addition to my collection! I've waited 20 years to find one that's as pristine as this one. And this one is branded and numbered. No question, it's one of the best in the country."

Jack always insisted that if he owned a piece, it was definitely the country's best!

"I'm going to feature it in my book. It's right over here." Jack led the men to the piece for viewing. He beamed with pride as he turned to see Dimitri's reaction.

Without hesitation, Dimitri pulled out the Russian MP-443 Grach Yarygin automatic pistol from his shoulder holster and shot Jack right between the eyes at point-blank range. The bullet blasted right through his head, punching a 9mm hole in the wall as blood and brains splattered the beautiful damask wallpaper behind him. The impact of the shot threw him backward, and he dropped onto the hardwood floor. Dimitri spun around in one swift move, and before she could move, he fired two shots into Scarlett. She tumbled off the sofa onto the floor, face down.

The Vors had to work fast, worried that the noise from the gunshots might have attracted the neighbors' attention. Using the auction catalog, they confirmed that the cabinet was from the Engle collection. They then grabbed a short hatchet and a pry bar and carefully tore the piece apart, searching anxiously for the flash drive. After 15 minutes of breaking the cabinet into small pieces, they realized the flash drive was not there. Cursing, the Russians left empty-handed and headed back to Cleveland.

Unaware that the visitors were murderers, Jack had invited his daughter, Gretchen, to meet the so-called Russian collectors, but she had an appointment and couldn't arrive at his house until after 1:00 PM. An obnoxious, overweight, unkempt woman with greasy black hair, she also believed she knew everything about Victorian furniture. That appointment saved her life. When she arrived at 1:00 PM, Gretchen found the front door ajar and let herself in. She saw the carnage and nearly fainted but instead became hysterical.

She managed to compose herself and dialed 911.

"911, what is your emergency?"

"I am at 926 Forest Hill Lane, and someone has killed my father and his wife! My God, help!"

"Please tell me what the situation is."

"I walked into my father's house, and he and his wife were dead on the floor, shot!"

"Are they deceased?"

"Yes, for God's sake, get someone over here now!"

The first to arrive at the scene was patrol officer Jim Barker from the Zone 2 headquarters of the Atlanta Police Department. Met by Jack's daughter, Gretchen, at the door, he immediately entered the home, checked the bodies, and confirmed they were deceased. Barker then called for backup to secure the house for evidence and contacted headquarters to summon the on-duty crime scene investigator. Standard police protocol was followed: a murder book was opened, and officers were dispatched to canvas the neighborhood to see if anyone had seen anything.

Police interviewed a retired neighbor who was watering his flower bed down the street when he saw a large black sedan with out-of-state plates leaving Jack's driveway. The neighbor recognized the make and model as a Mercedes S 560 sedan because he owned a Mercedes himself and admired the wealthy visitors at Hand's house. Sadly, the elderly witness didn't get the license plate number as the black car sped away. The murders made the evening news and stirred up a lot of talk, since there hadn't been a murder in Mt. Paran-Northside in recent memory.

Chapter 31

The most extraordinary antiquing experience in their forty years of collecting happened for the Penfields in the Deep South near Natchez, Mississippi.

It is 1859, two years before the outbreak of the Civil War. The South was an economic powerhouse built on slavery. Slave labor produced 80 percent of the world's cotton supply, surpassing tobacco, rice, and sugar in economic significance. It supplied cotton fabric production to both the United States and Europe. Eli Whitney's invention of the cotton gin in 1793 transformed cotton production, significantly reducing the time needed for processing it.

Richland Beau LeBlanc was a third-generation member of a French planter family that settled along the Mississippi River in the eighteenth century. Standing five feet ten inches tall, with blue eyes and blond hair, he was handsome at age forty. With plantations near Natchez along the Mississippi River, he owned 300 enslaved people and farmed over 2000 acres. LeBlanc was one of the country's largest cotton producers.

The LeBlanc townhome in Natchez, "Felicite," was one of the grandest in the South and rivaled any other private residence in the country at the time. The twelve-thousand-square-foot mansion overlooks the Mississippi River. Greek Revival in design, it was surrounded on all four sides by three-story white columns and was constructed by enslaved people in 1850.

It was a palace furnished with the finest antebellum treasures. Mrs. Arabella Georgina LeBlanc and her husband, Richland, shopped at the best decorative arts stores during their trips to New York City. Mrs. LeBlanc was a tall, beautiful woman with long black hair, brown eyes, and creamy white skin. One of their favorite acquisitions was the large fourteen-piece hand-carved rosewood double parlor suite made by John Henry Belter's shop. Notably, the suite included a pair of one-of-a-kind, massive sofas. By 1862, the LeBlancs had two lovely children; life and prosperity were good.

By the middle of the Civil War, one or more battles took place near Natchez. The city remained mostly undamaged, despite being shelled from the river by a Union ironclad ship in September 1863.

By July 1864, the Southern agricultural economy was collapsing. The Union Army, which was conquering the region, freed enslaved people fleeing the area. They also stationed thousands of soldiers in the South to restore order. Richland LeBlanc lost his fortune when the Union Army burned his last cotton crop at the port of Natchez.

One morning, a platoon of approximately 25 Union soldiers on patrol approached the house, and the commander, the unstable and corrupt Capt. Reginald Hatchett, ordered that the home be ransacked and burned. Capt. Hatchett did not occupy a place of respect among the Union commanding officers and was relegated to patrolling the outlying areas in and around Natchez. He hated Southerners and had been made aware of the valuables inside. He ordered everything, including LeBlanc's prized Belter parlor set with its two fabulous sofas, to be loaded onto three wagons and taken away.

"Captain Hatchett, I mean you no harm. Please spare our home so my wife and children will have a place to live," pleaded Richard LeBlanc. "I have lost everything."

"All right, Rebel, I'll spare your house," replied Hatchett.

During the chaos at the end of the war, LeBlanc was forced to sell the remaining belongings of the home that hadn't been taken, along with the house and land. Overwhelmed, he took his own life by shooting himself in the head with his pistol.

Since they disliked flying, Rosalie and Alex traveled by car to Natchez to attend an antique auction held by local auctioneer Reggie Anderson. A significant collection of important Victorian decorative arts, which had furnished Willoughby, a grand town mansion, was available for sale to the highest bidder. The owner passed away, and his will stipulated that all his belongings were to be sold at auction.

Among the many trips the Penfields took into America's Deep South, Natchez, Mississippi, stands out as one of their favorite destinations. They appreciate Natchez for its vibrant history and its unrivaled collection of pre-Civil War homes, both private and open to visitors. Because it was spared from the destruction that many other Southern cities faced during the Civil War, Natchez has preserved more antebellum homes than any other city, including some of the most stunning in the country.

They chose to stay at their favorite lodging, Mount Airie, a renowned mansion built in 1856 with Greek Revival architecture, surrounded by a colonnade of large white columns on all sides. Their room was decorated entirely with period antiques, including an eleven-foot-tall full-tester bed that was delightful to sleep in.

Willoughby was built in 1830 by Jarid Marshall, a successful cotton factor known as a broker. The mansion features a hipped roof, a two-story brick structure with two-story columns across the front and back.

On Friday morning, before the auction, the Penfields picked up their friends, Ned Samuels and Jeffrey Martinsen, from Washington, D.C., who had flown to Natchez via Atlanta to join them. The four eager collectors drove to the house, located in the center of town, to preview the collection. The boys and the Penfields registered for the auction and received their bidders' numbers. One can never miss the preview, soak in the atmosphere, and kibitz with other collectors.

The Penfields ran into Dave Petrocelli, and it was no surprise. As a seasoned collector, he never misses out on a major sale.

"Hey folks, how the hell are you?" I knew I would probably see you!" he exclaimed.

"Hi, Dave, it's great to see you!" As everyone was introduced, they shook hands and gave Rosalie a hug. "You know we would never miss a good sale. Natchez is one of our favorite places to visit. It's so historic," Rosalie replied. "Why don't you join Ned, Jeffrey, and us for dinner? We know a great restaurant that was once a historic stage stop. Great food. We eat there whenever we're in Natchez."

"Sure! We'll hook up after we've previewed everything!" After spending the whole afternoon inspecting everything for sale, they headed out for dinner. After an extraordinary meal, they said goodnight. Ned, Jeffrey, and the Penfields drove to Mount Airie to turn in for the night.

Always excited to attend an important auction like this, Alex found it hard to sleep that night. The next day, he was the first to wake up and placed his hand on Rosalie's cheek. "Good morning, my sweetheart," he said. "I'm famished. Let's get bathed and go downstairs for a great big breakfast. I swear I can smell it now!"

Calling Ned, he said they were already up and getting dressed. Everyone met downstairs and was greeted by the house hostess, Mrs. Gladstone. She is a lovely Southern woman, slim with brunette hair cut neatly above her shoulders, blue eyes, and a charming Mississippi accent. Her chef, a handsome Black woman named Bertha, was busy preparing a fabulous Southern breakfast of fried eggs, grits, bacon, and, best of all, homemade biscuits. There is nothing like homemade Southern biscuits.

"Oh, my God, it smells so good in here!" exclaimed Alex. "I have been looking forward to your lovely breakfast since last night!"

"Why, thank you!" replied Bertha." It's my pleasure."

After enjoying Bertha's wonderful breakfast, the Penfields and the boys arrived at Willoughby on Saturday at 10:00 AM to find a large crowd of eager auction-goers. They always make a point to arrive an hour early to examine everything thoroughly.

The auction was a one-day event starting at 11:00 AM, during which everything would be sold as is, where is, on that day. Since the auction took place on-site, each object that came up for sale was brought outside under a large tent and auctioned off. Chairs for over a hundred attendees were in place and filled with bidders. Auctioneer Reggie explained the terms of the sale. As the auction began, excitement filled the air, bidding was fierce, and the prices skyrocketed. The Penfields had their eye on a beautiful, six-foot-wide, and just under eight-foot-tall three-door, classical-style mahogany armoire that was allegedly one of the house's original furnishings, circa 1825. The side panels were made of solid Cuban mahogany, and the faces of the doors were veneered with highly figured fiddle-back mahogany. The piece naturally disassembled into its parts for moving. They were also interested in bidding on two early Cornelius & Baker solar lamps from the 1850s. Each light was fitted with a quality period shade. Although there were not many pieces that interested the Penfields, they relished being there, taking in all the action. As always, Alex could not stay seated, prowling the auction and examining all the merchandise.

Two hours into the auction, one of the Cornelius & Baker lamps was offered for bid. It featured an ornate tripartite base and an elaborate period ball shade. It had never been electrified.

"This is a good Cornelius lamp. Do I have $400? Yes!" The bid came from a bidder in the back of the room.

"$500?" "Yes!" shouted Alex.

"$600?" "Yes!" exclaimed the bidder in the back of the room.

"$700?" "Yes!" shouted Alex.

It looked like the bidder in the back of the room had had enough. "Sold! To Alex Penfield!"

An hour later, the auctioneer brought up the fancy three-section mahogany armoire.

"This is one of the best I have seen. It is a piece of Southern antebellum history. It is believed to be original to the house. Do I have $3000?" "Yes!" as several hands went up.

"4000?" "Yes!" shouted Alex.

"5000?" "Yes!" It came from another bidder.

"6000?" "Yes!" shouted Alex.

It seemed that the competitive bidder had run out of steam. "Sold! To Alex Penfield!"

Alex turned to Rosalie and hugged her. "That will look great in our bedroom, my sweetheart!"

Finally, forty-five minutes later, the second Cornelius & Baker lamp came up for sale.

"Do I have 500?" "Yes!" shouted Alex.

"600?" "Yes!" came from another bidder.

"700?" "Yes!" shouted Alex.

"800?" "Yes!" It came from the other bidder. "Shit!" exclaimed Alex. "That guy is going to make us pay. I'll hit him one more time."

"900?" "Yes!" exclaimed Alex.

"Do I have $1000?" asked the auctioneer. The other bidder hesitated and stepped out. "Sold! To Alex Penfield!"

"Those lamps will look great in our two guest rooms!" exclaimed a cheerful Rosalie.

In the meantime, Ned and Jeffrey kept busy bidding on a couple of lots and won the auction for a beautiful John Henry Belter armchair in the Rosalie pattern. By the end of the day, everyone was exhausted but happy to have taken part in the auction. The Penfields paid their bill and called to arrange the shipment of the armoire with a local trucking company that specializes in moving antiques. They packed the lamps for transport in the trunk of the Cadillac.

During the auction, a fellow collector named Lawson Madison started a conversation with Alex. Lawson was an interesting character, wearing a cowboy hat and a toy sheriff's badge. He jokingly explained that he was there "to keep order." Lawson noted that the Penfields are successful, aggressive bidders. After spending the day getting to know each other, he said, "Why don't you and your friends join us for dinner tonight? We know a great restaurant where we usually meet to celebrate our wins or commiserate over our losses. There will be my wife and me, Charlene, Blade and his wife, Clarice, and Doctor David Goldstein and his wife, Marsha. They are all serious collectors like yourself."

"Sure! We would love to! May we include our friend Dave Petrocelli? Maybe you know him. Please let us know where to meet you."

"Yeah, I know, Dave! The more, the merrier!"

Lawson led the group to their favorite watering hole, Joey's Bar. When they arrived, they sat with Lawson and his wife, Charlene, across from Alex and Rosalie. Blade and his wife, Clarice, sat beside the Lawsons, facing Penfield's friends Ned and Jeffrey. Dr. David Goldstein and his wife, Marsha, sat next to Blade and Clarice. Across from the Goldsteins sat Dave Petrocelli. This group of friends owns millions of dollars worth of valuable Victorian collections from around the country.

After everyone was seated, the waitress arrived and took cocktail orders. Naturally, the first topic was, what did everybody buy? The discussion of everyone's acquisitions sparked a lively and engaging conversation.

Although the bar is a smoke-free establishment, Lawson pulled out his cigarettes and started to smoke. The restaurant management looked the other way since he was a long-time loyal customer. Alex couldn't help but notice that Lawson was giving him the evil eye when he asked, "Where are you folks from?"

"We live in the small, quiet suburban town of Gates Mills, about forty miles east of Cleveland, Ohio," he replied. "How about you, Lawson? Where do you folks hail from?"

"We live in Oxford, located in Southwestern Alabama," said Lawson.

Alex continued, "I come from a family with a multigenerational connection to the Deep South. My grandparents on my father's side lived in Stamford, Texas, where he worked as an accountant for a cottonseed manufacturer in the 1920s. There, he was recruited to be a member of the Ku Klux Klan. He may have joined the Klan's 66 chapter later, after he moved his family to Dallas. His father, my great-grandfather, fought for the Confederacy in Hood's Texas Brigade."

That caused Lawson to raise his bushy eyebrows, and after an engaging discussion about his hobby of collecting antiques, he asked, "What religion are you?"

A devout atheist, Alex replied with a straight face, "We are Orthodox Hedonists." That quieted Lawson after he cast a suspicious look at the Penfields.

As the evening progressed, everyone engaged in stimulating conversation. Lawson, a rotund man, worked as a real estate agent, while his wife, Charlene, was a homemaker. Blade Ward, physically fit, was a prince of a man who, along with his wife, owned a successful plumbing business. Dr. David Goldstein, a personable and accomplished orthopedic hand surgeon, was married to Marsha, who was also a homemaker.

Before and during dinner, the Penfields and everyone else drank one or more cocktails to celebrate their newly acquired antiques. Early in the meal, Lawson declared that he did not drink alcoholic beverages, but near the end of dinner, he proceeded to down several rounds of brandy to "flavor his coffee."

By the end of dinner, it was clear that Lawson had become intoxicated, and the liquor had loosened his tongue. In a bragging tone, "I have heard for many years of the existence of a fabulous Belter sofa that matches the one in the Victoria and Albert Museum in London. Rumors are that it is somewhere in Alabama or Mississippi, but no one knows for sure."

That comment intrigued Rosalie and Alex. At the end of the evening, the joyful party broke up, and everyone said their goodbyes before heading their separate ways.

Chapter 32

Early Sunday morning, after the auction, the Penfields took their good friends, Ned Samuels and Jeffrey Martinsen, to the Natchez airport, where they boarded a puddle jumper flight to Atlanta for a connection home to Washington, DC.

Later that morning, the lovebirds set out for a bicycle ride. Avid riders, the Penfields have installed a bike rack on the back of their Cadillac to transport their bicycles. They love to ride local trails whenever they go on vacation and bring their bikes along, as they plan to spend a couple of days riding at various venues around Natchez. The weather cooperated with the forecasts, granting them sunny skies and warm temperatures. Over the years, the Penfields have logged over 10,000 miles on their bicycles, riding multiple trails across the country.

Rosalie evaluated various trails and recommended they ride the Church Hill/Natchez Trace Loop Trail, which starts about 10 miles outside Natchez. This 22-mile trail features several historic sites. The route includes passing by Christ Church, a Gothic structure built in the 1790s, along with its historic cemetery. Wagner's Grocery, built in 1837, is an abandoned building that still stands and once served as the local post office. Temple Mound is an ancient Indian burial mound used between 1300 and 1600. Mount Locust is a visitor center housed in one of the oldest plantation houses, dating back to around 1790. The area also includes numerous plantation houses, such as Cedars Plantation and Springfield Plantation, built between 1786 and 1791, where Andrew Jackson was married.

A couple of hours and ten miles into the ride, "Hey, Rosalie, are you getting hungry? There's great scenery here along Cole's Creek. What do you say we stop and have lunch?"

"Hey! I see a nice picnic bench up ahead. Let's stop there," Rosalie replied. Alex equipped their bicycles with bike-carrying bags that were large enough for their picnic and water. Rosalie loves picnics and prepares gourmet sandwiches, potato chips, and fresh grapes for the luncheon. With the lovely meal and the scenery, one could not ask for anything more.

Suddenly, they heard a man screaming for help, his mournful pleas coming from a secluded area in the nearby forest. Alex jumped up, ran to his bike, and grabbed his Smith & Wesson Model 19 from his bike bag. The .38-caliber, six-shot revolver with a 2 1/2" barrel is suitable for protection. Alex felt safe carrying a weapon because they chose to ride in an unfamiliar out-of-state area. Since Ohio has concealed-carry reciprocity with Mississippi, it is perfectly legal for the Penfields to possess the gun.

Following the sound of the screaming for help, they arrived at a clearing in the forest where a young Black man was tied up to a tree. Three men were savagely beating him with steel pipes. Alex immediately noticed that two men were wearing shirts with emblems of the Swastika and the Ku Klux Klan. A rope had been thrown over a thick branch with the intent of lynching the young man.

Alex whispered, "Rosalie, stay back; get down out of sight." He raised his gun to a firing position and pulled the hammer back. Shouting, "Get away from the young man! Drop the pipes and put your hands up! I will not hesitate to kill every one of you!" Fortunately, they were in an open section of the forest, and Alex could see clearly that just the three men were involved.

One of the men reached for a gun on his belt, and Alex pulled the trigger and shot him in the chest. The attacker was thrown back and hit the ground, mortally wounded. Just then, a second man pulled a gun from his backside belt and fired, narrowly missing Alex. He returned fire, hitting him in the face, and the man died before hitting the ground.

To the third man, Alex yelled, "You! I've called the police, and they are on the way!" He replied, "You don't know who you are screwing with, Mack! You're going to be very sorry!" The man backed off slowly and suddenly ran off into the underbrush.

While Alex stood guard, watching for the assailant to double back, Rosalie ran in from nearby and untied the man from the tree. He collapsed onto the ground. Mortally injured from the beating, the man identified himself as Jeramie Steele. "Oh my God, thank you!" Breathless, he said, "Listen to me! I am an investigative reporter working for the Free Press in Jackson. We're located 104 miles northeast of Natchez. I have been working for months investigating a corrupt Natchez police captain named Johnson Dagget and other local police officers who are members of the Ku Klux Klan. I have produced an extensive dossier on them. They protect local criminals and share in the profits of producing and selling methamphetamine."

The reporter exclaimed, "Do not go to the local police! They're all corrupt! Get yourselves to the FBI in Jackson! Now!" Meanwhile, Rosalie called 911 and ordered emergency services to the scene.

Jeramie said, "I'm hurt bad and don't think I will make it. I was intimately involved with Captain Dagget's daughter. We fell deeply in love. He found out about us and ordered those criminals to beat and kill me! He does not know about the dossier, however."

Rosalie exclaimed, "I've called an ambulance. We've got to get you out of here!"

"Don't bother; I may die, and if I do, please do me a favor. You have got to get the dossier. It is a 75-page document sealed in a water-tight plastic box and is buried on the west side of the base of General James Rothstat's grave in Natchez Cemetery. Locate a short stick protruding about an inch out of the dirt. That's where you dig up the box. The documents contain instructions for downloading a copy of the paper from my computer for publication. For God's sake, find the other copy in the box and get it to the FBI. I have run out of time."

At that moment, Jeramie coughed up a large amount of blood, indicating serious internal injuries, and suddenly stopped breathing. Alex yelled, "Jeramie! Don't leave us now!" He quickly started CPR, pressing hard on his sternum in an attempt to revive him, but it was no use. He was gone.

As the sounds of emergency vehicles, including one of Sheriff Dagget's henchmen, came into view, the Penfields hurriedly fled the scene on their bikes, raced to the trailhead, threw the bikes into the car, and sped away in the Cadillac. Luckily, the remote bicycle trail was thick with trees and undergrowth, fully hiding the couple.

Chapter 33

Racing out of Natchez, the Penfields head onto Mississippi Route 28 and speed down the highway, heading northeast toward Jackson. Using her cellphone, Rosalie immediately contacts the FBI and connects with Agent Jason Stephenson. She explains the incident in detail.

"Stay on that highway, keep moving, do not let anyone stop you, including local police. I have dispatched a team of agents to meet you."

Rosalie hung up the phone and asked Alex, "Who in the hell were those guys trying to kill poor Jeramie?"

"From what I saw of the emblems on their shirts, it looks like they were local Klansmen and Nazis. You may have heard me tell Lawson about my grandfather the other night. Family legend claims that he was a member of the Ku Klux Klan in the 1920s and 1930s, while the family lived in Stamford and Dallas, Texas. Years ago, I did some research on this."

Alex continued, "The KKK was one of this country's first terror groups. It was founded in late 1865 by six former Confederate Army officers embittered by losing the Civil War. The Klan was an attempt by Confederates to win through terrorism what they had been unable to win on the battlefield. The group harassed the freed African Americans and anyone else perceived to act against their conservative philosophy. White supremacy is their fundamental creed. The Klan faded out by the 1870s, as the country grew tired of their violence."

"By the turn of the twentieth century, the Klan reared its ugly head again. Millions of immigrants from all over the world were pouring into the country. Many people worried that foreigners were swamping the country. America's involvement in World War I brought an unsettling effect on the land, creating hatred, suspicion, and distrust of anyone foreign. This era saw the beginning of efforts in the Deep South to deny African American people political, social, and economic power. Most segregation laws date from that period. A series of lynchings of African American people by white mobs occurred during this time. The combination of legalized racism and the constant threat of violence led to significant Black migration to Northern cities."

"The new Klan represented a fervent conservatism: pro-American, which for them meant anti-Black, anti-Jewish, and most importantly, anti-Catholic."

"The national headquarters in Atlanta established an innovative marketing department to travel across the country and recruit members. It became a major revenue source, earning millions in membership fees and selling those ridiculous costumes. By 1921, they had recruited 100,000 members, which grew to one million by 1922. By 1925, the organization had a nationwide reach with anywhere from two to five million members and the support of millions more. Membership consisted of middle-class White American men and their families, including small-business owners, salespeople, ministers, professors, accountants, clerks, farmers, doctors, and lawyers."

"The Klan preached the restoration of 'true Americanism' and offered members a platform that demonized African Americans, Catholics, Jews, Mexicans, Asians, and any other nonwhite immigrants. It grew primarily in response to issues of declining morality typified by divorce, adultery, defiance of Prohibition, and criminal gangs in the news daily. It also responded to the growing power of Catholics and American Jews and the proliferation of non-Protestant cultural values."

"They condemned Communism or any other form of leftist politics, adultery, alcohol consumption, birth control, and the teaching of evolution in public schools. From the 1910s through the 1930s, Klansmen carried out hundreds of beatings, whippings, and countless murders."

"The Klan portrayed itself as a fraternal organization, giving members a sense of belonging to something special. They allegedly sponsored many community activities such as parades, picnics, baseball teams, public concerts, and 'Ku Klux Klan Day' at the State Fair of Texas."

"For every Klansman who joined for the opportunity to bully, threaten, and beat African Americans, immigrants, and adulterers, dozens of other members sought community and civic involvement. Many aimed to forge business and political connections with other middle-class white people and for the chance to be publicly proud of being White, Protestant, and native-born American. They even got politicians elected!"

"They looked absurd yet frightening as they paraded around in long white robes with a circular red patch featuring a white vertical cross with a drop of blood at its center. According to Klan heritage, this represents bloodshed to protect the white race. To complete the costume, everyone wore a pointed hood! The bastards even burned crosses on their enemy's property!"

Rosalie was deeply shaken by the thought of her husband's family's past, but was impressed by Alex's recollection of American history. Alex was passionate about the subject, regardless of where the issue led him.

Chapter 34

Jacob Pence was the man Alex chased off at the scene of Jeramie's beating. He ran to his pickup truck and drove to Wanda Dagget's house. She is the daughter of Sheriff Johnson Daggett. Jacob and Wanda dated for a year before she met Jeremie Steele. Wanda works from home, managing accounting tasks for an offshore oil drilling company, and spends eight hours each day in front of a computer. Wanda is slim, tall, and statuesque, with long blonde hair and blue eyes. She was the prom queen in her senior year of high school and was very popular. Although she has never been educated beyond high school, she is proficient in accounting and computer skills, making her well-suited for her work.

Like Wanda, Jacob also grew up in Natchez but never went past eighth grade, spending his adult years in low-paying, labor-intensive jobs. He is uneducated; his only edge is his good looks. Tall, slim, muscular, dark-skinned, and with brown eyes, Jacob can make any young lady's heartbeat race. He walked up the steps and knocked on Wanda's front door. When she answered, she stepped outside onto the porch and said, "Jacob, what in the hell are you doing here?"

He answered, "Wanda, I just want you to know that Joe Bob, Frank, and I killed that Black son of a bitch you're so in love with! I had to put an end to your nonsense!"

She fell to her knees, "You no good, dirty bastard! How could you! I loved that man! He was something that you could never be! He was educated, kind, and thoughtful!"

Jacob replied, "He was also Black! How could you fall in love with someone like that?"

Wanda stood up, stepped back into her house, and slammed the door in his face. She ran to grab her purse, dashed to her garage, started her car, pulled out, and sped to the central Natchez police station where her father is based.

Rushing into his office, "You son of a bitch! You killed Jeramie! How could you? I loved him!" Wanda yelled as loudly as she could so everyone in the office could hear her.

"He was a Black man! You are in the Deep South! How could you get involved with him?" yelled Captain Dagget.

"I know what you do with that scum! You're mixed up with those Klansmen and Nazis making meth! I'm going to take you down!" shouted Wanda.

Later that night, as Wanda sat in her living room, her father, Sheriff Dagget, drove to his daughter's house and knocked on the front door. Opening the door, "What do you want?"

Stepping into her front room, he said, "You must listen to me. There are very dangerous people involved with the production of meth around here. I can't control them. I would hate to see something horrible happen to you. I love you very much, and these people have warned me they may kill you if you get in the way. They could kill me, for that matter."

"I don't care if they kill me!" shouted Wanda. "Your association with that scum makes you as evil as they are! If there's a way, I'll take you down!"

Chapter 35

Out on the highway, Alex accelerated the Cadillac to speeds over a hundred miles per hour on Mississippi Route 28 heading toward Jackson, which is 100 miles away. The Penfields hope they are not being followed. Rosalie immediately calls the FBI, hoping the agents will clear the way for them if they are stopped by local law enforcement. She's quickly patched through to Agent Stephenson.

"Mrs. Penfield, this is Agent Stephenson."

"Agent, I am worried that some local Podunk sheriff might intercept and attack us before we reach you. Can you stay on the line with us? We are very concerned."

"Mrs. Penfield, as soon as we got off the phone earlier, I dispatched a car with agents, and they are on their way at a very high speed to meet you. You should see them very shortly. Certainly, I will stay on the line with you."

About halfway between Fayette and Hazelhurst, the Penfields sped past a local sheriff parked on the roadside, hidden in some underbrush, reading the local newspaper and nursing a cup of coffee. He accelerated his cruiser, dashed onto the highway after them, and turned on his lights to pull them over.

A half-hour earlier, over the county police wire, it was announced: "To all police authorities based between Natchez and Jackson along route 28: This is Captain Johnson Daggett of the Natchez police department. Two fugitives suspected of murder are en route, traveling northeast in a late-model black Cadillac, headed towards Jackson at a high rate of speed. They are armed and dangerous. Approach with caution and be prepared to use deadly force to apprehend if necessary."

Grossly overweight, with a gut hanging over his gun belt, patrolman Erastus McCauley of Fayette caught up to the Penfields, who were racing at 90 miles per hour. He pulled within inches of the back of their Cadillac, with lights flashing and siren screeching. Fearing they might be shot at, Alex slowed down and pulled over to stop on the side of the road. As he stepped out of his patrol car, McCauley unholstered his Glock 19 9MM, fully intending to kill the couple.

Thankfully, within seconds, the FBI appeared, roaring in at 100 miles per hour with all lights flashing. An agent skidded the black SWAT Chevrolet Suburban to a stop. Four agents, armed with their Sig Sauer P229 Double Action Kellerman 45ACPs, jumped out, shouting, "Patrolman, holster your sidearm, back away from the subject's automobile, or we will shoot you! They are witnesses to a capital crime."

"These people are suspects in a capital murder in Natchez, and I am going to arrest them!" shouted McCauley.

Lead agent Tad Montgomery walked up to the sheriff, his sidearm drawn and glaring within inches of his face. "You will do no such thing, asshole! These are my witnesses, and I am taking them into custody under the protection of the FBI. We are already aware that these folks witnessed a lynching murder in Natchez. They reported it to the FBI, and the information was purposely miscommunicated over the local police wires."

After the local hick police officer drove off, Agent Montgomery asked the Penfields to join him in the Suburban and provide a statement. Alex recounted the incident: "Rosalie and I were taking a lovely bike ride on the Church Hill/Natchez Loop Trail outside of Natchez when we decided to stop for lunch. We heard screams coming from nearby and saw three men beating Jeramie Steele, whom they had tied to a tree, intending to lynch him. I grabbed my registered Smith & Wesson and stopped the beating by shooting two of the men after they drew their weapons on me. They had every intention of killing us."

Rosalie added, "As he lay dying on the ground after I untied him, he told us that he was a reporter who wrote a dossier exposing the illegal drug activities of local police officers and Klansmen. It is hidden at the grave of General James Rothstat."

"Let's go get it!" exclaimed Agent Montgomery.

The Penfields followed the FBI agents to Natchez and arrived at the Natchez City Cemetery. After tromping all over the area, they found General Rothstat's grave and, while looking around it, discovered the stick. Shouting to the other agents, Agent Montgomery ordered, "Grab those military collapsible shovels that are in the back of the Suburban!" After a few minutes of digging, the agents uncovered the plastic box that contained the dossier. "Bingo!" exclaimed Montgomery as the agents secured the dossier.

Agent Montgomery asked the Penfields to accompany the agents to Jackson to provide a statement. First, they went to Dunleith Mansion in Natchez to retrieve their belongings, check out, and settle their bill. For their safety, the FBI team escorted the Penfields to Jackson.

Back at FBI headquarters, the agents open the plastic box containing the documents produced by Jeramie Steele. The agents are amazed by the reporter's extensive work. The FBI has been investigating a group producing crystal meth distributed across the South for over a year. He has uncovered crucial information about a group calling itself the "Rebel Mafia." This confirmed the FBI's suspicion that Captain Daggett was connected to the Rebel Mafia and its widespread production and sale of crystal methamphetamine.

The FBI quickly carried out a major raid on the police headquarters in Natchez and arrested Captain Daggett. They detained several of his accomplices both inside and outside the police department. Upon learning of her father's arrest, Wanda Daggett stepped forward to inform the FBI that her father had also ordered the murder of her dear lover, Jeramie Steele.

All parties will face trial; the Penfields will likely be asked to return to testify. While under arrest and locked up in the Natchez jail awaiting a bail hearing, Captain Daggett hanged himself that night.

Chapter 36

As they sat in the FBI parking lot in Jackson, Alex mentioned part of his conversation with Lawson Madison. "I don't know if you noticed, but Lawson made an issue more than once of his not consuming alcoholic beverages. However, he drank at least six brandies to flavor his coffee during the meal, becoming intoxicated and quite chatty regarding a lost treasure. He claimed that an identical mate to the famous Belter sofa in the Victoria and Albert Museum in London exists and is located in a house somewhere in the Deep South, but nobody knows its whereabouts. You know the piece. It is the most magnificent example of Victorian Rococo Revival seating furniture and, if found, it would be worth a fortune."

"Since we are down here, what do you say we see if we can find it?" asked Rosalie.

"Hell, yes! Let's go! I have always loved your sense of adventure, Rosalie!" replied Alex.

The Penfields drove onto Interstate 20 heading west and embarked on the forty-minute trip to the historic city of Vicksburg, which is situated on the Mississippi River. They checked into the grand antebellum house known as Anchuca Mansion B&B. Having stayed there before, they requested and were given the most exquisite bedroom in the house. The room is lavishly decorated with pre-Civil War furnishings, including an eleven-foot-tall half-tester bed.

Opening their tablet, they Googled and accessed the Victoria and Albert Museum website in London, England. As they scrolled, they discovered images of the sofa. "My God, it is magnificent!" exclaimed Alex. "The sofa was purchased by Sir Alfred George Beech Owen, owner of Rubery Owen & Company, a multi-billion-dollar private family manufacturing business that is among the largest in Britain. The sofa was sold when his family's estate and its contents, New Hall Manor, were auctioned off in October 1982, following Sir Alfred's death in 1975. Oddly, the piece ended up in England. The museum states that he purchased the sofa sometime in the 1920s from an antique dealer. I wonder if that was in the United States or England?"

"The story gets even better! Somebody tipped off the major New York antique dealer, Ben Bernstein, that the sofa was about to go on the auction block. He bid at the auction, was the winning bidder through a transatlantic phone call, and bought the piece for just $38,385! What a bargain! The Victoria and Albert Museum, which desperately wanted the piece, invoked British laws against exporting significant antiquities and works of art. Britain's Minister for the Arts was notified about the sale and denied Bernstein an export license to take it out of the country. When Victoria and Albert officials appealed to the Minister, they declared the Belter sofa 'a document of international importance both technologically and stylistically.' The Minister gave the Victoria and Albert Museum eight months to raise the funds to buy the sofa from Bernstein. Both parties agreed on a sale price of $60,000, which matched the highest price ever paid for a Belter piece sold in November 1980. These pieces would sell for much more today!"

Chapter 37

The next day, the Penfields set out in search of the lost Belter treasure! They decided to begin their search in Mississippi by visiting several dealers with whom they had done business. Their first destination was the Riverview Manor shop in Vicksburg, owned by Clyde Emerson and Dawson Hayes. Clyde is a thin, personable man and an impeccable dresser, while Dawson is more standoffish, with deep blue eyes and a portly build. Their shop is filled with high-quality merchandise and a wealth of Victorian decorative art, making it challenging to navigate the place.

Rosalie spotted a beautiful Parian porcelain statue of a maiden with a butterfly on her index finger. The figure was in perfect condition, with no chips. "Clyde, how much is the young girl with the butterfly?"

He answered, "You can have her for $150."

"Okay, I'll take it," she said as she brought the piece to their sales counter.

Alex noticed that both men had gathered at the sales counter and saw an opportunity to ask them about the Belter sofa. "Have you gentlemen ever heard of someone who allegedly owns a Belter sofa that is the mate to the one in the Victoria and Albert Museum in London?"

"No, but if I did, I would have already chased it," replied Clyde.

After bidding the gentlemen farewell and wishing them good health, the Penfields drove east to the Jackson area to visit Florence Harper. Her shop is called Capitol Antiques, located on Pearson Road in Pearl. She is a personable middle-aged woman of slight build with short gray hair, and Rosalie and Alex have done business with her before. She offers a decent general line of merchandise. The Penfields purchased a good Starr, Fellows & Co. solar lamp with a period shade for $500. They also questioned her about the Belter sofa, but had no success.

Florence asked, "My ex-husband has some lovely pieces he wants to sell. Would you like to go over and see them?"

"Sure! We are always willing to look if you have the time." The Penfields followed Florence to her ex-husband, Truman Harper's, house in Pearl.

Although Truman was out of town, he authorized Florence to sell the pieces on his behalf. Alex and Rosalie were thrilled to see his pieces, having purchased an excellent rosewood parlor desk made by John and Joseph Meeks in 1855. "I will give my furniture mover your name and phone number so you folks can arrange for them to pick up the desk," Alex said.

"Regarding the whereabouts of the alleged hidden Belter sofa you described, I recommend you visit my friend, Vaughn Tierney. He owns a warehouse on the outskirts of Pearl. He is a picker who sells to many dealers. As you know, pickers buy antiques from various sources and resell them to dealers or retail customers. Coincidentally, he told me that he has been contacted multiple times by an older woman who has discussed her collection of antiques but refuses to let him visit her house to see them."

"Thank you very much, Florence. It was great to see you again. We'll go over and visit Vaughn." The Penfields followed Florence's directions and dropped into Vaughn Tierney's warehouse. He is a fit man, not the least bit overweight. Tall, with long brown hair and dark eyes, he looked like he had been lifting heavy furniture all his life. After walking through the place, they realized there was nothing they could add to their collection. Sitting down to speak with Vaughn, Alex explained the situation of the Belter sofa. "Florence was right. Once in a while, I get a call from an elderly woman who describes a quite impressive collection, but I can't get her to let me see it. I think that she is lonely and needs someone to talk to. I have also heard of a rumor about a great set of Belter furniture, but I have had no luck finding it."

"Well, it was nice meeting you, and thank you for your time. We will stay in touch," Alex said.

From the Pearl-Jackson area, the Penfields drove north to Sawyer's Warehouse Antiques in Greenwood. The business specializes in antebellum-era antiques, offering high-quality merchandise with a focus on furniture. The owner is Rufus Hayes, a short, overweight man with gray hair and dark blue eyes. He does not appear to be in good health, which is understandable given the conditions in his warehouse. It is bizarre: a large space with dirt floors covered in old carpet, and the place is thick with insecticide fumes used to keep insects away from the carpeting. "Alex, I can't stay in here. The fumes are making me sick," exclaimed Rosalie.

"Oh, I agree, I'm getting woozy myself," replied Alex.

After a brief conversation with Rufus, who knew nothing about what the Penfields were after, they dashed out of the building to save themselves.

After visiting two other shops without success, the Penfields decided to call it a day.

That night, back in their exquisite room at Anchuca Mansion in Vicksburg, the Penfields received a call from their friend Ned Samuels. "Hey, it was fun visiting with you folks at the auction in Natchez! We love what we bought there. I have a favor to ask. I was browsing Josephine Dawson's website today and noticed a lovely rosewood parlor cabinet. I'm looking for one to put in our front parlor. Since you're in the area, I was wondering if you could stop by and take a look. Can you give me a call with a condition report?"

"Of course, I can, Ned. I'd be happy to help. We've exhausted our leads here in Mississippi and will move to Louisiana tomorrow. I'll call you as soon as we get to her shop."

"Thank you, Alex; you know that we love you and Rosalie."

Chapter 38

The next morning, after a delicious Southern breakfast of ham, eggs, and more homemade biscuits, the Penfields said goodbye to their gracious hosts at Anchuca Mansion. "Alex, if I haven't gained 10 pounds here, eating all this Southern food, I'll be shocked!" Rosalie said. "We need to get back home, start working out again, and eat more vegetables!"

As they left Vicksburg, they merged onto Interstate 20 heading west and crossed the Mississippi River into Louisiana. Continuing west, they took U.S. Route 65, then turned south onto Louisiana Route 28, followed by Route 167. After traveling 169 miles into Cheneyville, they found themselves deep in the rural, little-known heart of Louisiana.

After such a journey, the Penfields are ready to end their travel day and are happy to arrive at a charming B&B called Mayfield Hall. It will serve as a perfect base for searching for the Belter sofa. Doctor Bradley and Florence Harrison own the property.

"Hello, my name is Alex Penfield, and this is my wife, Rosalie. You have a beautiful property here!" A fantastic story was to follow.

"It's a pleasure to meet you. I'm Florence Harrison." Mrs. Harrison is a slim, attractive middle-aged woman with graying, shoulder-length hair and hazel eyes. "My husband, Bradley, and I bought a 500-acre plot of farmland, and upon exploring the place, we discovered that at one end of the property, buried in a sizeable stand of trees and brush, was a perfectly preserved plantation home circa 1840s. We did not even know it existed. After a couple of years of clearing the site of underbrush and restoring the home and outbuildings, we decided to open a bed and breakfast, along with contracting out the farming of the acreage."

Upon checking in, the Penfields were assigned a delightful outbuilding for their stay.

Bradley Harrison is a veterinarian who practices from an office located in an outbuilding on the property. He is a tall, fit, and slim man with steel-blue eyes and a full head of gray hair. He and his wife have a well-cared-for assortment of lovable pets, including two dogs and several friendly cats. As cat lovers, the Penfields immediately invite them into their cabin and receive plenty of affection from the kitties. The innkeepers' rule states: Cats cannot stay the night, and eventually, everyone is ushered out.

After a good night's sleep, around 7:00 AM, the Penfields begin to hear the cats pawing at their door, eager to be let in for more affection. In the kitchen of the main house, Mrs. Harrison and her friendly Black maid Sylvia serve Rosalie and Alex a delicious breakfast of eggs, grits, locally sourced ham, and, of course, homemade biscuits.

Off they go to search as the Penfields drive to Bunkie, a small town fourteen miles southeast of Cheneyville with 3400 residents. They walk into the charming shop named Dawson Antiques, owned by Jessie Dawson. A petite woman in her sixties, she is very friendly. She specializes in Antebellum-era antiques. "Good morning, Jessie. I'm Alex, and this is my wife, Rosalie. Our friend, Ned Samuels from Washington, D.C., asked me to examine a parlor cabinet of yours that he spotted on your website."

"Sure, it's right over here," replied Jessie. "Mr. Ned is a nice man, but very demanding."

Upon close inspection, Alex noticed that the plinth, the board supporting the cabinet, is badly damaged due to a worm infestation. This is a common issue with old furniture in the Deep South. Meanwhile, the Penfields looked around her shop and found nothing to add to their collection. Additionally, her prices were noticeably high. When describing the long-lost Belter sofa, she was unfamiliar with the piece and offered no clues about its location.

After leaving the shop, Alex called Ned from the parking lot and said, "The piece is totally wrecked, as the worms completely ate up the plinth. I would advise passing on it."

"Whoa, thank you so much, Alex. You saved us a lot of trouble. We'll keep looking."

Next, the explorers drove west, got onto Interstate 49, and headed south to Lafayette, which is forty-one miles from Bunkie, to visit Harley Quinn's shop. He works full-time in offshore drilling but maintains a shop selling Victorian antiques as a hobby. As the Penfields enter, they notice that his shop is mainly filled with furniture. Meeting Harley, he embodies the image of a man who works on a drilling rig: barrel-chested, stocky, with sun-darkened, rough skin, piercing blue eyes, and a firm handshake. After exchanging greetings, the Penfields looked around the shop but found nothing to add to their collection.

"Harley, we heard a rumor about a great Belter sofa sitting somewhere in the deep South. Do you know anything about that?"

"We heard the same rumors about it, have even searched for it, but have had no luck finding it."

"Thanks for your time. We will stay in touch," Alex replied. Back in the car, "Hey! It's lunchtime! I saw a local dive down the road as we came in. Let's go for shrimp po-boys! Maybe they can make us a muffuletta to snack on later." For all the miles traveled together on their antiquing adventures, the Penfields always looked for a small local dive to eat at. The food was always better there.

That afternoon, the treasure hunters headed east on I-10 to Baton Rouge, then north on Route 61 to St. Francisville to visit Keaton Parker. An hour and a half later, they arrived at the complex, a term that describes the place since the man's business covers five acres. It was once a chicken farm, but now it is home to seven or eight 50-foot trailers. Every imaginable object is displayed outside, and a barn showcases better items inside. Of course, nothing appealed to Alex and Rosalie, but they needed to talk to Keaton to see if he knew anything about the missing Belter sofa. "You're looking for what? I never heard of anybody tromping all over hell's half acre looking for a damned sofa!" exclaimed Keaton.

Alex replied, "Thank you very much, sir. We'll be on our way."

"I don't know if they hate us down here for being Yankees or if these dealers really don't know where that sofa is," Alex remarked to Rosalie after getting in the car. "I have my suspicions."

"They may not like us, but they always take our check," replied Rosalie.

With the cocktail hour approaching, the Penfields took Route 61 south out of town, turned west onto Route 1, and traveled along Route 71 to Cheneyville, ending a day of searching with no luck. Traveling through central Louisiana is an adventure because the countryside is entirely covered with thick forest.

"Imagine that this entire area was once cultivated for cotton a hundred years ago, and now it has been completely reclaimed by the forest," Alex remarked.

Chapter 39

Around five o'clock, the Penfields pulled into the Mayfield Hall courtyard and saw Bradley outside tending to some chores.

Stepping out of the Cadillac, they caught his attention. "We cannot tell you how much we are enjoying our visit. You have a lovely B&B here. As long-time cat lovers, we really enjoy being in the company of your kitties. They are so friendly and lovable," said Rosalie.

"Thank you. As a practicing veterinarian, I am pleased to provide good care for them."

Alex commented, "We love coming down to this part of the country to sightsee and hunt for antiques to buy."

"So, what brings you folks to this part of the state? Typically, everyone heads over to Natchez or New Orleans for antiques," Harrison inquired.

"We are searching for a long-lost, fabulous Victorian sofa made by a renowned American cabinetmaker. We've heard a rumor that it might be located somewhere in central Mississippi or Louisiana. We are retired business people who love collecting antebellum-era Southern Victorian antiques. Our hobby is a major part of our lifestyle, and we have enjoyed it for over forty years," Rosalie explained. "Hunting for long-lost treasures is a thrill for us."

Alex added, "We have been all over hell's half acre for the last two days and have hit a dead end."

"I'm finished with my chores for now. How about joining my wife and me on our screen porch at the back of the big house? I have a nice bottle of Chardonnay that we can share. Walk over with me." As the Penfields sat on Harrison's screen porch, Bradley entered the kitchen to open the wine bottle and retrieve four glasses. Bradley's wife, Florence, joined them. With the wine served, Bradley proposed a toast that the Penfields would find their treasure. The conversation was enjoyable for all.

"I have a client, an elderly woman named Charlotte Montgomery. She owns four cats, and they are my patients. She is poor, and I feel sorry for her.

Periodically, I treat the cats, and she often compensates me by letting me explore her house and choose a small antique piece to take home as payment. She lives alone and rarely invites people into her home. I believe she possesses many wonderful antique pieces, but I don't know enough about them to describe them accurately. She lives alone in a grand, albeit run-down, plantation house in the southern countryside of Cheneyville."

Alex asks, "Just for the fun of it, if I showed you a picture of the piece we're hunting, would you be able to tell us if the woman owns anything like it? We've run our butts off; who knows where that piece may turn up."

"Sure, I would be happy to try."

Alex jogged over to their cabin and retrieved an 8x10 glossy of the sofa reproduced from the Victoria and Albert Museum website. Taking a look, Bradley said, "I think that Miss Charlotte owns one just like it! She is desperately poor and should be willing to part with it, as she has so much more in the house."

"Oh my God!" exclaimed the Penfields at once.

"I certainly could look in on her cats, since it's been a while." Bradley retrieved his cell phone from his pocket and called Charlotte.

"Miss Charlotte? It's Doc Harrison calling. How are you? Good. We're just fine. I have some free time tomorrow and was wondering if I could come over to look in on you and your cats. It's been a while. Good. We have a lovely couple staying with us right now, and they are avid antique lovers. Would you mind if they came with me? They would love to meet you and see your grand house. Great! We will bring lunch for everyone. How about eleven o'clock? Good! We will see you then." After closing his cell phone, he said, "It so happens that Miss Charlotte sounded lonely, and that's probably why she consented to let you folks come with me."

Chapter 40

Up and at it early because the kitties were thumping at the door needing love, the Penfields could hardly contain themselves. It is always exciting to visit a historic property like Miss Charlotte's, one that the public never sees. Alex did not sleep well, as he was too excited. Rosalie slept better. They strolled over to the back of the big house for breakfast and were greeted by Florence and her helper, Sylvia. They prepared a lovely breakfast for everyone, which included fried eggs, thick-sliced bacon, grits, and Sylvia's famous homemade biscuits. "Ladies, I cannot tell you how wonderful your breakfast is!" exclaimed Alex.

The Penfields loaded into Bradley's Chevy pickup and set off to visit Miss Charlotte and her grand mansion. Sylvia had prepared a lovely lunch to take with them, packing it in a charming basket. Driving through central Louisiana to see Miss Charlotte felt like a dream. Beautiful, thick forests of evergreen trees and deep, lush undergrowth covered every inch of ground along their route. Suddenly, Bradley turned onto an isolated driveway that one could easily overlook; only someone who knew it was there would notice. The Penfields saw a long driveway lined with ancient hardwood trees that wound up to the front of the house and circled a once-gorgeous, now crumbling marble fountain that hadn't run for years. In the center of the fountain stood an exquisitely carved putti holding up a pair of doves.

Stepping out of the doctor's truck, the Penfields gazed at what was once a grand Southern antebellum mansion. Surrounded by massive, two-story white columns topped with ornate capitals and tall windows, the sight took their breath away. A vast amount of overgrown greenery cloaked the house. It almost seemed abandoned. They noticed that the mansion was falling apart, literally in a dilapidated state. Bradley commented, "Miss Charlotte will never leave the house, as it is the family homestead, and it is all she has ever known."

The threesome stepped onto a creaking front porch under a grand portico. Alex rang the old mechanical doorbell, admiring the pair of ten-foot-tall, solid mahogany doors. A couple of inset crystal door lights display the initials F on the left door and M in Victorian script on the right panel.

A few moments later, Miss Charlotte opened one of the massive, three-inch-thick doors and invited everyone inside. Bradley introduced her to the Penfields. She is a petite woman, standing at five feet two inches tall, with gray hair neatly piled on top of her head. She has stunning blue eyes and is elegantly dressed. Pleasantries are exchanged at the front of the center hall. "Miss Charlotte, you have a beautiful home that is truly grand. Thank you very much for inviting us. Alex and I greatly appreciate this." Rosalie handed Miss Charlotte a hostess gift of wrapped fancy chocolates they had bought on the way over. Bradley then brought in the basket Sylvia prepared for the luncheon. "Excuse me. I will tend to the cats and carry the basket to the kitchen."

Alex spoke, "Rosalie and I have been serious collectors and students of Victorian decorative arts for over forty years. We love the architecture of the great Southern antebellum homes."

"Well, thank you. It's always a pleasure to share this with people who appreciate it," Miss Charlotte replied. A good rapport develops as she describes each object in the center hall, which runs through the downstairs from the front door to the back door of the house. Every inch of the walls is covered with antique French Zuber wallpaper. Notably, a magnificent Joseph Meeks heavily carved mahogany classical pier table sits against the west wall. A pair of Duncan Phyfe side chairs flank each end of the pier table. She then guides the Penfields into a front room by the front door. "This room was my grandfather's office, where he conducted the plantation and family business." The room is furnished with her grandfather's ornately carved Renaissance Revival walnut desk, chair, and grand bookcase. The room remains cluttered with papers and documents.

Miss Charlotte then took the Penfields across the hall into the double grand salon, which runs from the front to the back on the east side of the house. Upon entering the room, the Penfields behold something few serious Victorian collectors will ever see. Inside is a fourteen-piece matching set of breathtaking John Henry Belter Cornucopia pattern Brazilian rosewood Rococo Revival parlor furniture, including the long-lost sofa. Made in 1856, it is almost unheard of in its height, measuring five feet. It's eight feet wide and four feet deep. Every square inch of the top of the laminated curved back is profusely hand-pierced and carved with flowers, leaves, and berries. Some of the flower blossoms are as big as one's fist. No words can do justice in describing its grandeur; it is that fabulous. The heavy seat rails and legs are profusely carved with flowers and leaves from solid Brazilian rosewood. No other piece of Victorian furniture rivals it.

"Please, sit down on the sofa," exclaimed Miss Charlotte. The Penfields found it hard to contain their excitement and had to hold back their gasps of delight. "Please tell us about your Belter parlor furniture in this room. How did your family come by it?" Alex asked.

Miss Charlotte began by recounting the story of her great-grandfather, Confederate Major Frederick Montgomery.

"He was moving his company of about 80 soldiers south along the Natchez Trace, just ten miles outside of Natchez. The company was returning from the battle at Tupelo in July 1864, heading south, and was ordered to conduct hit-and-run guerrilla raids on Union troops at night to avoid capture. As his company reached a rise, his advanced scouts reported a smaller force of 25 Union Army soldiers heading north ahead on the Trace with three large wagons in tow."

"Major Montgomery determined the platoon was headed for a railroad junction up the Trace. He ordered his company into battle formation and instructed them to move down the hill and attack just as the Union Army platoon reached an open meadow. A bloody battle ensued, and the Major's forces overpowered the Union forces, killing Capt. Reginald Hatchett. In the chaos, the Confederates captured the wagons. After driving off the remaining Union soldiers, Major Montgomery ordered the wagons to be uncovered, and they discovered the treasures. Not knowing who owned them, he confiscated the loot, calling it the spoils of war. He and his troops then transported the wagons to his farm in Bunkie, Louisiana, where they stayed hidden in his barn until he returned."

"While he was away at war, my great-grandmother, Josephine, and their enslaved workers continued to produce cotton. Josephine was a strong, overweight woman who knew how to manage the farm. Fortunately, thanks to the Major's connections, Josephine could somehow smuggle their cotton past any blockade and ship it out of the country to paying customers overseas."

"My great-grandfather and his company continued to conduct various raids across Louisiana and Mississippi until the war ended in April of 1865."

"My God, what a great story," exclaimed Alex. He was nearly out of breath after reliving the battle Miss Charlotte described. "Shall we have that lovely luncheon that Florence Harrison made for us?" The foursome moved to the exquisitely furnished dining room and enjoyed the meal at the grand classical-style mahogany dining table.

Over lunch, Miss Charlotte continued, "During the war, Major Montgomery was clever enough to put the proceeds from his cotton crops into gold. He entrusted it to a gun dealer friend who traveled back and forth to England to acquire shipments of guns for the Confederacy. While there, the gun dealer made several deposits in one of the central banks for safekeeping until the war ended. At the war's end, the Major retrieved the gold, which was worth the better part of a million dollars. He and his wife moved here, acquired over a thousand acres, and built this grand house. For years, he operated a successful cotton farm using sharecroppers, many of whom were formerly enslaved people."

"He and my great-grandmother made trips to New Orleans and New York to acquire additional furnishings for the house. He never did find out who the wagon loads of furnishings belonged to, as so many plantations were burned."

Alex replied, "There is an identical mate to your sofa in the Victoria and Albert Museum's collection in London, England. It was definitely part of your suite, right down to the matching fabric. Do you know how the sofa was separated from the rest of the suite? According to the Victoria and Albert Museum, wealthy British businessman Sir Alfred George Beech Owen purchased the sofa in the 1920s from an antique dealer. It does not state whether he bought it in England or the United States. Do you know anything about this?"

"I do. Sometime in the 1920s, my grandfather, the General's son, had a bad crop year and needed money. He sold the sofa to a dealer in New Orleans. Maybe Mr. Owen saw the sofa while visiting New Orleans and purchased it."

After lunch, Miss Charlotte invited the Penfields and Bradley to tour the upstairs and view its remarkable antique collection. As the group climbed the grand staircase, Alex couldn't help but admire its construction of solid Cuban mahogany. The second floor features four bedrooms, two on the east side and two on the west. Once again, a center hall runs down the middle of the upstairs. All four rooms are furnished with exquisite Victorian antiques, including two with stunning half-tester beds.

Back in the grand salon, after more than three hours of visiting with Miss Charlotte, the Penfields had established a good rapport with her. To avoid overstaying their visit, "Miss Charlotte, you have been a wonderful hostess. Rosalie and I cannot thank you enough for your hospitality and such a lovely afternoon. Would you mind if we visited with you again briefly before we head back home?"

"I also enjoyed our visit, and by all means, please come back before you leave for home."

Chapter 41

The Penfields and Bradley climbed into his pickup truck for the trip back to Mayfield Hall. As they admired the beautiful countryside, Alex brought up the topic of their offer to buy the sofa from Miss Charlotte. "I certainly do not wish to offend the dear woman, but what do you think of our offering to purchase the Cornucopia Belter sofa from her? I can't believe we found it! She does have a valuable second sofa in the Belter Fountain Elms pattern. Although we strongly believe it would sell for $300,000 at auction, Rosalie and I are willing to offer her $500,000. We plan to enjoy it in our home for a short time and then donate it to the Cleveland Museum of Art. It is too fabulous to keep in a private house. Like the one in the Victoria and Albert, the piece should be shared with the world."

Bradley raised his eyebrows and exclaimed, "I am astounded that the piece is so valuable. I have watched all four cats lounge on it for years!"

"You have my word as a gentleman that I am providing you with accurate information. I do not need to try to steal from that woman. We can afford to pay the actual value of the piece." Alex continued, "If Miss Charlotte consents to sell the piece, we can wire the funds to her bank account that same day if she agrees."

Bradley replied, "That is more money than that woman has ever had, and she could be comfortable for the rest of her life. Let's schedule a meeting with Miss Charlotte to discuss the sale of the sofa. She will be able to make all the necessary repairs to the house, and, what's more, she will still have the rest of the rosewood parlor furniture to enjoy. I have appointments tomorrow, so let's schedule a meeting for the day after tomorrow. Let me give her a call. "Miss Charlotte? It's Doc Harrison. I'm wondering if the Penfields and I can see you the day after tomorrow? We have something particularly important to discuss with you. You can? That's great. How would, say, one-thirty be? Good! We will see you then."

The next day, eager for a bit of fun, the Penfields set out on Interstate 49, heading south to explore the magnificent houses along the River Road south of New Orleans. The River Road is situated atop a vast alluvial fan of land formed over millennia, where the Mississippi River flows into the Gulf of Mexico. Throughout a long day, they toured the splendid plantation homes of Destrehan, San Francisco, Houmas House, Nottoway, and Oak Alley.

Chapter 42

Alex struggled to sleep, feeling anxious about meeting Miss Charlotte the next day. At the scheduled time of 1:30, the Penfields and Bradley arrived at her front door. She was delighted to see everyone and led them into the grand salon. While seated on the magnificent Belter sofa, Alex said, "Miss Charlotte, Rosalie and I would like to speak with you about something important. Respectfully, we wonder if you would honor us by selling us this Belter sofa. Based on our over 40 years of experience in the auction market and after consulting with several experts, we believe the piece would sell for $300,000 at auction. However, we would be willing to pay you $500,000 for it. We can arrange for the funds to be wire transferred to your bank account in full today."

Being a proud Confederate descendant, Ms. Charlotte replied, "Oh, no, I couldn't. Although you have certainly made a handsome offer, this sofa has been in my family for over 150 years. My great-grandfather obtained this furniture during the Civil War."

Bradley intervened. "Ms. Charlotte, consider what the money will do for you. It will cover the necessary restoration of the house and provide you with a comfortable living space for the rest of your life. The sofa will become part of a great collection of decorative arts in the Cleveland Museum of Art, a world-renowned institution. You will be sharing the piece with thousands of visitors in perpetuity. You still have a beautiful second sofa and many other pieces left in this great room to enjoy."

After several minutes of silence, one could see the wheels turning in Miss Charlotte's mind. She asks Bradley, "Are you going to start charging me for taking care of my cats?" Alex says, "Miss Charlotte, I will write a check to Doc Harrison for $2,000 to cover the cost of caring for your cats for the foreseeable future."

She replied, "Maybe I can get more for the sofa if I send it to auction in New Orleans."

Bradley spoke up, "Miss Charlotte, you would face the expense of shipping the piece down there; it could get damaged and might not fetch $500,000. They have made you a fair offer. I think you ought to take it."

After several minutes of hemming and hawing, Miss Charlotte agrees to sell the sofa to the Penfields. "All right, I'll sell it to you!" The Penfields are thrilled. Everyone shakes hands and shares hugs. She gives Alex her bank account number at the Farmer's Bank of Bunkie. He uses his cell phone and immediately calls one of his brokers, Ideal Investments. From her grand salon, he instructs that $500,000 be transferred to her bank account.

"Miss Charlotte, we will give the sofa a great home at the Cleveland Museum of Art. I propose we pick up the sofa tomorrow morning at ten thirty. We must take Bradley back to Cheneyville and get a trailer." On the way to Cheneyville, Rosalie got on the phone, found a U-Haul dealer in Alexandria, and reserved an enclosed trailer. After dropping Bradley off at the farm, the Penfields rushed to Alexandria, rented the trailer, and hooked it up to the Cadillac for the journey back to Ohio.

While traveling back to Mayfield Hall, Alex called Bradley. "Hey, what do you say the four of us go out to celebrate tonight with a lovely dinner at Café Vermillion in Lafayette? Our treat."

"We need to discuss something important with you. How about seven o'clock? Great! Rosalie will make our reservations. See you then."

Upon arriving at Mayfield Hall, Alex unhooked the trailer from the Cadillac. At seven, the four of them headed out for dinner. After celebrating with a toast from a nice bottle of champagne, Alex asked the Harrisons, "What can we do to show our appreciation for helping us get the sofa?"

"Well, we could use a new barn, which will cost about $20,000. We would really appreciate your helping out with the cost," the doctor replied.

Alex said, "We will do better than that. Rosalie will write you a check for the whole amount tonight!"

Chapter 43

By the next morning, the funds had arrived in Miss Charlotte's account at the Farmer's Bank. As Alex requested, she called and spoke to the branch manager, Rufus Tierney, to verify. A rotund man with greasy, slicked-back hair, he wore an ill-fitting suit, and his gut hung over the waistband. "Hello, Rufus, it's Charlotte Montgomery calling. Thank you, I'm fine. I am calling to check if a deposit has been made into my account. It's a wire transfer from Ohio."

"Well, let me see, Miss Charlotte," he says, as he goes online and enters her account number. "Hmmm. Oh, my God!" Shocked, he asks, "Yes, ma'am! $500,000 has been deposited into your account. Where in the world did all that money come from?"

"Well, Rufus, I've decided to sell an antique sofa from my collection. However, I feel a little sad because it once belonged to my great-grandfather. A lovely couple from Ohio bought it from me. I need the money, which will go a long way toward fixing up our family's plantation house and securing my future."

He replied, "Oh, Miss Charlotte, how could you! There goes a piece of our history! Shame, shame!"

"Listen, Rufus, it's my antique collection, and I will do what I must!"

After ending the call with Ms. Charlotte, Rufus picked up the phone again and called his nephew, Duke Harper. Duke is a longtime drifter who struggles to hold a job. He earns money through odd jobs and sometimes dabbles in pot and other illegal drugs. He's always available, as he typically just sits around in his rundown shack. Duke is part of the local Ku Klux Klan Klatch and has committed numerous crimes and hateful acts, targeting the nonwhite community. He wears filthy jeans and an unwashed T-shirt with a KKK logo. The shirt is too short to cover his large, unsightly gut that hangs over his waistband. The man stinks. Rufus yelled, "Get your worthless fat ass over to Miss Charlotte's and stop the loading of her sofa. Some damn Yankee has swindled it out of her."

Duke grabbed his holstered Ruger .357 Ruger Blackhawk, threaded his belt through the holster loop, and strapped it to his waist. He drew the gun from the holster and pushed the release button, causing the six-shot cylinder to swing out. It was fully loaded with ammunition. After closing it, he reholstered the gun, waddled out the door, and started his broken-down 1970 Chevelle with a great puff of blue smoke.

Meanwhile, the Penfields arrived with the trailer hitched to the back of the Cadillac. Bradley followed them with two men in his truck to help load the sofa and ensure everything went smoothly. As they parked in the turnaround driveway, Miss Charlotte greeted them in the front yard. Fortunately, the weather cooperated; it was a beautiful, sunny day.

Just as the Penfields and their crew were loading the sofa onto the trailer, Duke came storming up the driveway and slammed on his brakes, sending up a cloud of dust. Jumping out of his truck, he stormed over to Alex and got in his face. Alex cringed at the smell of Duke's stinking breath as he exclaimed, "That sofa is a piece of Confederate history, and you're not taking it anywhere!"

"What's it to you, asshole?" replied Alex. "Our legal purchase of this sofa does not concern you! Who the hell are you, anyway?"

"I'm a member of the local Klan Klatch, and you're not taking that sofa away!"

Alex yelled to Rosalie, "Call the police! Now!" She immediately started dialing 911.

Bradley senses that this situation could escalate into violence, so he sprints to his pickup to grab his Colt .357 revolver.

The situation abruptly escalated as Duke stepped back, drew his .357 Blackhawk from its holster, cocked the hammer into firing position, and aimed the weapon at Alex's face. Realizing Duke might kill Alex, Dr. Bradley shot, hitting him in the head and killing him instantly. Duke collapsed where he stood.

Within minutes, a local Cheneyville police cruiser raced up the driveway with the siren blaring and lights flashing. Coming to a screeching halt, the police officer jumped out of the car. "What the hell is going on here?"

Alex and Bradley calmly explained what had happened, and Miss Charlotte corroborated their story. The officer contacted the coroner's office and requested that a van and a coroner come to Miss Charlotte's to retrieve Duke's body. He then instructed Bradley, Miss Charlotte, and the Penfields to proceed to the police station to file a report.

Before driving to the police station, Alex, Bradley, and his two helpers finished loading and wrapping the sofa for safe transport and secured the trailer.

After completing the necessary paperwork and giving a statement at the police station, the Penfields, Bradley, and Miss Charlotte were told to meet with the city prosecutor at the Cheneyville Municipal Court. Each of them provided their statements and was told they would be contacted if additional information was needed. The city prosecutor stated, "At this point, I view this incident as a case of self-defense. The victim was a known troublemaker with an extensive criminal record."

The Penfields drove Miss Charlotte home and said goodbye. Bradley and his two assistants went back to Mayfield Hall.

After enjoying one of the greatest adventures in collecting antiques for over forty years, the Penfields were ready to head home. The next morning, they said goodbye to Bradley and Florence Harrison. Cleveland, here we come!

Chapter 44

Ned Samuels and Jeffrey Martinsen were excited to become the new owners of a beautiful piece from the Engle auction, which had just been delivered by their movers. Ned and Jeffrey proudly own a grand Victorian Italianate row house from the 1870s, located next to the Embassy Row district of Washington, D.C. Ned works as an estate attorney for a prominent law firm in Washington, D.C. Jeffrey is a retired art professor from Howard University. They are very close friends of Alex and Rosalie.

The Penfields played a vital role in bringing Ned and Jeffrey together. It all started when the magazine 19th Century Homes published an article about Jeffrey and his collection of Victorian bird domes. In the 19th century, the English enjoyed creating taxidermied bird collections displayed under glass domes. At the time the article was published, Jeffrey was single and lived in Annapolis, Maryland, just outside Washington, D.C. Alex saw the article and reached out to him. The two collectors struck up a conversation, and a strong bond formed. Alex assured Jeffrey that he and Rosalie would visit him the next time the Penfields were on the East Coast.

A few months after contacting Jeffrey, the Penfields arranged a visit with Ned, who was also single and unattached. Alex and Rosalie had been close friends and fellow collectors with Ned for several years. With graying brown hair and intense hazel eyes, Ned is a brilliant and passionate collector. He already owns the magnificent Victorian row house now occupied by the couple. Additionally, Ned is an avid collector of Victorian-era Jacobean Revival decorative arts. The Penfields looked forward to spending special time with Ned, and Rosalie hoped to purchase some Medallion silver flatware pieces from him.

While we're here, we'd like to visit a collector in Annapolis who owns a collection of Victorian bird domes. The collector mentioned that he has many domes for sale, and we might be interested in buying a couple. How about the three of us drive over to see him? We'd love to see his collection," Alex proposed to Ned.

"No, you folks go see him. I'll stay here to catch up on some office work I brought home."

"Oh, come on, Ned. It'll be fun. You need to get out of the house on this beautiful day. Besides, it's always important to connect with other collectors. You'll never know what will come of it," Alex replied.

After some prodding, Ned conceded, "Oh, all right, I'll go." Alex called Jeffrey and arranged for the three to meet him the next day at 1:00 PM.

The adventurous trio arrived a bit late, and Jeffrey was noticeably annoyed when he met them. He was hosting out-of-town guests and had sent them out for the afternoon. Jeffrey glared at the visitors as they exchanged introductions. Alex apologized for the delay, and Jeffrey soon softened, kindly offering them a tour of his beautiful home and collection. The Penfields looked at the assortment of bird domes for sale and bought two. Even Ned joined in by taking one home for himself.

In the meantime, Ned looked as if he had been struck by lightning. The Adonis Jeffrey had captured Ned's attention. More than anything else, he was drawn to Jeffrey, who was incredibly attractive and well-built, with wispy blond hair and deep blue eyes. Ned shyly asked for Jeffrey's phone number so they could stay in touch. After the Penfields left town, Ned invited the unattached Jeffrey to dinner, and the rest was history. The romance blossomed, and the union of the two collectors was like pouring gasoline on a fire.

Dating blossomed into love, and Jeffrey moved in with Ned after a few months. It marked the union of two beautiful lives and the beginning of collecting some of the country's finest Victorian Rococo and Jacobean revival decorative arts. Jeffrey has an exceptional ability for decorating and color, and he led the effort to transform their row house into a showplace. They added a stunning conservatory at the back of the home, as Jeffrey has a remarkable talent for growing exotic tropical plants and propagating orchids. After same-sex marriage became legal in Washington, D.C., the couple was married amid much celebration.

Ned and Jeffrey were the winning bidders for the rosewood library table from the Engle auction, which had recently arrived to display in their rear parlor. That room showcases their collection of extraordinary, museum-quality John Henry Belter Rococo Revival rosewood parlor furniture, upholstered in sumptuous silk damask fabrics. It reflects Jeffrey's influence on the couple's collecting, as his favorite style is the exuberantly carved Rococo Revival furniture. The front parlor, on the other hand, reflects Ned's influence on their collection, decorated with more massive English late 19th-century Jacobean revival dark oak parlor furniture that the couple had imported from England.

Before taking the rosewood library table upstairs to the back parlor, the boys pulled out the drawer and gave it a thorough dusting. They then turned the table upside down to clean the underside and remove any potential cobwebs. At that moment, they noticed the clasp mailing envelope that Westley Engle had taped to the bottom of the wooden top. It was still intact. Jeffrey carefully peeled the duct tape from the top and took off the envelope. They opened the envelope and pulled out a set of documents. The top page read, "I have made a grave mistake, and please forgive me for what I have done. A computer flash drive of deadly consequence is hidden in my collection and must be found. Follow the clues listed below, locate the symbols, and save humanity before it is too late."

"Holy shit, what the hell is this?" asked Ned.

Meanwhile, the Russian criminals kept breaking in and terrorizing more collectors across the country without success. They were no closer to finding the flash drive. Local police investigations into their violent acts in each city led to reports being filed with one or more federal crime reporting agencies. Incident reports started appearing in the National Crime Information Center database. This database has been called the lifeline of law enforcement—an electronic hub for crime data accessible to nearly every criminal justice agency nationwide, 24/7. It helps law enforcement officers catch fugitives, find missing persons, recover stolen property, and identify terrorists. The database also allows officers to work more safely and provides vital information to protect the public.

The Nationwide Suspicious Activity Reporting Initiative is another agency that receives reports of Russian crimes. The initiative is a United States government program that collects and shares information about suspicious activity incidents reported by individuals across the country. It builds on the work law enforcement and other agencies have been doing for years, including gathering data on behaviors and incidents related to criminal activity. The program operates without the usual restrictions on collecting data about individuals without reasonable suspicion or probable cause. The reporting initiative has established a standardized process allowing agencies to share information about suspicious activity, which helps detect and prevent terrorism-related crimes.

Reports of suspicious behavior, observed by local law enforcement or private citizens, are forwarded to state and major urban fusion centers, the Department of Homeland Security, and the FBI for analysis. Sometimes, this information is combined with additional data to evaluate suspicious activity within a broader context. The U.S. Department of Justice primarily oversees the program.

Much of the illegal activity was eventually traced back to the Engle collection based in Cleveland. After numerous reports of murder and violence committed by the Russians, the Department of Justice shared the collected information with the FBI Cleveland office. Agent Robert Armstrong was assigned to the case and quickly gathered a team of investigators to examine the reports. Armstrong stated, "After so many murders and the destruction of furniture pieces, it is needless to say that they are all connected. Without property taken, it is obvious that somebody is trying to find something, but what?"

Chapter 45

The news of the brutal murder of a key government defense contractor, along with what is believed to be related murders, even reached Agent Ronald Grimsley's desk at the CIA.

A hardened man, Grimsley has dedicated his whole career to espionage. His mindset ignores moral limits when it comes to using murder, torture, or coercion to meet the agency's goals. After earning a degree in computer science from college, he joined the U.S. Army. Grimsley started as a second lieutenant and quickly rose to the rank of major, serving in Army Intelligence with a focus on counterterrorism.

The time he spent in Army Intelligence laid a solid foundation for the next phase of Grimsley's life. He was always a man drawn to adventure. After his last tour of duty, he decided to retire. The following chapter in his life involved applying for and being accepted into the CIA.

The success of the British Commandos during World War II encouraged U.S. President Franklin Roosevelt to create an intelligence agency based on the British Secret Intelligence Service, also known as MI6. MI6's achievements led to the formation of the Office of Strategic Services (OSS) by a presidential military order issued by President Roosevelt in June 1942. Soon after World War II ended, in September 1945, President Truman signed an executive order to dissolve the OSS. For a short time, intelligence duties were split between the Departments of State and War.

In January 1946, President Truman established the National Intelligence Authority, whose operating arm was the Central Intelligence Group, a direct predecessor of the CIA. On July 26, 1947, President Truman signed the National Security Act, which created the National Security Council and the Central Intelligence Agency. The National Security Council was formed as part of the Executive Office of the President of the United States. It functions as the main forum for addressing national security, military, and foreign policy issues, involving senior security advisors and Cabinet members. The Council's role has been to advise and assist the President on matters related to national security and foreign policies.

The main reason for creating the Central Intelligence Agency was the rising tensions with the Soviet Union after World War II. The 1949 Central Intelligence Agency Act authorized the agency to use confidential financial and administrative procedures and protected it from most restrictions on federal funding. The act also protected the CIA from having to disclose its "organization, functions, officials, titles, salaries, or numbers of personnel employed."

Ultimately, the two primary responsibilities of the CIA were covert action and covert intelligence gathering. One of the primary targets for intelligence gathering was the Soviet Union, which had also been a priority for the CIA's predecessors. They aimed to learn everything about the Soviet forces in Eastern and Central Europe - their movements, capabilities, and intentions. The CIA possesses no domestic law enforcement authority, and in the case of domestic incidents, it would report to local authorities or the FBI.

For over 70 years, the CIA has worked to keep the United States safe from both domestic and international threats; however, it often has come at the expense of morality, lives, and resources.

At the peak of the Vietnam War in 1969, President Nixon's Secretary of State, Henry Kissinger, instructed the CIA to surveil leaders of the anti-Vietnam War movement. This measure included wiretapping.

The CIA and other agencies have sent suspected terrorists to countries known for using torture over the years, whether or not they intended to enable it. Torture, including practices like waterboarding, was performed with the knowledge or approval of U.S. agencies.

The most expensive covert operation in U.S. history was Operation Cyclone. The CIA supplied and trained Islamist insurgent groups called mujahideen to fight against the Soviet Red Army's military intervention in Afghanistan. From 1979 to 1989, the CIA provided over $2 billion in weapons, logistical support, and training to the mujahideen in support of the Democratic Republic of Afghanistan.

At that time, the scattered insurgent groups were fighting against Nur Muhammad Taraki's government, an Afghan communist and KGB asset who had taken power in a Soviet-backed coup in 1978. The CIA believed that Operation Cyclone would divert significant resources from the Soviet military, which they might otherwise use against its increasingly restless Eastern European client states.

The CIA's involvement in Afghanistan began in 1979 with an authorized budget of $500,000. By 1987, the funding had skyrocketed to $700 million annually to procure equipment and provide logistical support for the mujahideen.

Some viewed the long-term legacy of this program as highly controversial. Many of its original architects considered it a success, as it certainly contributed to weakening the Soviet Union and perhaps accelerating its eventual collapse. The lack of oversight with which the CIA distributed weapons and military aid resulted in numerous heavily armed militant Islamist factions left to vie for power after the Soviet Union withdrew. Many figures involved in the U.S.-backed struggle against the Soviet invaders would later become notorious terrorist commanders, including Jalaluddin Haqqani, leader of the Haqqani Network, Mohammad Omar, leader of the Taliban, and Osama bin Laden, leader of al-Qaeda.

The CIA has been accused of using torture, funding, and training groups and organizations that later participated in killing civilians and other non-combatants. For 60 years, the CIA has attempted and succeeded in overthrowing numerous democratically elected governments, conducting human experimentation, and carrying out targeted killings and assassinations.

In the decades after World War II, the CIA and other agencies recruited over a thousand former German Nazis to work as spies and informants during the Cold War. Nazi scientists and engineers were taken from Germany for their technological skills after the war ended. The most famous among them was Wernher von Braun, known as the father of modern rocketry and space exploration.

For many years, the CIA misled Congress about its use of waterboarding and other forms of torture, and they sometimes acknowledged these actions. The agency is legally required to inform Congress of any covert programs it starts; however, it has repeatedly failed to do so.

Throughout his 20 years at the CIA, Agent Grimsley has taken part in numerous covert operations that raise questions about their legality.

The CIA, the Russian KGB, and their Bratva collaborated on numerous operations over the years. After considering his situation, he called Russian mobster Maksim Kuznetsov at his mansion overlooking the Black Sea in Georgia to see if he had any helpful information.

On an encrypted line, Grimsley exclaimed, "Good morning, Maksim. How are you, my friend? It's been too long since we spoke."

"I am good, Grimsley. What can I do for you?" the Russian crime boss suspiciously replied.

"Maksim, here at the CIA, we are trying to track down any information on the murder of an important Cleveland-based computer scientist working for one of our aircraft contractors. I know you have a strong group of Vors working there, and I wonder if you can help us?"

"Well, Grimsley, it turns out I have been talking to my Bratva in Cleveland about that very issue. Your computer scientist lost $100,000 in one of my poker games. That night, he drowned his troubles in vodka, and in his drunken state, he revealed that he was working on perfecting advanced bombing missions using pilotless drones. Needless to say, this would be very interesting to my country. He offered a computer flash drive in exchange for the $100,000 owed to us. It seems he backed out of the deal, and we suspect the flash drive is hidden somewhere in his antique furniture collection."

"Maksim, I know our scientist met a violent end, and his house was ransacked. I have a strange feeling that this was the work of your Vors. We want that flash drive back, and if you find it before we do, we want it intact and unopened. We will repay you for that man's gambling debt plus interest, say $500,000?"

"Oh, no, my dear Agent Grimsley, I can get several million dollars for the flash drive."

"Well, dear Vor, what price do you put on your daughter's life?"

Shaken, the Vor replied, "What do you mean, Grimsley?"

"I mean, dear Vor, we know that your one and only daughter is a graduate student at Vassar College studying art history. Beautiful girl, Maksim. She has a lovely apartment in an exclusive area outside Poughkeepsie, New York. Living there under a false identity, she uses the name Tatyana Novikov. An attractive young man named Rodney Anderson is living with her. He is quite well endowed, and they screw like crazed weasels almost every other night. We have agents monitoring her every movement in case she might be employed doing work for you."

"You dirty bastards!" replied Kuznetsov.

"Listen to me very carefully, Maksim: You have made a fortune conducting various operations for us over the years. You were well paid for your services. I have seen undercover photos of your daughter. She is beautiful: slim and statuesque, with large breasts, blue eyes, and gorgeous, long blond hair. We know that her natural hair color is brown. Do not ask me how we know that. You either do as we say, or your daughter will end up in the Hudson River in small pieces. I guarantee it."

Taken aback, "All right, I will contact my crew there and make sure they retrieve and return the flash drive intact." Always greedy, "Wire me the $500,000 you offered, and I will consider us even. And don't you touch my daughter. I am trying to give her a better life than I had."

The next day, Maksim talked on the phone with Cleveland crime boss Andrei Lebedev.

"Andrei, I have made a deal with the American CIA to retrieve the flash drive for them. My contact is an idiot, and I am shaking them down for half a million bucks!"

"But dear Vor Kuznetsov, you know that we can get millions from one of the terrorist groups for that flash drive."

172

"Do not tamper with the flash drive. Do as I say, Andrei; it's personal, and I do not have to explain it to you."

Chapter 46

Ten minutes after discovering Westley's document taped to the underside of their newly acquired desk, Ned and Jeffrey were on the phone with Alex and Rosalie. "Hey, folks, you won't believe what we found under the writing desk tabletop," Ned said.

"A C-note? A twenty-dollar gold piece? I give up, Ned. What?"

"It is a note in which this guy, Westley Engle, says he has hidden a flash drive somewhere and begs the finder to locate it immediately!"

Alex replied, "Uh-oh, I might know what that is. The good news is that it is not in your piece of furniture. Text us pictures of all the pages right now, and send the original overnight. I will call the FBI as soon as we are off the phone."

While Jeffrey sent images of all the pages via text, Ned asked Alex, "Why is a flash drive hidden in a piece of furniture?"

"Ned, you may have heard us talk about Dr. Westley Engle. He was a dear friend and the former owner of the piece. He was an AI engineer working for the government. Two nights before he was murdered, he came to our house for dinner. Westley was visibly upset and finally told us he was in big trouble with some dangerous guys. I know they killed him, obviously trying to get their hands on the flash drive. One of his pieces hides the flash drive. Unfortunately, we are probably the only people who know this."

"Alex, what can we do? You know Jeffrey and I will help in any way we can," Ned said with conviction.

"I'll let you know; God help us!" Alex said in a worried tone as he hung up the phone.

As promised, Alex called the Cleveland FBI office and reached the officer on duty. He explained the situation and was connected to Agent Robert Armstrong, who was in charge of the case. He is a very fit man in his late thirties, tall with light brown, closely cropped hair, blue eyes, and a sharp dresser. After a brief overview, Agent Armstrong said, "Mr. Penfield, I need you to meet me at the office right away. How soon can you get here?"

"I will be right down. Have I got something for you!" shouted Alex. So, Alex and Rosalie drove west out of Gates Mills on Mayfield Road, got onto northbound I-271, and merged onto the Shoreway heading west toward downtown Cleveland. After passing the Inner Belt, they took Route 2 and exited at East 9th St., heading south. They turned left onto Lakeside and drove to the FBI headquarters at 1501 Lakeside Avenue. They were greeted at the front reception desk by Agent Armstrong.

The Penfields were escorted into a conference room by Armstrong, where they met two agents from the task force. The Penfields presented the agents with texted copies of the documents that Ned and Jeffrey had retrieved from underneath Westley's table. Alex explained, "Rosalie and I were very close friends and fellow collectors of Doctor Westley Engle. After his wife was killed in a car accident, he sank into a personal downward spiral. His deep grief manifested itself by participating in high-stakes poker games around the area. The last time we saw Westley was at our home. He was a dinner guest for the evening. His spirits were low, and after much cajoling, Doctor Engle confessed to getting himself into trouble at a recent poker game. He had lost $100,000 to a group he described as dangerous individuals and was seeking a way to extricate himself from the situation by repaying them. He offered no further information regarding the circumstances. We offered to loan him the $100,000, and unfortunately, that never happened because he was murdered shortly after that."

Alex continued, "You probably already know Doctor Engle was an independent AI engineer working under a government contract. Unfortunately, we knew nothing more than that. The document before you is a list of clues and a map to locate a piece of furniture from his collection that I believe contains the flash drive. He used a technique that I taught him called symbology. Rosalie and I have spent the last forty years becoming experts in collecting and interpreting Victorian decorative arts from the era. During that time, I fell in love with and mastered the art of Victorian symbology. That is the technique of interpreting the language of the design, carvings, and ornamentation of 19th-century decorative arts. They came to speak a language of their own. What we need to do now is get a list of the furniture pieces sold at the recent auction. We can locate that piece of furniture using Doctor Engle's clues."

"Mr. and Mrs. Penfield, you would be doing the country a great service if you would allow us to recruit you to join this effort for the community's safety," said Agent Armstrong.

"We would be happy to help. We will find the piece."

That afternoon, Agent Armstrong and a backup agent arrived at the offices of Integrity Auction Company. The company president, Jason Hunt, met with the agents. "Mr. Hunt, we believe that the murder of your specialist, Mr. Jameson, is related to our investigation. Therefore, we need a list of the furniture pieces sold at your recent auction." Jason Hunt was happy to comply and instructed his IT person to load the entire furniture inventory onto a flash drive, which he then handed over to Armstrong.

Naturally, the Federal Bureau of Investigation was also unaware of the Central Intelligence Agency's efforts to locate the flash drive.

Meanwhile, Ned Samuels and Jeffrey Martinsen were nervously aware of what they now knew. They feared that dangerous visitors might come looking for what they believed was hidden in their writing desk. They didn't have to wait long. Two nights later, Vladislav "The Wolf" Volkov and Mikhail "The Eagle" Orlav stood in an alley near Ned and Jeffrey's row house. Typical of an East Coast urban row house neighborhood, the front of Ned and Jeffrey's house faces the street and is connected to other homes by shared sidewalls to form a "row."

It was an extremely dark night, with not a sliver of moonlight to illuminate the alley. Around 2:00 AM, the Russian criminals found the carport in the backyard that faced the alley behind Ned and Jeffrey's house.

Dressed entirely in black Russian military Special Forces uniforms and equipped with weapons and gear, the Vors climbed over the carport roof. Without making a sound, the pair dropped into the backyard. They approached the back of the house and crept silently up to the conservatory door. Orlav pulled out his set of lock-picking tools. Using the tension wrench and a selected pick rake, he opened the door in seconds, as it was a simple lock style. They were unaware that the entire property had a sophisticated security system. When the Vor opened the door, it instantly triggered an alarm in Ned and Jeffrey's bedroom, which was a buzzer rather than a siren that goes off outside. Ned, being a light sleeper, sat straight up in bed, listening. He had been expecting trouble like this.

The Vors moved carefully through the lush foliage in the conservatory, weaving between Jeffrey's rare orchids and past the 1860s English wrought iron terrarium, and stepped lightly to the back door of the house. Once again, Orlav pulled out his trusty lock-picking tools and began working on the deadbolt. It was a newer model, so it took a bit longer. After several minutes, he managed to shift the bolt, opened the door, and they entered the house from the rear, stepping into the dining room. The Russians moved in single file. Ned was already out of bed and had gone downstairs. He sat silently on the silk-upholstered round pouf settee in the front parlor, across from the dining room. In the dark, he observed, waiting as they crept forward. When the Russians were well into the room, Ned asked the intruders, "What do you two think you are doing in my house?" There was no reply from the Russians as they stepped closer to Ned.

"Take one more step, and I'll blow your fucking heads off!" The Russians moved forward. Ned stood up and fired his Model 27 .357 Magnum Smith & Wesson revolver three times, hitting Orlav in the chest and face. The big Russian was thrown back and dropped to the floor. Volkov reached into his shoulder holster for his MP-443 Grach Yarygin 9mm pistol. That pause cost him his life as Ned pumped two shots into him. Neither Vor wore a bulletproof vest that night, and both men died instantly.

The appeal of firing the Smith & Wesson Model 27 .357 Magnum revolver is that a double-action handgun like this can fire as quickly as you can pull the trigger and will never jam. It turns out that Ned spent his entire childhood growing up in California, shooting guns with his father and brothers at their ranch, and he became very skilled at handling firearms.

Jeffrey immediately called the D.C. police, and when they arrived, they were amazed at Ned's marksmanship, especially for having shot the Vors so accurately in the dark. Later, Sgt. Steve Horowitz, the lead homicide detective, arrived and examined the bodies before calling the coroner to take them to the morgue. He opened their torn, bloody jackets and saw the Russian-made MP-443 Grach Yarygin handguns lying nearby. He noticed the edges of terrible tattoos peeking out from the tops of their shirts. "These guys are Russian criminals! Look at their tattoos! What the hell are they doing here?"

Now thoroughly shaken and repulsed by the bloody mess in their exquisite dining room, Ned and Jeffrey began to connect the dots. They asked Detective Horowitz to take a seat and calmly recounted the entire story about Westley Engle and the secret document. This marks the first time the Russians have entered the picture.

Detective Horowitz replied, "You know, I did see something come over the wire regarding home invasions with murders and broken-up antique furniture."

Chapter 47

The day after the FBI recovered the list of Westley's furniture pieces sold at Integrity Auctions, the Penfields returned to the FBI's offices to work on finding the flash drive that Westley had hidden in the collection. With all the images uploaded into their computer system, Alex reviewed them, comparing them to Westley's clues. The document contained a set of cryptic passages that described decorative elements on various pieces in the collection. At the end of the document, it read, "Locate each piece, follow the trail, and you will find the flash drive."

Alex explained, "What Westley did in creating this set of clues was very clever. First, if the Russians had gotten the document before we did, they would have had to find someone knowledgeable about the symbols. Secondly, without knowing what the symbols meant, they would have had difficulty choosing the right piece to search."

As Alex and Rosalie began their research, Agent Armstrong entered the conference room and said, "DC police just advised our office that a pair of Russian thugs attempted to burglarize the home of your friends, Mr. Samuels and Mr. Martinsen, last night."

They gasped simultaneously at the thought of their dear friends being threatened and dragged into the mess. Before either could speak, Armstrong assured the Penfields, "Don't worry. Your friends are safe. Mr. Samuels shot and killed both intruders in their dining room as they were entering the house. Interestingly, they were what is known as Russian Vors. Criminal mobsters."

"That sounds like Ned! I would never want to be on the wrong end of a gun he's holding. Rosalie, would you mind calling the boys and seeing how they are?" Alex was extremely concerned about their DC friends but needed to start reviewing the images.

"Of course, Alex. How terrifying! You stay here and get right to work," replied Rosalie. "I'm going to give them a call," she said as she picked up her cell phone and walked out of the conference room.

Armstrong said, "The Russians are after that flash drive, too. So, we've got to beat them to it."

Alex went to work and looked at the first clue. He read aloud, *"A certain green leaf has long been a symbol of victory, success, and triumph."* Westley probably referred to laurel leaves or laurel wreaths, which are symbols of eternal glory, special achievement, success, and triumph. Laurel leaves crowned victors of athletic competitions in the Olympic Games."

Alex scrolled through the images. "There it is! Lot number 465 is the Renaissance Revival walnut sideboard. It was located on the west wall in Westley's dining room. Look at the laurel leaves carved in the crest at the top of the piece. During the Victorian era, sideboards like this graced the homes of families led by successful businessmen. It was an expensive piece, and the laurel leaves represent his victories in business. The carved game birds, fruit, and carvings symbolize a life of abundance. The flash drive could be hidden anywhere in this piece because it's fitted with drawers and doors."

He read the second clue, *"It is a symbol of the sea and sometimes symbolizes fertility. It is associated with the goddess Venus (born of the sea), often depicted in paintings carried to the shore in one. Look for it at the top of the piece."* Westley referred to the scallop shell. "We must find a piece with a shell carved in the crest." He scrolled through the images and found one. "There it is! Lot number 155!"

"I know that piece! Rosalie and I lusted after it for years! It's the rosewood Rococo Revival parlor desk made by John and Joseph Meeks. Look at the pierced, carved crest. It's decorated with a large, stylized shell carving flanked by acanthus leaves and flowers. The piece also has an abundance of melon ball finials fitted at the edges of the horizontal shelves. A rope-twist carved edge surrounds the marble top. The furniture maker aimed to glorify nature. Rococo is named after the French words "rocaille," meaning rock, and "coquille," meaning shell. Carved flowers and acanthus leaves were added to the crest for ornamentation. The melon ball finials are distinctive because they feature an outside edge of carved spheres. That was a specific detail created by Meeks."

"It has a drawer that, when pulled out, the face drops down to form a writing surface. The secretary's interior is fitted with open compartments and small drawers where Westley could have hidden something. Below, there is a pair of doors that open to a larger interior space below. If the object is larger, it would easily fit in there!"

"Good job!" Armstrong exclaimed.

They moved on to the third clue. Alex read, *"It is a fearsome, dangerous animal, an emblem of fertility, fearlessness, strength, and stubbornness. A favorite game animal whose meat is prized and is also a symbol of hospitality."* He continued, "Westley must have referred to the wild boar's head at the top of the backboard of the other Renaissance revival sideboard on the east side of his dining room. The boar's head carving on the backboard, along with the gamebirds, fruit, and nut carvings on the doors, and pulls of the lower cabinet, all represent hospitality, good cheer, and wealth."

Alex anxiously continued, "I know that piece. Let me find it in the inventory; I'm scrolling, scrolling, and there it is! Lot number 567. That sideboard could hide anything. There are four drawers above and a large space below."

"Let's see the next set of clues," said Armstrong.

"'Mirrors reflect light, which allows them to reflect the world around them. They enable one to look deep into oneself. Every lady will look gorgeous sitting at this,'" read Alex. It was Westley's next clue, and it took Alex a while to figure it out. Then it hit him. "There is only one piece of furniture in the collection with a mirror that you sit in a chair to use: The rosewood Rococo Revival dressing table! It is another fabulous John and Joseph Meeks-made piece that allowed the lady of the house to sit in her boudoir and make herself beautiful."

Alex scrolled through the images and found lot number 488. "It is a magnificent piece made for the lady of the house from a wealthy family. I remember Westley telling us that it came from a famous plantation house on the Mississippi River. It has a drawer fitted with an interior of dividers, and it could easily hide a smaller object."

Although Agent Armstrong struggled to relate to antique furniture and the nuances of the clues, he was delighted that Alex could decipher Westley's meticulous hints.

"We have to be getting close," Armstrong exclaimed.

Alex read the following clue aloud: *"Find the symbol of truth, humility, protection, and courage. Associated with the Knights Hospitallers.'"* He said, "That has to be the Maltese cross, symbolizing the Knights Hospitallers who fought in the Crusades during the medieval age. The eight points of the cross represent their obligation to be truthful, have faith, repent sins, be humble, strive for justice, show mercy, be wholehearted, and endure persecution."

Scrolling through dozens of images, Alex suddenly realized, "There it is! It's the Pottier & Stymus Renaissance Revival parlor cabinet. The crosses are carved into the doors! Lot number 540! It has a large compartment behind the door that will easily hide what we're looking for."

Next came another clue. *"It holds pieces used in a game of chance, including cards and chips. Commonly used in the parlor, it was born in Massachusetts.'"* Alex pondered, "Let me see, it must be a card table. The only one I can think of is the Salem, Massachusetts-made mahogany game table in his bedroom. Believe it or not, he never used it as a game table, but instead put his television on it so he could watch TV from his bed. Wait! I saw Westley open that table once, and he showed me a compartment to store cards and chips. That's it!" Scanning through the images, he located it as lot number 327. He said, "It has a space large enough to hold the flash drive."

"Well, here's the last clue, Armstrong." Alex read, *"It is an ancient symbol for good luck and has four leaves. It has come to symbolize harmony, symmetry, and proportion. Look for eight of them and find the drop.'"*

"Was Engle referring to four-leaf clovers?" Armstrong asked.

"Possibly, but maybe he was describing that shape otherwise known as a quatrefoil."

"What the hell is a quatrefoil?"

"It comes from the word *quattuor,* which means four, and *folium,* which means leaf. Put the phrases together, and you have quatrefoil. So, the second clue of having eight of them could lead us to the right piece of furniture," Alex said as he scrolled through the images.

Then Alex saw it, hitting him like a bolt of lightning. "Oh, my God! It's the secretary bookcase, lot number 519. That's the piece that Rosalie and I bought from Westley's collection! It has eight quatrefoils in the lattice on the doors!" The thought of the flash drive being in their furniture shakes him to his core. "The upper section behind the doors is an ample space with shelves for displaying books. The lower section features a drop-down panel that serves as a writing surface. Inside, there is a set of small drawers and slots for envelopes. The small drawers could certainly hold a small object. However, the last clue reads, *'Find the drop.'* What the hell does that mean?"

Chapter 48

The Russian Vors continued to search for the flash drive, spreading terror wherever they went. Using the list of buyers from the auction, they decided to visit an East Side Cleveland antique store called Gerstein Antiques. Esther Gerstein and her two sons, David and Selig, own the shop. Esther has been a key figure in the Cleveland antique dealer community for nearly fifty years. She brought her sons into the business when they were in high school. Working around the shop -- vacuuming the floors and dusting the merchandise -- the boys eventually became partners with their mother. Esther is a short, dark-skinned Jewish woman with bright orange hair who wears oversized horn-rimmed glasses and is tough as nails. David is small and slim, with dark brown eyes and hair; he is effeminate, gay, and single. Selig is taller, dark, chubby, and stuck in an unhappy straight marriage. None of the Gersteins had formal training in fine arts, per se. Instead, they were merchants who mastered the art of buying and selling, developing a keen eye for excellent pieces.

The Gersteins were successful and aggressive businesspeople who were not particularly well-liked in the industry. They were tough and looked out for one another to a fault. Despite disliking the Gersteins, the Penfields conducted significant business with them because of their high-quality antique pieces. The Penfields often brought friends and family into the shop, where they generally made purchases. Over twenty years, Alex and Rosalie, along with their families and friends, spent more than $100,000 at the shop. As the Penfields' collecting grew to a higher level, they eventually outgrew Gerstein's offerings.

Ultimately, the Penfields and Gersteins had a falling out over a piece of furniture. Gerstein's greed caused them to overlook the valuable business they had built together over the past twenty years. It cost them their relationship with the Penfields, along with their families and friends. Thanks to the internet, the Penfields found many alternative sources to get quality furniture without dealing with the Gersteins.

Russian Vors Yaroslav "The Hawk" Solkolov and Dimitri "The King" Vasiliev walked into the Gersteins' shop. Unaware to the Gersteins, the thugs were searching for one of the pieces Westley had left clues about: the classic mahogany, Massachusetts-made game table. David and Selig were managing the store in their mother's absence. The Vors sneaked around the store for a few minutes, browsing the merchandise, until David approached and asked, "May I help you?"

"We want to see the game table that you purchased at the Westley Engle auction," said Solkolov.

"It's not for sale right now. We just unloaded it and still have to price it," replied David.

Vasiliev approached the front door, pushed on it, and locked the deadbolt.

At the sound of the rattle and the click of the front door deadbolt, brother Selig entered the room. "What's the problem here?"

With a menacing look, Solkolov replied, "You are going to show us the game table."

"Who the hell do you think you are? Didn't you hear my brother tell you we haven't priced it yet? It's in the back room, and it's going to stay there until we damn well decide to put it up for sale!" exclaimed Selig.

Vasiliev said, "I think we've had enough of dealing with these two." With that, he pulled out his switchblade, opened it, approached Selig, and jammed the seven-inch blade into him just below the sternum, slicing into the lower part of his heart. He dropped to the floor and died within a minute.

Terrorized, David turned to the men and shouted, "Wait! I will show you the table!" Shaking and having just wet his pants, he led the Vors to the back room where the table was stored. With the men standing in front of the table, Solkolov pulled his 9mm MP-443 Grach Yarygin from its shoulder holster and shot David in the back of the head. The impact threw him, his brains and blood, against the wall as he collapsed to the floor. The Vors pulled the top off the table's base, threw it on the floor, and were enraged to find the hidden compartment empty. "Fuck!" yelled Vasiliev. The Vors kicked the table over and quickly ran to the shop's back door, unlocked it, and escaped into the alley and out of the area.

An hour later, Esther drove up the alley to her parking space behind the store and noticed that the back door was ajar. "What's the matter with those boys? They left the back door open!" She stepped inside and, to her horror, saw David sprawled on the floor. Feeling faint, she screamed for Selig but received no answer. Then, running to the front of the store, she saw him lying on the floor in a pool of blood. Esther cried in Yiddish, *"Oh, meyn got! Meyn zin!"* She collapsed on the floor in total shock. "Oh, my God! My sons!" she sobbed.

Moments later, she composed herself and called the police. "911, what's your emergency?"

"I'm at 4841 Fernwood Boulevard. My name is Esther Gerstein, and I am the owner of Gerstein Antiques. Someone has murdered my two sons in my shop!"

"Are they still breathing?" asked the dispatcher.

"I don't think so! Hurry!"

Patrol officer Jason Cohen of the Cleveland Heights police department was the first to arrive at Gerstein Antiques, just before the distant wail of a racing ambulance's siren. He entered the shop and examined the bodies of the two slain men to confirm their deaths. The officer then secured the scene with yellow tape both in front of and behind the building. Homicide detective Lt. Larry Forester was called in and arrived ten minutes after the ambulance. "Lieutenant, I've secured the scene, and the paramedics have confirmed two deceased males, one stabbed and the other by gunshot."

"Thank you, Officer Cohen."

Forester's first action was to contact Sgt. Albert Procter of the Cleveland Heights police department. A veteran of the force, he is trained as a crime scene technician responsible for processing the scene. He arrived within thirty minutes.

After Officer Procter examined the bodies and the surrounding areas, he called the Cuyahoga County Coroner. He ordered that the coroner's assistant be sent in a van to remove the bodies for transport to the morgue for examination by the medical examiner.

Detective Forester also examined the scene. The only items out of place were a spent 9 mm shell casing, the overturned tabletop, and the flipped game table base lying beside David Gerstein's body. After the paramedics managed to calm Esther down, Forester proceeded to interview her. "This whole scene revolves around that piece of furniture. What can you tell me about that?"

"We purchased it at the Westley Engle auction held by Integrity Auction Company. You know, he was the computer scientist who was murdered a while back. We brought the piece to the store and were getting it ready to put on display."

"Yes, many strange things have happened with this man's collection. But unfortunately, your sons' murders are not the first to be linked to this. Do you have video surveillance cameras connected to your security system? Maybe they recorded the murders."

"Yes! Yes! I do!"

Police information technology expert Jason Rubin was called in from the county and arrived at Esther's shop within an hour. He proceeded to retrieve videos from her security system. Fortunately, she had installed two security cameras: one covering the main showroom and the other the back storeroom.

The IT specialist downloaded the footage from the last two hours and transferred it onto a flash drive.

"Mrs. Gerstein, I would like to ask you not to view these images. You have been through enough, and if the murders are on the tapes, they automatically become evidence for the prosecutor." Officer Cohen escorted Mrs. Gerstein to her office.

Jason Rubin then plugged the flash drive into his laptop and pressed play. As he fast-forwarded the video, Rubin, Officer Cohen, and Detective Forester were shocked to see the two large thugs arrive, kill the brothers, tear apart the game table, and leave. Detective Forester exclaimed, "We now know who the hell we are looking for!" The detective then removed and tagged the flash drive as evidence before driving back to headquarters to file his report.

Chapter 49

After working through all of Westley's clues, Alex turned to FBI Agent Robert Armstrong and said, "Robert, those are the pieces the agents need to find. You should go back to the Integrity Auction Company and get the names and addresses of the collectors who bought those pieces. We need to track where they went and send local agents after them. It's not uncommon for the winning bidders to be located all over the country. So, some of those pieces might currently be on trucks heading to unknown destinations!"

"The first place we have to go is back to our house and search the secretary bookcase!" yelled Alex.

"Let's go. I'll round up a team of agents and we'll follow you over there," Agent Armstrong replied.

Rosalie and Alex dashed out of the FBI building, sprinted to their Camaro 2SS, and buckled up. The Camaro 2SS is one of America's fastest and most powerful production cars. The car boasts a 450-horsepower, over 400 cubic inch V-8 engine, a six-speed manual transmission, and the ability to accelerate to 100 mph in just five seconds. For added sex appeal, the Penfield Camaro features a convertible top and is painted in candy-apple red.

As the engine roared to life, "Hold onto your butt, Rosie! Let's see these FBI agents keep up with us!" Alex hurried east along Lakeside Avenue to the Innerbelt, then entered the freeway going north on I-90, heading east toward Gates Mills. With the FBI in pursuit, the couple quickly reached speeds of 90 miles per hour. Just east of East 266th Street, I-90 sharply curved south, then back east. At the I-271 interchange, they moved south, weaving through traffic while slowing to 80 miles per hour. Alex could only think that the FBI had radioed ahead to the highway patrol, alerting them of their emergency, and hoped the Penfields did not injure anyone rushing home to Gates Mills.

The Penfields exited I-271 at Mayfield Road and sped eastward. As they approached the intersection at SOM Center Road, the traffic light turned yellow. Alex accelerated the Camaro and ran the red light. At least ten car lengths behind, the FBI agent driving the follow-up vehicle had to stop because the light was already red. The Penfields continued east on Mayfield Road into the scenic Gates Mills. They turned right onto West Hill Drive, then left onto Old Mill Road. Next, they made a sharp right onto Berkshire Road, followed by another right into their driveway halfway down Woodstock Road. "I swear you were trying to kill us!" exclaimed Rosalie.

"I love this car!" replied Alex. "Sorry if I scared you, Rosalie. I got carried away."

As they approached the house, Alex tapped the garage door opener on the visor and pulled into the garage. They both jumped out of the car. Alex unlocked the deadbolt on the mudroom door and pressed the garage door opener button to close it. In their haste, the couple rushed inside the house and slammed the door shut without looking back. They didn't notice that as the garage door closed, the next-door neighbor's cat, Callie, seeking a visit and a treat, walked underneath and triggered the child safety sensor, causing the garage door to reopen. The Penfields left the mudroom door to the house unlocked in their hurry to check out the secretary bookcase now in Alex's basement studio. Meanwhile, the cat patiently waited at the doorstep.

At that exact moment, Vors Solkolov and Vasiliev drove east on Cedar Road. Now it was the Penfields' turn to be terrorized or killed. Armed with their copy of the Integrity Auction furniture buyer list, they headed to the Penfields' home in search of the flash drive. First, they turned left onto Woodstock Road and looked for the Penfields' address. Spotting their house, they were pleasantly surprised to see the garage door open. They quietly moved the large black Mercedes S 560 just past the house and parked on the street in front of the next-door neighbor. Jogging up to the mudroom door, they realized it was unlocked. "This is going to be easy, my friend," Vasiliev whispered. In their rush, they forgot to wear their bulletproof vests.

The Vor intruders quietly opened the door to the mudroom, and Callie slipped into the house ahead of them. The cat darted into the kitchen through the doorway on the left. Without giving the cat a second glance, they heard the Penfields' voices coming from the basement just down the steps to their right. They crept slowly down the stairs into Alex's studio and moved forward until they saw Alex and Rosalie standing in front of the secretary bookcase.

Moving very slowly, like predators stalking their prey, both Russians drew their MP-443 Grach Yarygin pistols, and in an instant, they rushed toward the Penfields. Solkolov grabbed Rosalie from behind, wrapped his forearm around her neck, and pressed his pistol to her head. Vasiliev aimed his gun at Alex. It had been a long time, but Alex could feel a terrible rage building inside him. Seeing his beautiful Rosalie in such danger, he knew he had to keep control.

"We are here for the flash drive," Vasiliev shouted.

"The desk is locked; let me get the key," responded Alex very calmly. He turned around, stepped to the tool cabinet against the wall behind him, and pulled open a drawer. In one motion, Alex grabbed his .357 Ruger Blackhawk revolver, spun around, and fired a single shot into Solkolov's forehead. The bullet and his brains splattered against the back wall. He stiffened and was dead before dropping to the floor. Rosalie slipped through his death grip, shaking with terror. Alex dropped to one knee without hesitation as Vasiliev fired at him, but the 9mm bullet went over him and hit the cabinet behind him. Alex fired off three rounds into Vasiliev's chest. The impact of the shots threw him backward and onto the floor. He lay on his back, wounded but not dead.

Alex could not control his rage at this point. He walked over to Vasiliev, still alive and struggling on the floor. "Mother fucker!" He kicked his gun away and fired one more round right between his eyes, splattering skull and brains everywhere. Lastly, he walked over to the dead Solkolov and fired his last two bullets into his chest, making a second bloody mess on the floor.

Like their friend Ned Samuels, Alex was highly trained with firearms, having spent his childhood shooting and hunting with his father, a World War II gunner and armorer. As a result, he always kept a gun on every floor of the house for protection against intruders.

The four FBI agents rushed into the basement studio just a moment later, their Glock G-19s drawn. With his heart pounding so hard it felt like it was about to burst from his chest and trying to calm himself, Alex shouted, "Where the hell were you guys? You missed all the action!"

"The last couple of shots were fired just as we entered the house! You left us in the dust on the freeway and then at the red light at SOM Center Road! Your speeding could have killed yourselves or somebody else!"

"So, give me a ticket!"

Armstrong could tell that Alex was not in a frame of mind to be antagonized any further.

Armstrong grabbed his cell phone and called the Gates Mills police department to report the shooting and requested a patrol officer and the crime detective on duty. Patrol Officer Roger Sims arrived first and stretched yellow tape across the front of the house. Then, with the arrival of homicide detective Lt. Steve Walter, the crime scene investigation began with interviews of Alex, Rosalie, and Agent Armstrong. While everyone examined the bodies, they were shocked by the grotesque tattoos covering the men. "More damned Russian mobsters!" said Armstrong. "We are going to go get the head of this crew!" Later, Lt. Walter radioed the Cuyahoga County coroner's office and issued an order to remove the bodies.

Chapter 50

While the coroner photographed and documented the gruesome scene at the Penfields' home, his team prepared to remove the bodies. Everyone's attention then shifted to the secretary bookcase. Agent Armstrong said, "Well, Alex, shall we see if the flash drive is in the bookcase?"

Alex knew he had the right piece to search, but what did Westley mean when he said, *"See the drop,"* Alex asked himself. He lowered the drop-down writing surface and examined the exquisitely crafted interior, which featured African satinwood and Brazilian rosewood. Then, aloud, he described what he saw to those present: "As we move from left to right, the interior is fitted with a pair of drawers made of satinwood with rosewood fronts set one on top of the other. Next comes a narrow vertical slot used for envelopes and papers, and a wide cavity in the center fitted at the top with a decorative carved drop. Then, there is another narrow slot. Lastly, there is another pair of matching drawers stacked on top of each other on the interior's right side. Another exquisite detail is the ivory drawer pulls." Of course, everyone had already pulled all four drawers open to find them empty.

While carefully inspecting the interior, it felt as if Westley was talking to Alex, *"See the drop, see the drop!"* As if directed by Westley, Alex ran his hand over the face of the ornately carved rosewood piece of trim fitted to the top of the large cavity in the center. "Is this the drop he is describing? Could this be the front of a fifth drawer?" He ran his hand under the drop, looked, and discovered that, sure enough, there was the bottom of a fifth drawer! "Oh, my God! There is another drawer there! We didn't even notice it was there when we bid on the piece!" He tried to pull it open, but it would not budge. Then, feeling under the drawer, he discovered a round hole drilled through a horizontal rail behind the drawer front. He pushed up at what felt like a latch on the drawer bottom, and as he pulled on the drawer face, the drawer began to slide open!

189

Alex exclaimed, "It's a secret drawer for storing valuable articles or documents. It was a common practice during the Victorian era." As he pulled the drawer open, everyone was shocked to see the flash drive! For a moment, they stood in stunned silence.

Rosalie said, "Bless dear Westley, what a clever place to hide the flash drive from the Russians. They would never have found it!"

A few days later, professionals cleaned up the blood, and life went back to normal for Alex and Rosalie. The daily visits from Callie the cat became very comforting for the couple. She seemed to know they needed her purring and cuddling, and the Penfields rewarded her with special treats and new toys. Next, Alex started the difficult task of cleaning and touching up the secretary bookcase. Knowing that it once belonged to their good friend Dr. Westley Engle, restoring it felt like an honor. It would be displayed in a prominent spot in Rosalie's office.

A month later, the Penfields received a call from FBI agent Robert Armstrong. He proudly told them they had been chosen to receive the Attorney General's Award for Meritorious Public Service. The award recognizes the most important contributions made by citizens or organizations that have helped the department fulfill its mission and goals. Alex and Rosalie were invited to Washington, D.C., to attend the annual ceremony where they would receive the highest public service award given by the Justice Department. The award would be presented to the Penfields for providing crucial evidence and deciphering Westley's symbols to locate the flash drive. "I hope you two will accept this award; you'll never know what you have done for the FBI and our country," said Agent Armstrong.

At the same time, the FBI's Cleveland office and the FBI in Washington, D.C., worked diligently to locate and dismantle local Russian organized crime operations, including illegal poker activities. One day, there was a firm knock at the front door of crime boss Andrei Lebedev's Beachwood home, known as "The Swan." Standing at the door were Agent Armstrong and two other agents. "Andrei Lebedev, you are under arrest for conspiracy to commit murder, loan sharking, and illegal gambling. You attempted to obtain secured property for profit illegally."

"You've got nothing on me!" Lebedev shouted.

"Sir, two Mercedes S 560 automobiles were used in the crimes of murder and attempted murder in Cleveland, Ohio; Dover, Ohio; Atlanta, Georgia; Washington, D.C.; and Gates Mills, Ohio. We have the two vehicles in our possession. First, witnesses will identify these vehicles at those locations during the crimes. These two cars are registered to Acme Enterprises, one of your shell corporations. Second, we have witnesses who will connect the four dead Vors to you as your employees." The agents led a cursing Lebedev away in handcuffs to be booked at the Cleveland FBI office.

Other operations included raiding illegal poker games at the Hotel Belvedere and Hotel Stanton. The FBI increased its efforts against other unlawful Vor enterprises and made numerous arrests. They initiated deportation proceedings against all Russians remotely connected to any of those businesses.

Regarding Agent Ronald Grimsley, this incident was documented and probably led to his forced retirement from the CIA.

Weeks later, the Penfields traveled to Washington, D.C., to accept the Attorney General's Award for Meritorious Public Service. The Attorney General presented the award during a ceremony honoring the recipients at the Great Hall of the Robert F. Kennedy Justice Department Building in Washington, D.C.

They stayed with their friends, Ned and Jeffrey, in Washington, DC. The four celebrated their success, marksmanship, survival, and, most importantly, their friendship.

TRAPPED

www.ingramcontent.com/pod-product-compliance
Lightning Source LLC
Chambersburg PA
CBHW071909220626
47052CB00002B/276